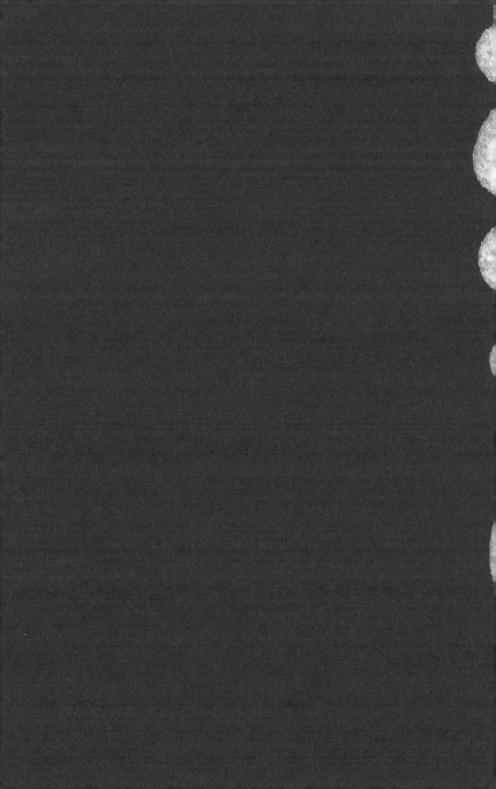

CALM
AT
SUNSET,
CALM
AT
DAWN

Paul Watkins

CALM AT SUNSET, CALM AT DAWN

HOUGHTON
MIFFLIN
COMPANY
BOSTON

Copyright © 1989 by Paul Watkins

For information about permission to reproduce
selections from this book, write to
Permissions,
Houghton Mifflin Company,
2 Park Street,
Boston, Massachusetts 02108.

Library of Congress Cataloging-in-Publication Data

Watkins, Paul, date.
   Calm at sunset, calm at dawn / Paul Watkins.
      p.   cm.
   ISBN 0–395–50959–9
   I. Title.
PS3573.A844C35   1989   89–32471
813'.54—dc20   CIP

PRINTED IN THE UNITED STATES OF AMERICA

Q 10 9 8 7 6 5 4 3 2

CALM
AT
SUNSET,
CALM
AT
DAWN

1

~~~
≈≈≈≈≈≈≈≈≈≈≈≈≈≈≈≈≈≈≈≈≈≈≈≈≈≈
≈≈≈≈≈≈≈≈≈≈≈≈≈≈≈≈≈≈≈≈≈≈≈≈≈≈
~~~

I SPENT my time in the frozen air.

The walls were covered with ice.

I sat on a wooden crate, staring through a thick plastic curtain that separated me from the rest of the East Bay Fish Packing Plant.

Through the foggy screen, I watched a Vietnamese man unloading salmon from an air freight box. The salmon had come in from Alaska that morning.

The man lifted each silver-gray fish from the ice and set it in a plastic tub. Now and then he looked around, to see if anyone was watching.

Once I saw him bring his face close to the pink, gutted flesh of a salmon's belly and smell the meat.

I knew what he was thinking.

When he came to the last box, he set one big salmon aside. When he thought no one would notice, he cradled the fish in his arms and crept out of the warehouse.

The floor manager let the Vietnamese man get ten paces into our parking lot. Then he grabbed a mop and chased him across the compound, out into the street, past the dockside restaurants and halfway up the main road out of Galilee. All this time, he was slapping the man with the mop.

Finally, the Vietnamese dropped his fish on the hot black road and kept running.

The floor manager walked back with the salmon. He smoothed away the dirt as if the silver scales were coins that needed polishing.

Then two trawlermen dragged a swordfish off one of the boats.

The first man held its tail and the other gripped it by the sword. They heaved the fish onto a cutting table and fed it to a band saw.

I watched the swordfish turn into a puzzle of steaks.

The cutter set its severed head upright on the floor, sword pointing at the ceiling. A boy weighed the fillets and packed them into tubs. In red marker, he wrote down the day's date and type of fish.

The boy had to stand on a box while he worked. He had a birth defect that made his legs about the length of a man's forearm. Normal feet. Normal upper body. But his legs were stumps, taken up mostly by the chubby balls of his knees.

I had the worst job at the East Bay Plant. I sat in the freezer all day preparing orders for shipping. Even in a heavy jacket, I was always cold.

I had instructions to wipe off the old dates marked on tubs of fish and replace them with today's date. That way, the market receiving their order thought they were getting fish fresh off the boat. Sometimes the tubs had been sitting there for weeks. On the cardboard shipping boxes was a picture of a trawler hauling in its nets and below that the East Bay motto: "Always Fresh Today."

The floor manager said if I ever told anyone about changing the dates, he would beat me up and fire me and make sure I never found work on the docks again.

I rode the bus home to Narragansett each afternoon at five, my palms smeared red with ink.

Everything I owned smelled of fish.

Clothes I'd never worn to the Plant smelled of fish.

Fish scales fell out of my hair each time I scratched my head. Even after showering and washing and combing, they still flickered down onto my shoulders.

In my dreams, I became a fish and swam down to the wreck of my grandfather's trawler in the deep water off Block Island. I finned along dark corridors, staring at the algae-covered skulls of his crew.

The curtain blew open and a boy named McFarlane tripped into the room. He fell face down on a sack of oysters.

The floor manager strode in, lifted McFarlane by the collar and set him up against the wall. "I swear to God I'll fire you right now!"

"Go ahead, Ramsey." McFarlane squinted down at the little red-haired man. "You can't find anyone else who'd take my place."

McFarlane's job was to wheel a trolley back and forth between the Plant and the dock. On his trolley he carried fifty-gallon drums of fishguts left over from the cutting line. He dumped the guts in the bay.

"I could get one of the Vietnamese to do it." Ramsey stepped back and wiped his hands on his trousers, trying to remove the stench of guts that McFarlane always carried with him. "The Cong will do anything I tell them to do. At least, they would if you didn't chase them all away!" Then Ramsey jumped forward again, remembering his anger. "I'll fire your ass!"

"What did he do?" I didn't bother to get up from my crate.

Ramsey wheeled around. "How come you aren't working?"

"I'm waiting for orders."

"I'll fire you too!"

"Tell me what he did and then fire me."

Now that Ramsey had stopped bullying him, McFarlane took a crumpled sandwich from his pocket and began to eat.

Ramsey walked to the plastic curtain and stared through it at the warehouse floor.

"So what did McFarlane do? Are you going to tell me or not?"

Ramsey sighed. "He puts on a pair of green trousers and a green jacket and he goes up to where the Cong are working and stands there like a Department of Fisheries officer. Then he yells, 'Freeze! I want all of you to show me your work permit cards!' "

"They took off like a stampede." McFarlane laughed with a small snuffling sound.

Ramsey nodded. "And of course none of them have any work cards because they're all illegal immigrants."

"That's why the company only pays them a buck fifty an hour." McFarlane picked a gaff hook off the wall and used it to tap his knee and test his reflexes.

"So they all took off through the side door and ran away into the swamp and off down the road and drove away in their cars . . ." Ramsey sat down next to me on the crate. He didn't look angry anymore.

"They ride about twenty to a car." McFarlane picked bread crumbs off his jacket.

"Did they come back?"

"Some of them did." Ramsey turned away from the plastic curtain. "The ones who figured out who it was."

"They were saying 'Mafawene! Mafawene!' " McFarlane blinked slowly and grinned.

"But Vic's not going to think it's funny. Soon as he finds out" — Ramsey leveled his finger at McFarlane — "you'll end up packed away in one of these tubs."

Vic Vogel was owner and general manager of the East Bay Company.

If I asked him a question for which the answer would be yes, he'd say, "That's a rog." If the answer would be no, he'd tell me, "Negatory."

He hardly ever came down to the working floor. Instead, he watched us from a room built up near the roof. It had a huge glass window. The secretaries worked there.

Vic hired Vietnamese people to work on the squid line, packing the pale pink bodies, like sausages with eyes, into boxes marked "East Bay Company" and "Always Fresh Today." Vic and Ramsey called them the Cong straight to their faces.

They wore blue bath hats and their clothes were always stained black from squid ink, which dripped off the conveyor belt and spread across the wet concrete floor. Sometimes ink reached all the way to the other end of the fishhouse. I watched it seep slowly under the blur of my ice room curtain.

Whenever the real Department of Fisheries officers arrived on inspections, the Vietnamese disappeared.

Ramsey would order McFarlane and me to stand at the conveyor belt. We pretended to box squid while an officer, carrying a gun and a billy club, paced through the warehouse with his hands behind his back, nodding and moving on. Always nodding and moving on.

Squid piled up at the end of the belt. They slapped down to the floor and lay scattered with bath hats dropped by the Vietnamese.

I heard that some of them used to be rich in Vietnam. Some had been officers in the South Vietnamese army. One man claimed he'd been a general. He wore a fake leather jacket with "Mr. Sensible" written in white paint on the back.

I squinted at Ramsey's handwriting on an order form.

It looked as if he'd been taught to write by making letters out of matchsticks.

The order was for a hundred one-pound bags of oysters. Each bag had to be weighed individually on a tiny kitchen scale, which was all Ramsey would let me use.

On the seventy-ninth bag, Ramsey walked in. "Order's canceled."

I looked up. "You're fucking kidding."

"Never do." He spun on his heel and walked out.

I stood up from my crate and pounded the walls. Slabs of ice crashed to the floor. I stamped my feet in the slimy water and yelled at the gloomy-eyed fish laid out in rows like cannon shells. None of what I yelled made sense. I picked up a frozen flounder and spun it across the room like a dinner plate. Then I slumped down on my crate and sat huddled in my coat, listening to trolleys drag past outside the freezer.

McFarlane's blurred face appeared on the other side of the screen. "Secretary wants to see you."

"Did she say what for?"

"There's been some layoffs. Maybe you're next."

I held out one of the yellow slips of paper. "Fill this order for me, will you?"

McFarlane took the yellow slip. "Will do."

When I first arrived at the East Bay Company, I saw how people spent their time breaking each other down.

It all worked on instinct. You had to carve out a space for yourself and make sure people left you alone in that space.

My space was the ice room.

McFarlane's space was his trolley and the fishgut barrels.

During my first days, McFarlane came to the ice room and gave me a hard time, telling me to do his job while he took a break.

I knew if I gave in and did what he said, that soon I'd be little more than a slave. He'd have me crushed into a space so small I wouldn't be able to breathe .

So I was as mean to him as I knew how to be and he backed down. In time, I started moving into his space and keeping it for my own, as if it had always been mine.

Emily met me halfway down the stairs that led to her office. She was one of the secretaries. She was also Vic Vogel's daughter.

I couldn't understand how such a pretty girl came from such an ugly man.

She ran her fingers through my hair and said we were going to the depot again.

The depot was a warehouse where the East Bay Company stored spare equipment for the fishhouse. It was also where the Cong disappeared to whenever Fisheries men came by.

I knew Emily before I came to the Plant. I had known her for years. Over a couple of months in our last semester at high school, I knew her very well. This didn't last. I stopped knowing her very well and went back to just knowing her. But now things were starting again.

When I began the job, I didn't know she'd be working for her father at the Plant.

People said she and Vic were too close. He pawed at her and slapped her bottom when she walked by. I heard a rumor they weren't even related.

We walked out to a parking lot behind the warehouse and sat in her rusted black Camaro. We left the doors open. A smell of low tide blew in off the beach.

Heat curled up from car roofs.

Trawlers jammed the dock, most of them empty.

Fishing had been going badly for a while now. Around Christmas time, Ramsey said, the boats used to come in loaded down with yellowtail flounder. Trawlers hit schools of them so large their nets tore out. Then the yellowtail disappeared. Nobody caught more than a couple of hundred pounds a trip, and these fish were small and sickly.

It happened sometimes, Ramsey told me. The fish would vanish for years at a time and then suddenly reappear in sizes bigger than anyone had ever caught before. Nobody seemed to know why.

*

Most times Emily and I left for the depot, we never arrived.

Usually we drove in the opposite direction and spent our afternoon on the sun deck of a restaurant in Narragansett, drinking dark beer in the shade of big umbrellas.

Sometimes we just sat talking in the parking lot.

"I could get you a raise, you know." She straddled where I sat in the Camaro, knees pressed into the seat on either side of my waist. She hooked her hands behind my neck and scratched at my head with her nails, making goosebumps show on my arms.

"You could get me killed if Papa Fish finds out how many times we leave for the depot and how many times we actually get there. If I was him, I'd fire me too."

"Don't call him Papa Fish. Only people who hate him call him that." She pulled off her sweatshirt, showing the dent of her belly button and the smoothness of her stomach, and leaving only a tank top with no bra. She moved the hair away from her eyes. "Which depot shall we go to today?"

"Any depot where it's happy hour."

She looked past me at the watch on her wrist. "Too early for happy hour."

She started the car and drove out of Galilee. "So when are you going to ask me out on a date, James Pfeiffer?"

I laughed and smiled, then turned my head away. A few minutes later, when she asked me again where I wanted to go, I looked at her and realized the same awkward smile was still stitched to my face.

She stopped the car in a parking lot near the Dunes Club in Narragansett. We sat with the windows rolled down, hearing the sea roll and crack on the shore beyond the dunes.

The club hadn't opened yet for the season. It was still too early for summer people. Too early for the rich boys dressed like poor boys, who spent their time skateboarding up and down the Narragansett boulevard.

"I'm going to have a hard time clocking out. It's almost four-thirty already." I took off my watch and wound it, the leather band dotted with fish scales. "Everything'll be closed when we get back."

"I have the key. I'll just write your name down. Nobody checks." She was in charge of the payroll as well as the phones. She leaned past me and flicked a cigarette out the window.

"And how are you going to raise my salary without getting both of us killed?"

"Easy." She leaned over and kissed me once. "Six dollars." She kissed me again. "Seven dollars." Again. "Eight."

"You should give your dad some credit." I twisted the key in the ignition and turned on the radio. Then I reached outside and played with the coat hanger aerial to find a station clear of static. "Your dad knows what's going on."

"Starting to lose your nerve?"

"No, I'm starting to lose my job."

My father said you couldn't trust Vic Vogel. He told me Vic wasn't smart but he was sly. He never did anything for anybody else that wasn't first weighed up and primed for payback.

Emily offered me a cigarette and I shook my head. Then she offered me a stick of gum and I didn't want that either. "My dad likes people who like his daughter. So make me like you, Pfeif."

She looked tanned for this time of the year, pale the way I was only in the webs between her fingers.

I knew she'd been down at the salon, lying on one of those purple-glowing beds and wearing plastic cups on her eyes so as not to go blind from radiation.

"If I didn't have this job, things would be different, Emily. If my father hadn't found me work at the East Bay Plant as a punishment for getting kicked out of college, then things wouldn't be the way they are. But this is a last straw for me. I just can't afford to get fired. When it's over, I promise things can be different."

She started the car and spun it as we left the parking lot. "Don't worry about when things are over, James Pfeiffer. They're already over." She talked over the sound of gravel cracking off the axle. "This has nothing to do with my father or your father. This is all to do with you and me."

A couple of times a day, I walked across the warehouse floor to fetch more shipping containers.

Past the cutters, slicing apart mackerel and scup with long knives and singing to the music on their Walkmans. They flipped the peeled skin and heads into barrels next to them and fed lozenges of pale meat to the belt. At the head of the belt was a tank where the fish were washed in a weak chlorine solution, then shoveled onto the belt by a woman who used to be a belly dancer. Her nose had caved in from years of snorting cocaine.

I walked past the birth-defect boy, who stood marking tubs with red ink.

Past the jabbering Vietnamese.

The box room was above the fishhouse floor. An old woman named Claudette worked the place by herself.

She never allowed anyone up there. If I wanted a box, corrugated cardboard with wax lining and "East Bay Company" printed on the side, I took a broom handle and banged on a trap door in the ceiling. Then Claudette would open the trap door and throw down as many boxes as I wanted.

No one answered when I pounded at the trap door, so I walked out of the building and up a small iron staircase to the box room entrance.

The door was heavy and armored and blue, propped open to let in the breeze. I walked in. Rows and rows of musty-smelling cardboard stretched out in front of me.

Claudette caught up with me at the end of an aisle. "How many times I got to tell you, you can't come up here! Vic won't allow it! You want a box, you bang on the trap door!" She pointed at me, as if there were others standing nearby and she needed to single me out. "I know you! I know your face from a dozen other faces!"

"I banged on the trap door. No one answered." I looked around while she figured out what to say next.

Clean, I was thinking.

No fish, I said to myself.

It must take less than fifteen seconds to fold one of those boxes together and East Bay uses only about two hundred boxes a day. Hardly any work at all.

I know why you don't let anyone up here. So they can't see how little work you do. I nodded, still looking around.

She knew what I was thinking. She yelled at me again to get out.

"Vic sent me up here to work for you." I spat out the lie. The words fell like marbles from my mouth.

"I don't need any help. You tell Vic I don't need help."

"I'll do all the work. You won't have to do anything. Just tell me what to do and I'll do it." I spoke quickly, the sentences running together.

She tipped her face to one side, a red baseball cap wedged onto her head. "When'd he tell you this?"

"Today. Just now. Just tell me what needs doing and I'll do it. You go ahead and take a break. You look tired."

"It's hard work." She eyed me, trying to see through the lie so she could send me away and keep the box room door locked from now on.

"I'm ready to work. Just tell me what to do, Claudette."

"Well." She plodded across to an open space where she folded the boxes. "Alls you got to do is make boxes." Then she wheeled around and pointed at me again. "But it isn't so easy as you think!"

*

To cover the tracks of the lie, I told Vic that Claudette had asked me to help her in the box room on a permanent basis.

Vic rested his elbows on his desk and touched the tips of his fingers together. Then he stood up, edged over to the coffee machine and poured himself a mugful, thick and black like creosote.

On the wall behind his desk was a chart of fish caught in New England waters and a calendar with women in bathing suits standing on the decks of trawlers. In big letters and in several languages under this month's picture was "Protect Ocean Cables."

Vic raised his eyebrows, a solid line of hair running across the base of his forehead, which Ramsey called Unibrow. "Normally, I wouldn't agree to something like this. But I like you, James."

This was an even bigger lie than the one I'd just told him.

He rubbed his knuckles back and forth across his gritted teeth. From the look on his face, it seemed to me he thought I had some information on him. Now he was afraid I'd hurt him with what I knew. "I run this company. You know that, don't you, James?"

"Yes."

"People do what I tell them to do."

I nodded.

He waved me away.

As I reached the door, he stood and cleared his throat. "So how are things with you and Emily?"

"Things aren't with me and Emily, Mr. Vogel."

He hiked his trousers up into his balls. "Glad to hear it."

I told Ramsey that Vic had transferred me to the box room to work for Claudette. "Vic said it was 'definite confirmed.' "

"This isn't right." He dropped his cigarette into a barrel McFarlane was wheeling past. "I'm going to check up on this."

"Vic's the boss. What can I say?"

"Shit is what you can say. Shit and shit and shit! Who's going to work in the ice room? I can't ever get people to work in there. I'm going to check on this." He set down his pen and walked off the warehouse floor.

I knew he wouldn't talk to Vic. They hated each other.

Vic would have fired him ages ago, but Ramsey belonged to a union, and besides, he knew the way Vic ran his business. They'd both been at the place so long there was nothing left to do but hate.

Later, on my lunch break, as I walked out to the warm dust of the parking lot, I saw Ramsey standing on the end of the pier. He was talking to McFarlane. McFarlane leaned on his trolley and barked, "Why should I?"

"It's only for a little while." Ramsey slapped him on the shoulder. "I'll get one of the Cong to dump your barrels."

McFarlane tipped the barrel on its side. The load of fishguts fell away in a slow spread of oil and scales. Little flounder eyes stared up from a tangle of empty skin, sad and distant and sinking into the green of the bay. "This is my job." He set the barrel upright on his trolley. "I'm good at it. And I can't stand being in the cold."

"It's only for a little while," Ramsey was saying. "Just a little, little while."

Claudette and I sat on the roof of the East Bay Plant making boxes.

I clocked her in for work at nine. She showed up around ten with doughnuts and coffee.

By that time, I'd have made all the boxes for the day.

For the rest of the time, she made stews in a crock pot with ingredients she'd brought with her from home.

I peeled carrots and potatoes while she thumbed through cookbooks.

We took turns sitting by the trap door.

When someone banged on the door, we waited a minute before opening, and then sounded impatient, as if we had no time to spare.

At four, when the stew had simmered for a few hours, she poured some into a bowl for me and took the rest home to her family.

"You're the one who's screwing Emily, aren't you?" She leaned back in her chair, baseball cap shading her face.

"No, I'm not. What makes you think that?" I squinted at her through the glare off the packing house roof.

"People say you are."

"Well, I'm not." I put a box on my head to shield my eyes from the sun.

"She acts as if you are." She leaned across and rested her hand on my knee. Her skin was wrinkled and blue-veined with brown spots. "I know what you're worried about. You're worried Vic is such a jealous father that he'll rip your head off and stick it on the flagpole." She nodded at the pole outside the front office.

"I have a girlfriend someplace else." This was another lie.

"So how come you're always driving away with her in the car?" She snorted through her sharp nose. "I see everything from up here on the roof."

"Just don't spread any rumors, Claudette. I could do without that."

"It's Emily who spreads the rumors."

"Why? Do you know why?"

"Maybe she wants to get her father mad at you. You know, some people say they aren't even father and daughter."

"I heard that."

"I seen some things from up here that would make you think about it." She emptied a can of mushroom soup into the crock pot and added white wine from a thermos.

*

I walked up the Escape Road to my bus stop. It was called the Escape Road because, in hurricanes that sometimes ruined Galilee, it offered the only way out to safety.

Sun hung in yellow beams across bulrushes growing at the roadside.

I turned to look back at Galilee, its dockyard spiked with the raised outriggers of fishing boats.

Emily's Camaro was coming toward me from the Plant.

I turned and started walking again, hoping she would pass on.

But she stopped. She opened the passenger door and told me to get in.

I rested my hands on the hot roof of the car and leaned down. "I need to talk with you. People have been saying things about us that will lose me my job. It's not the job I'm afraid of losing, Emily. I'm afraid of what my father will do to me."

"I have to talk to you as well, Pfeif. So get in."

For a while we didn't speak.

She drove us out to the lighthouse at Castle Point and parked the car next to a building where wedding receptions took place most weekends in the summer.

"You have to quit." She fed herself a cigarette and lit it with a lighter that hung on a leather strap from her rearview mirror. Then she sat back and puffed smoke, waiting to see what I'd say.

"Is this all because we're not friends like we used to be? Because I didn't get this job just so I could see you? So you go get me fired?"

"That's not the reason."

"Then what is?"

"I can't tell you right now."

"My father's going to kill me when he hears I've been fired." I put my hands behind my neck and squeezed at the muscles. "He'll pull me apart."

"I'm just telling you for your own good that you have to quit."

"What did you tell your dad about us?"

"Nothing. Nothing to tell."

"I've been hearing some rumors."

"If you've been hearing any rumors, they probably came from Claudette. That's all she ever does. Make up rumors."

"It was Claudette who told me."

"There you are."

"So why do I have to quit? Because we're not getting along like you wanted us to?"

"I'm telling you this because I like you. Understand? Let's not talk about it anymore. Just collect your pay and go."

I opened my mouth to speak, then sighed and closed it again. I looked at the evenness of her face and her dark eyes and for a moment I couldn't remember why we didn't get along anymore.

I walked into Vic's office the next morning.

Emily was there. As soon as she saw me, she turned away and began to write up the day's fish prices on a blackboard.

"I'm sorry, Mr. Vogel. I have to quit, at least for a little while. My mother . . ." I told Vic my parents needed me to work full time at home.

"Don't worry about it." He grinned at me, Unibrow riding up on his skull. He went to get my time card and began figuring my pay on a pocket calculator.

Emily turned around behind him, smiled at me. Her teeth were very bright. She mouthed "Fuck me."

"I hope this isn't a problem, Mr. Vogel."

"Hell, negatory. I understand. You say hello to your dad for me." He stood and shook my hand. Then he pulled out a checkbook, the checks decorated with scenes of geese in a swamp at sunrise, and wrote one for me. "I rounded it up a buck or two." He moved his fist out slowly until it rested on my chin. "Take care, James."

*

My father and mother sat on the sofa listening to what Emily had told me about having to quit. I said I didn't know any more about it than that.

They sat there side by side waiting for the rest, but I'd already told them everything.

"Is that it?" My father narrowed his eyes.

"Yes, sir."

"Not much of a story." He looked at his fingernails.

"No, sir."

He scratched the back of his neck and sighed. Then he pointed at me and through me and out into the back yard. "Paint the garage."

I sat in my room at the end of the day, hearing a lawnmower buzz grass on a lawn across the street. People flip-flopped down to the beach after getting off work. Sounds of car radios rose into my hearing, were loud and then faded again.

I took the blanket off my bed and pulled it over me where I sat in my chair by the window. It came down to my knees. The only light that reached me was a dark, quiet Hudson Bay green.

For a long time, I sat under the blanket, trying not to think.

Two days later, Emily called and said she wanted to talk.

I was standing on a ladder painting the garage when her Camaro pulled into the driveway. Flecks of white paint peppered my hair and my shoulders.

I got in her car and we didn't speak until we reached the parking lot of the East Bay Plant.

"Why are we going in the back way?"

The car smelled of burnt marijuana and beer.

"You'll see." She stopped at the far end of the parking lot, away from the Plant.

A crowd had gathered at the main gate. The cutters and the

packers and the Cong. I saw Ramsey and McFarlane. They leaned against a truck, sharing a cigarette.

The gate was closed and a sign had been bolted to it. The sign was too far away to make out the words.

"Dad filed for bankruptcy yesterday." Emily opened the car door and stretched her legs. "The feds are looking for him now."

"Where is he? And your mother?" I heard shouting over by the gate.

"Bahamas, I think. And the reason they're all so pissed off over there is because their last paychecks bounced. Yours may have been the last good one Dad ever wrote."

"What do the feds want him for?"

"Oh, illegal employment, embezzlement of funds, income tax evasion. They read me a list over the phone this morning. I said I didn't know where he was."

"Where are you going to go?" I caught the sound of breaking glass. The Cong had started pelting offices on the second floor with stones from the parking lot.

Emily chewed at her lip as the windows shattered one after the other. "I'm going to live with my uncle and aunt in Newport. I don't know what else to do. I have some money he put in my bank account before he left. I don't know when they're coming back." She didn't look sad. Only tired. "Just wanted you to know the reason I made you quit. Didn't want you to think it had anything to do with me. And the thing about going bankrupt is that you can't tell anyone or the creditors drop down on you like vampires. If I told someone and Dad found out, I think he'd have killed me just like he'd have killed anybody else."

"They're going to tear the place down."

"I know it. I would too, if I was them. I brought us here to see the show."

Leaving Galilee, we passed a black and white police car, lights flashing, going in the opposite direction.

Emily dropped me off at the breakwater by Narragansett Beach. It was a moon high tide. Water slapped deep against the stone wall.

I leaned through the open door and kissed her on the cheek. "We'll meet up soon."

She shook her head. "It's a shame about us." Then she put her car in gear and drove away fast down the road to Newport.

For a moment I stood in the road watching her car.

It occurred to me that she was one of the few friends I had, and if we left things the way we'd just left them, I'd probably never see her again.

I sprinted after the black car, felt my breath rush in and out through my clenched teeth.

I had no idea what I'd say to her.

The car slowed briefly. The cat's eyes of brake lights flashed red in exhaust fumes as it turned onto the Newport road. Then it picked up speed and was gone long before I reached the corner.

I walked back, sweat sticking my shirt to my chest. I sat on the breakwater, dangling my legs over the stone wall until the water reached my feet.

Then I wandered home and painted the garage until it was too dark to see anymore.

2

My grandfather washed up on a Block Island beach.

This was in the winter of 1959.

Two fishermen found him rolled in seaweed at the high-tide line. His mouth was full of sand and hermit crabs lived in the pockets of his coat. His boat and the rest of his crew completely disappeared.

My grandmother asked that he be laid to rest near where they found him, so he was buried on the cliffs at a place called Mohegan Bluffs. After the funeral, they set a bronze plaque in the ground.

Captain Augustus Weber. 1910–1959.
F/V Matador left Galilee, R.I., Nov. 12.59.
And was never seen again.
Requiescat in Pace.

Sometimes in late autumn, around Indian summer, my mother took the Block Island ferry. She walked out to the bluffs and set flowers on his grave.

My father had been a fisherman since age twelve.

At twenty-four, he bought his own boat.

On his thirtieth birthday, a wave washed him overboard somewhere off Montauk. He drifted for ten hours before another fishing boat picked him up. A shark swam circles around him in the last hour before he was rescued. As a man reached down to pull him from the water, this shark swam from under the boat and butted my father's chest so hard it broke three ribs. The fish never bit him. People said he had lost his mind by the time they brought him on deck.

When he returned to shore, he promised my mother to give his sons a way out of fishing. All our family had done for generations was run trawlers off the New England coast.

He stayed on as a trawler captain because he couldn't find a way to make better money than in fishing. Without the money, he figured, he couldn't keep his promise.

He put my older brother Joseph through college and business school.

After my first year in high school, he sent me to a summer program at a place called St. Regis Prep in New London, where I stayed for three weeks before being sent home.

I had a recipe for brewing beer from an old cookbook.

I made a mixture according to the instructions and hid the sealed bottles under some floorboards in my room.

A week later, in the middle of the night, the bottles exploded one after the other. They blew the floorboards up and sprayed ugly-smelling fermented yeast all over my bed and the walls and the ceiling.

People told me they could smell it in the dorm across the road.

I realized later that I'd known I would be caught. I knew if I didn't get caught making the alcohol, then I'd get caught drinking it. And I knew I'd be kicked out.

When I arrived home from St. Regis, my father sent me to work with a friend of his named Gunther.

Gunther ran a trap boat out of Newport. He had nets set down a couple of miles off shore from the Newport mansions. The nets were huge, complicated funnels that trapped whole schools of fish.

*

My father thought that by keeping me on the docks and on a fishing boat with the drunks and burnt-out people Gunther hired, I'd see what kind of life was waiting for me if I didn't follow his advice.

At first I did hate the job. If he'd waited a few days and then allowed me to quit, I would have.

But he kept me there too long for what he had in mind. By the end of that summer, I had learned to like the trap boats.

I got used to the smell of Gunther's dock. Fish. Diesel. Damp wood. Grease. The mustiness of chopped ice.

And I got used to the hours. Waking at four in the morning to catch an early bus to Newport and falling asleep to the sound of evening news downstairs.

Gunther took the first twenty people who showed up at his dock each day. We had to be there by six o'clock. The pay was forty dollars. Each of us had to get his name on the sheet of yellow paper Gunther pinned up, a thick red line twenty spaces down the page. After several months of work, a person could have his name put on the list of regulars, which would be written on the sheet before it was posted. All a regular had to do was arrive by six and write a check mark next to his name.

Some of the regulars lived in the hulk of a boat that Gunther had moored next to his dock. He always talked about fixing it up but never got around to the job. The regulars slept in the bunks, on burlap sacks and old sleeping bags. Each morning in the half-light, they crawled like rats from the hatches and port-holes, draped in their filthy clothes.

His work boat was named the *Baby Boy*. It left the dock at six-fifteen, towing four aluminum skiffs used for pulling up the trap nets.

The regulars sat with Gunther in the wheelhouse or huddled for warmth near the engine pipes in places they had claimed as theirs. Newcomers sat on the stern in shiny new rain gear — or no rain gear at all if they didn't know what they were doing.

Fishermen who worked at Gunther's were known by others on the docks as men who had no place else to go. They were men who had seen bad accidents or been in one and couldn't bear to be away from land for long, but who knew no other trade except fishing. Or they were like me and too young to go out on the trawlers.

By the time we reached the nets, the sun would already be up. Dazzling like smashed glass on the water. Hurting our eyes in the glare.

The skiffs paddled around to each corner of the trap and we hauled in the nets. We clawed our hands through weed-fuzzy twine until the fish were gathered in a small enough area that they could be scooped into the *Baby Boy*.

The net stank from fish that had tried to force their way out through the gaps, became stuck and died.

Rainbows of oil spread on the surface long before the fish began to show.

Then water frothed with mackerel. They barreled from one end of the net to the other, ramming the sides so hard that our skiffs dipped down with the force against the twine. Fat, purple electric rays paddled to the surface. Sharks beat their way through silver sheets of menhaden.

Gunther scooped his catch onto the *Baby Boy* with a thing like a huge butterfly net. Fish spilled over the deck until there was no room for a crewman to stand except waist-deep in the middle of them, feeling the twitch of hundreds of fish as they died in the pile.

Sometimes the net held more fish than the *Baby Boy* could hold, and Gunther had to set some loose.

I learned from the regulars to bring tin foil with me, along with a lemon and salt. We searched through the mass for any fish we wanted, filleted it with knives we all carried, then wrapped it in the foil with lemon and salt. We baked them on the engine pipes. The pipes were thick with grease from years of cooking.

At Gunther's dock, we unloaded the fish from his boat, boxed them in ice and were done by midday.

I worked next to a man called Kelley, shoveling ice. He stole any black bass he could find in our catch once the boat was on its way home, careful not to let Gunther see him.

Black bass were the most valuable fish Gunther ever pulled from his nets. Kelley stuffed them in a plastic bag and hid them in his overalls, then sold the fish later to a local restaurant.

He didn't pay any taxes. Instead, he collected his money in cash and hid it someplace on the dockyards in a Tupperware box. He said he couldn't even remember his social security number.

Kelley talked about the big money a person could earn on trawlers, making two- or three-week trips off-shore.

The trouble with working off-shore trawlers was that they wouldn't take a new crewman unless he had experience, and there was no way except on the trawlers for a new man to gain experience. Least of all from my father, who never let me set foot on his boat except when he wanted it cleaned.

I made up plans for having a boat of my own one day. I found ways around doing the dirty jobs that Gunther made the burn-outs do because they couldn't be trusted with anything else.

On the way out each morning at sunrise, I sat in the wheelhouse and made Gunther tell me how his trap nets worked, what sort of boat a person would need to pull nets, how big a crew a captain had to have. Gunther explained everything as he weaved his boat between the scattered lobster-pot buoys.

Years before, my brother Joseph and I bought a lobster pot and set it down on a thirty-foot length of rope a quarter mile off Narragansett Beach. In the evenings, we borrowed a rowboat from one of the beach clubs. It was used for rescuing people who had drifted out too far. If we found a lobster in the pot, we stuffed it in a big iron kettle and rowed back to shore. We cooked the lobsters on the beach, in salt water, on fires made from driftwood. We were careful to place the boat back exactly as we had found it, overturned in the dunes with the oars stored underneath. Joseph and I talked about running our own lobster boat someday.

Every summer through my high school years, I worked for Gunther. I became one of the regulars, and could have run the boat as well as Gunther.

My mother and father didn't stop me, but they made things difficult at home.

Summer became a time of slammed doors and sighing, with things not said and ugly lengths of silence at the table.

While my father was in port, he'd let me take a couple of hours' rest from Gunther's before driving me down to the Galilee docks and putting me to work on his boat. It was a ninety-five-foot, steel-hulled trawler named the *Glory B*. As long as I lived at home, he said, there would be chores to do.

Dad liked to keep his engines ticking over at the dock.

He gave me a bucket of water and told me to scrub out the engine room. He had me cleaning pipes that didn't need to be cleaned and scrubbing the floor, which had been scrubbed so many times the paint was worn off.

I'd climb down a steel ladder to the engine room and see him watching me from the deck. He wore baseball hats with foam padding on the front and plastic mesh at the back. He wore his hats until the mesh holes were completely clogged with engine grease and dirt.

On my knees scrubbing and scrubbing, the two vast Cat engines thundering in neutral on either side of me, I'd look up sometimes through trickles of sweat and see him at the top of the ladder.

When he saw me looking, he'd turn away.

Once I stood and yelled at him. "Why doesn't Joseph have to do this?"

His voice barely rose above the hammer of the engines. "Joseph has problems of his own."

I dropped back to my knees and kept scrubbing.

When I raised my head a few minutes later, he was still there. Just standing. Tall and thin and weathered.

Joseph had a plan to make a million.

The plan didn't work and he found himself heavily in debt. He lived at home to avoid paying rent on an apartment.

The plan came from a man he met in the restaurant of a hotel when he was in Massachusetts interviewing for the First Bank of Boston. This was in his last year at business school.

The restaurant had been doubling people up at tables because of crowds.

The man sat next to my brother. He said he was a dealer in solar panels, and told my brother about an idea to use little solar cells, like the ones you find in pocket calculators, to run an address file.

The file would hold phone numbers and addresses like any other, except this one would turn the cards automatically when you pressed a button, powered by a solar cell that could pick up its light from a desk lamp as well as the sun.

The man asked Joseph if he thought it would be a good idea. It was something he'd just thought up. Popped into his head only the night before. The man was dying for an opinion, he said. Would it work? Would anybody buy the thing?

Joseph told him maybe so.

The offer from First Boston didn't sound as good as this new idea to sell solar-paneled address files, so he turned them down.

When he got home he stole the idea, patented it and took out a big loan from the bank to begin production.

*

In the first weeks, while parts to the machine were being built, Joseph drove to different chain stores and tried to get them interested in buying. He hard-talked them the way he'd learned to hard-talk in business school. At home he read books about subliminal persuasion and martial arts books to get himself in the right frame of mind. He wouldn't leave the stores until they'd at least said maybe.

All through the autumn in my last year of high school, I watched his car pull in over fallen oak leaves in our driveway.

Each day it was the same.

The car would stop and for a while he'd stay at the wheel, staring at the lawnmower and old rakes at the back of the garage. His car looked dusty from being on the road.

Then Joseph would get out, set his briefcase on the hood and stretch, untucking his shirt with the movement.

He'd shut the car door with his foot, walk across the gravel driveway to the back door and disappear into the kitchen.

I watched this through the mosquito screen of my bedroom window.

I'd hear nothing for a bit and then the sound of the TV being switched on.

After that, I'd go back to lifting free weights at my bench, listening to the car click and mutter itself quiet in the garage and to Joseph in the kitchen telling my mother what he did all day.

The address file was mounted on a large box. This box contained the flat, purply solar panel screens.

The machine had to be directly in the light to work. When you pressed the On button, the file made a humming noise and the little pages flipped from A to Z. It had a red tab for marking the place where the file should start turning.

He contracted a local man to assemble the units and a company in Virginia made the parts. They arrived at our house in boxes of fifty, marked ROLOMATIC. FRAGILE!

It came in several colors, including camouflage, because Joseph thought he could get the Army interested.

After a few days of putting the Rolomatics together, the assembly man called Joseph and said he wanted more money.

So Joseph hard-talked him, too.

At home he started talking about Will to Power and the Ninja of the Nuclear Age.

Sometimes I'd wake up in the night and hear the humming of Rolomatics from down in our basement, where Joseph tested them with a heat lamp for keeping French fries warm. He didn't trust the man to assemble the units correctly, so he made spot checks. Sometimes he checked only ten. Sometimes three hundred.

Some of the local chain stores agreed to put the Rolomatic in their shops to see how it would make out, but told him he'd have to wait until spring before any appeared on their shelves. In the meantime, they wanted some promotional fliers made up.

We had eight thousand Rolomatics in the basement. They had a certain smell. New and sterile.

He set Mother to work making up slogans for the fliers, and paid an artist to draw the easy-to-follow instructions:

A woman's hand pushing the On button.

The face of a man with a big chin looking at the Rolomatic and smiling because he found what he was looking for in his file.

The Rolomatic on a neat desk top, along with a typewriter and telephone and a picture of someone's family.

Everything was black and white. Almost every sentence in the instructions had an exclamation mark at the end of it.

He decided on a slogan: "Rolomatic . . . Find Facts Fast!"

In the evenings when Joseph was home, he talked about the way he did his business.

No one could suggest a better way for doing something. No one could criticize.

Joseph stuck a message board on the basement door. It was

the kind you could write things on and wipe them off. At the top Joseph wrote "Suggestions." If we had anything to say, he told us, we should write it up there and he'd see to everything in due time.

Now suddenly everything he owned was precious and not to be touched.

It made me nervous to see how much he valued the things he set around himself. There wasn't anything I could use or borrow that he didn't see as abused or put back in the wrong place when I'd finished with it. Wasn't an argument I could have without him saying that he ran this house when Dad wasn't around, and if I didn't like that, I should think about moving on.

Joseph said he'd employ me when I graduated. My job would be to travel up and down the East Coast selling Rolomatics to big chain stores. I'd get a percentage. He'd show me the ropes.

He sold me two shares at twenty dollars apiece, sold some to my mother and father, then went down to the docks and sold some to my father's friends.

He rigged up an answering machine. When he made the recording, he asked my mother to type on her typewriter in the background to give it the feel of being a busy office.

Kids called up pretending to be Russians and Japanese and ordering six million camouflage Rolomatics.

When the chain stores displayed their spring inventory, they put the Rolomatics on their shelves. We waited for orders to come in.

Another address file arrived in the shops at the same time. It was called a Rolosomething as well. This machine was smaller and much simpler and had no solar cell.

Joseph said not even to give it a thought.

It turned out that the other Rolothing was marketed by the same man Joseph stole the idea from, only this man had abandoned his idea of solar panels and gone for something cheaper.

He called several times to say that Joseph was a thief and a bastard and that anyway the solar panel idea wouldn't work.

Joseph laughed an unnaturally long laugh and said we'd see about that soon enough.

Then he ran down to the basement and tested a thousand Rolomatics under his French fry lamp.

The Rolomatics sold well for about a week.

Then the chain stores began receiving complaints from people who said they had to hold the thing right up to a light to make it work. Sometimes file cards became stuck and the roller wouldn't turn. One business claimed the noise was offensive, like a poo-poo cushion being sat on. It was too big, they said, and sometimes it went off by itself.

Meanwhile, the other Rolothing sold so well it became almost a cult item. Anybody who was anybody had a Rolothing on his desk.

The chain stores took Joseph's Rolomatic off the shelves after a month.

We still had 7,500 units in the basement.

When the Rolomatics failed, my father bought back from his friends at the dock the shares Joseph had sold them. But he never told Joseph.

I found it out from someone at the East Bay Plant.

He had spent a long time listening to Joseph's plans, nodding slowly and quietly and continuously as Joseph mapped out the possibilities.

Now with the business gone under and Joseph in debt up to his skull my father began pulling me aside and telling me to walk with him after dinner.

"Alls I want from you is hard and honest work. No hocuspocus. No damn samurai self-help books like Joseph bought. Alls I ever think about when I'm out on the water is how proud I'm going to be of you one day. I'm giving you the raw materials and you shape them into a way of living that doesn't smell of fish and that keeps the family together. I wish my father'd have done this for me when I was young. Now, when you get a wife and kids, you can come home to them at the end of the day and still be making a living. Your mama and I don't have that. It's what we want for you. And when Joseph gets back on his feet, he'll have it too. I swear to God, I never did think those dinky Rolomatics would work. Between you and me."

I hated sitting down to dinner with my brother at the table.

The house began to smell very clean and disinfected. Nothing was ever out of place. Joseph wandered through the rooms arranging things in piles and categories. He stacked magazines exactly together and alphabetically in a basket by the sofa.

The Rolomatics in our basement seemed to me like insects, crawling over each other in the dark.

Once I found him in the laundry room, long after my mother and father had gone to bed. He was sitting on the dryer with a Rolomatic held up to a bare bulb that lit the room. He moved the blank cards back and forth, set the red selection tab and moved them some more.

"I fucked up," he said when he saw me. "I fucked up the American Dream."

From high school, I graduated to the University of Southern Massachusetts, where I stayed for one year before getting in a fight with another student.

I went up in front of the Executive Committee, and they kicked me out for the rest of the semester. Two months and the summer.

The fight started over a stolen camera.

I had taken up photography as soon as I arrived at college. Photography was the only class in which I received good marks. All my other grades went to hell because of photography.

At the end of the fall semester, my math report had said, "Don't give up!"

Under the grade on my physics final, the instructor wrote, "Absurd."

All my free afternoons I lived in the dingy developing room with another boy named Ronald Bartlett. He ran a portfolio business, for people on campus who were trying out as models. He did birthdays, weddings and fraternity parties. Bartlett had spent so many years in darkrooms that he even smelled like developer chemicals.

We worked in the soft glow of red lights. The room echoed with the sound of running taps and the rustle of paper in large plastic trays.

After a few weeks, tiny brown spots began to appear on my skin from the chemicals.

I photographed events for the school newspaper. Sports and charity drives and class reunions. For the first couple of months, I had to borrow a camera from a teacher. The director of photography let me work in the darkroom, mixing chemicals and helping people wind their film onto developing spools in the dark. I worked until I had enough to buy a decent camera, an old rangefinder Canon.

I'd go back to my dorm with a batch of prints and hang them on a clothesline strung across my room. Then I'd sit at my desk, staring at my other assignments until I had a stomachache. After that, I'd go out and take more pictures.

The film and developing paper were getting too expensive, even with my darkroom job, so I applied to a real estate company to take pictures of properties they had for sale. I handed over a portfolio of my best pictures. They said they were looking at a number of applications and would get back to me. A week later, they gave me the job.

The properties were never far from town. I took the bus or walked or borrowed cars and bicycles from friends.

I was in business two weeks before someone stole my camera.

No one had cameras to lend and I couldn't afford a new one. I phoned the real estate people and told them it would be a while before I could get hold of a new camera.

They said it was too bad and that they were giving the job to another student, named Bartlett.

Bartlett.

Now and then after the camera disappeared, Bartlett lent me developing paper while I rummaged through old negatives, trying to find photos to show in class. He used his own camera all the time and couldn't lend it to me.

When Bartlett was out working for the real estate company one day, I went to his locker to borrow some developing paper. The locker was closed with a padlock, but I knew the combination because he'd told me it had the same set of numbers as his birthday.

In the locker was the case for my camera. Not the camera. Only the case.

I walked into the empty developing room and sat on the floor, red lights all around. I weighed the case in my hands, feeling the leather texture printed on the black plastic.

Then I began walking to the place I knew Bartlett would be. He was taking pictures of a new block of condominiums at the other end of town. I walked, and after a while I started running.

By the time I reached the condominiums, I was sweating in streams down my face. I still held the case in the knot of my fist.

I found him winding a new roll of film in his camera. I stood sweating and breathing hard in front of him, holding out the case and not able to speak.

His eyes popped when he saw what I was carrying. "What were you doing in my locker?"

I tried to slow my breathing so I could talk. "Where's my camera?"

"How did you get into my locker?"

"Where the hell is my camera?"

"My locker and what's in it is my own business. I suggest you don't mention to anyone what you just did." He finished with the film and snapped the back of his camera shut. He had been crouching over the film to shade it from the sun. Now he stood.

"Give me back my camera." I threw the case in the mud, churned up by work boots and trucks. "Give me back my job."

"I don't have your camera. I'm busy. I have to go." He turned to leave.

I grabbed him by the arm and spun him around.

He stepped back. "Get your hands off me! Don't you lay a finger on me!"

Over his shoulder, I saw a workman on a half-built roof. He had stopped what he was doing and looked down on us.

"I'm going to ask you this one time, Bartlett. What did you do with my camera? Where is it now? And why the hell did you take it?"

"I found that case. I was going to give it back."

"When did you find it?"

"A couple of days ago." He sat on the hood of his car and put his foot on the bumper. He blinked fast and his mouth was twitching.

"You've seen me half a dozen times in the last couple of days, and all we talked about was my camera. You took it and you know it. How the hell could you do that? Did you want this job that badly?" My knees and my elbows were shaking.

"I applied for this job at the same time you did. It should have gone to me and you know it. I've been taking pictures years longer than you have."

"You have jobs all over campus."

"This is a real job."

"Why the hell did you steal my camera? Just tell me why you did it."

"Listen to me, Pfeiffer. You have nothing to go on. You have no proof."

"This is proof!" I picked my case out of the dirt and shook it in his face. "Right here!"

"All we have as proof, Pfeiffer, is that you broke into my locker. You took a job that you know should have gone to me. Now I have the job. Why don't you save up and buy a new camera?"

At first, I didn't remember hitting him. Suddenly he was just lying in the dirt, blinking up at the sky, with blood running slowly from his nose down the side of his face. My knuckles ached, as if they had been pulled apart and stuck back together the wrong way.

It wasn't for several seconds that I recalled my arm swinging out. I remembered how he had sat there for a moment without moving and I thought I didn't hit him hard enough. I hadn't ever hit anyone before. Now he's going to kill me, I thought. Then he slid off the hood and onto the ground.

I looked up and saw several workmen looking down at me. They muttered to each other.

"He stole my camera!" I shouted up to them.

Bartlett still lay on the ground. I picked him up and sat him back down on the hood. He fell off again. Blood from his nose had spread across his face and soaked his collar. He continued to blink straight in front of him.

I put him in the car and drove to the university clinic. While I sat in the waiting room, the campus police arrived.

They took me to their office and I sat opposite an officer who asked me to tell him the story, typing out what I said on a computer.

I tried to speak clearly. I tried to stay calm, sure that as soon as they found out the truth, they'd let me go and no more would be said. But in the back of my mind, I had a sense of things crumbling, of everything falling apart.

*

In the week leading up to the Executive Committee's inquiry, I became convinced nothing would happen to me once they found out what Bartlett had done.

On the day, I wore a jacket and tie and sat at the end of a table lined with professors.

The room was high-ceilinged and paneled with dark wood. Footsteps echoed in the hall outside. The place smelled of polish and old tobacco.

Bartlett wasn't there. I hadn't seen him all week.

"Now, James." The man at the head of the table was an English teacher named Mr. Mahoney. "You maintain that Ronald Bartlett stole your camera. Is that true?"

"Yes. He stole it." I fiddled with the top button of my shirt. It was cutting into my windpipe.

"Can you prove he stole it?" Mr. Mahoney asked all the questions. Six or seven other professors took notes, looking up now and then to see my face as I talked.

"I found the case for it in his locker."

"Ronald Bartlett says you're lying. He says there wasn't any case in his locker." Mr. Mahoney held up a typed statement from Bartlett.

"I found my camera case in his locker. That's what happened." I lifted my hands from where they rested flat on the shiny wood table. I looked at the sweat marks of my palms and finger tips on the polish.

"Now why would someone who presumably was your friend steal a camera from you?"

"I guess he was angry he didn't get the job. I don't know why he stole it." I wondered then if I had ever been friends with Bartlett, if it hadn't just been me trying to make friends with him all the time.

"Even if he did steal your camera, what makes you think you have the right to hit him? Why didn't you come to us?"

"That would be like running to my mother."

"What if you'd killed him, James?"

"Then he'd be dead, Mr. Mahoney."

None of this was going the way I thought it would.

"Mr. Pfeiffer, you are in a lot of trouble, and if you don't take us seriously, we will make you take us seriously."

"Isn't anybody going to talk about him stealing my camera?"

"If we were sure he did steal it, then we'd talk about it, James." Mr. Mahoney took the cuff links from his shirt and set them on the table in front of him.

I fixed my eyes on the little gold tablets joined by tiny gold chains. Then I looked at the committee, fanning my eyes across their faces.

I said I was telling the truth.

I waited in the hall while they decided what to do.

I stood with my hands in my pockets, acid-stomached and a feeling in my throat as if someone had his hands around my neck.

Then a member of the Executive Committee came out and told me I was being sent away for the remainder of the semester. He said I should consider myself lucky only to get that. Bartlett's parents had threatened to take me to civil court if I didn't get kicked out for a semester or expelled altogether.

I had twenty-four hours to be gone.

When I arrived home, I spent a week in my room. Mostly I lay on my bed and stared at the ceiling.

My parents didn't blame me for hitting Bartlett.

"But this could have been avoided!" my father said over and over until my mother told him to say something different for a change.

I caught him staring at me sometimes, a worried look on his

face. I knew he thought I'd got kicked out of college on purpose, the same as at St. Regis summer school.

At the end of that week, my father brought me to the East Bay Plant.

I started living in the ice room.

I started talking to the fish.

3

WHEN THE East Bay Plant closed down and Vic Vogel had run away to the Bahamas, I went back to working for Gunther in Newport.

"Where's Kelley?" I asked at the dock. "Doesn't Kelley work here anymore?"

They told me Gunther had caught him stealing fish and fired him.

Kelley was gone. A crewman on a trawler now. Working the deep-sea boats.

I thought of the trawlers as I rode out with Gunther each morning.

Kelley always said he'd work off-shore.

My father practically lived out there. The more I thought about it, the more angry I became. It didn't seem possible to me that he would return and keep returning to a job he said he hated.

I thought about rumors of strange things that happened out to sea. Rumors of killer whales suddenly surrounding a boat in places where killer whales had not been seen before. Rumors of old ships that whole crews saw with their eyes but that never showed on radar. Rumors of boats on which crews heard singing in the fog, but, again, nothing ever showed on radar.

It seemed to me that my father had found something so precious he couldn't bear to share it with his sons.

*

When the *Glory B* next left port and I knew there would be no chores for me at home, I started walking after work to a fish-house named Sabatini's on Severn Street. The trawlers tied up there. It was only a short walk from Gunther's.

I asked anyone I could find if there was a place for me on a boat. I was honest. Told them I had no experience.

The trawlermen weren't rude to me. They said to come back tomorrow.

When I came back the next day, either they had left the dock to make another trip or they told me again to come back tomorrow.

Soon nothing else mattered except finding a job on a trawler. I had no idea what my parents would do to me if I went out to sea. I wasn't thinking about it.

The next time I walked on the dock, I told the trawlermen I knew how to fish, careful only to ask at boats I hadn't checked with before.

I lied all the time for days.

The only boat that would take me was a wooden-hulled scalloper named the *Ocean Horse*. It was run by three Portuguese men.

The woodwork had been scraped into garbage and never re-painted or refinished. The steel rigging was corroded. Brown bubbles of rust showed through the oily black paint.

The boat had only one scallop dredge, a triangular piece of metal maybe sixteen feet long with a chain bag attached to the end for gathering scallops. Most scallopers carried two dredges.

The captain and two other men were splicing the dredge cable when I walked on and asked for work.

The captain told me to splice the cable for a while and he'd think about it.

I started to splice and an hour later, when the crew took their lunch break, I was still splicing.

The men came back three hours later, checked the cable and

said it looked all right. Then they told me they didn't really need a crewman and burst out laughing.

I told them if they didn't give me a job after all this work, I'd unsplice every damn piece of cable I'd worked on while they were gone. And I tried to look out of my head, hoping they'd think I was nuts enough to do it.

I stood looking down at my boots, hands cramped into fists, while their laughter sounded across the dock.

Then the captain told me to be on the boat at ten o'clock that evening because they were leaving on the night tide.

I was walking away from the dock when a man drove up on a motorcycle. He asked if I'd just signed on to work for the Portuguese.

"I'll tell you." He cut the engine on his machine and scratched at the blond tufts of hair under his armpits. He wore Buddy Holly glasses with thick lenses. After he'd gone, the only thing about his face I could remember were the glasses. "You don't want to work for them."

"I want to work for anybody. If you can get me a job on another boat, I'll take it."

"Well, maybe I can't do that, but I'm telling you, no one wants to work on that boat because they lost a man overboard two weeks ago and didn't even try to save him. That's just the way the fucking Portagees are. See the way they was laughing at you? That's the way they was laughing when the man went overboard."

"Where's the man now?"

"Hell. I don't know. Floating around off Martha's Vineyard, I guess. If he floated. They can't get anyone to work for them, and there's good reason for it. Just don't go. Work at a burger place. Work for Sabatini."

I walked to Gunther's in the rain. I asked him for some time off.

"How come?" He sat in his office, gnawing on a sandwich. The floor was ankle-deep with old receipts.

"I found myself a job on a trawler."

He nodded, chewing. "And you want me to give you back your job if it doesn't work out. Is that it?"

"Yes, sir."

"Did you lie to the crew?"

"Yes, sir."

"I lied too, my first time on a trawler." He grinned. "I wasn't much older than you."

"So you'd take me on again?"

"Six A.M. on the dock. Same as always."

"Thank you, Gunther."

He went back to eating his sandwich.

Only my brother Joseph was home when I called.

I asked him to tell Mom and Dad I'd be home in a week.

"How come you want to make trouble?" He talked over the sound of television in the background.

"I was offered a job and I'm taking it."

"You're making trouble, James."

"Will you tell them for me? I just want to see for myself. Dad can't grudge me that."

"He can and he will."

I stood with my head tucked under the tiny roof of the phone stand, shielding myself from the drizzle.

"Please deposit fifty cents."

"I have to go, Joseph. I'll see you in a week."

"All right. Pray for mercy when you get home."

"You pray for me too."

Fog on water in the night.

I watched squid jetting up from under the dock and into the glare of dock lights, then jetting down again.

No one showed up at ten. Not by midnight either.

I'd bought new rubber boots from the army-navy store, and

had my waterproofs from working at Gunther's that morning. But I had no clean clothes or a hairbrush or a toothbrush.

Sitting on a crate next to the boat, I peeled strips of wood from the rotten bow. I made up my mind that if no one showed by two, then it would mean they were playing another joke on me. I promised myself I'd break all their windows, snap off their radar mast and do any other damage that came to mind before I ran away and never came to the docks again.

The thought of going home without the job made me miserable.

I was asleep on my face on a pile of old fishnet when someone set his boot on the back of my head and pressed down. I couldn't move.

"I don't have any money." I said each word slowly and clearly.

The Portuguese captain took his boot off my head and rolled me over with his toes.

I helped carry groceries onto the boat. Potato sacks filled with sweet bread rolls. Cans of fava beans and iced tea. Spaghetti sauce. Liverwurst.

The captain picked up the bundle of my waterproof gear and threw it in a bunk underneath his. He told me his name was Tony. The engineer was also named Tony. The third Portuguese crewman didn't tell me his name. He only told me he was tough and I should watch it. He was short, with arms too long for his body and a chin like a brick with a thin strip of skin stretched over the edges.

The last I saw of Newport was a cluster of lights on the horizon, falling in twos and threes into black water. Five minutes later, I could no longer remember the direction back to land.

Captain Tony pulled me by the elbow out of my bunk at four in the morning and said it was time to work.

I choked on his breath.

I didn't find out until after I made it back to port exactly how the dead man died. They had me doing the same thing that killed him.

In order that our dredge wouldn't come up too fast from the water and crack a hole in our boat's flimsy wooden hull, I stood at the stern and shouted when the cable had almost wound in. Bands of colored tape were tied on the metal cord at ten-fathom intervals. I gripped a cleat screwed into the rim of the boat and leaned over the side, calling out markings as they came from the water.

The man who did my job before me had tried to lean over the side without holding the cleat.

It was stormy. He slipped and fell in, floundered in his heavy waterproof gear. The man's boots filled with water, and by the time the Portuguese turned their boat around, he had disappeared.

I hung on to the cleat and watched the heavy vein of cable twist out of the sea. The waves boiled black beneath me in the darkness before dawn.

When the dredge came over the side, I moved across the deck, gathering any fish that had been brought up along with the scallops. Yellowtail. Fluke. Dabs.

I washed the fish by throwing them in a wire basket, spraying the slime off them with a deck hose and stirring their bodies around with my boot.

Then I climbed down into the ice room. It was a space below the deck partitioned off with stalls, as if it had been designed for horses.

I used a pick to hack ice and make a bed of it in one of the stalls. I spread the fish on the bed, covered them with more ice and did the same with the scallops, which the Portuguese bagged on deck in cream-colored sacks.

I waited for Captain Tony to inspect my work before climbing back out to the warm air and the light.

There was no talk. None of the men spoke with me except when they had to. I found myself talking to the dredge or to fish, insulting the boat as I hung from my cleat, watching for the cable's fathom markers.

At night, while the two Tonys slept, I kept watch with the third crewman. He still hadn't told me his name. He only let me know again how tough he was.

After twenty minutes on watch, Tough slapped me on the back and went to bed.

I watched him for a minute, trying to figure out if he should be staying awake with me or whether he had the right to go to sleep.

I waited to catch his eye, but he didn't look my way. He smoked a cigarette and ate some olives, staring by the light of his cigarette at pictures of naked women taped on the ceiling of his bunk with Band-Aids.

Everything around me was reduced to solid black beyond the wheelhouse window, which exploded into silver and white whenever waves crossed our bow.

Captain Tony had given me a compass bearing to keep, but I couldn't hold it.

I got seasick about once every half hour until there was nothing left to throw up. But I still hung over the side, fingers dug into the wood for grip, gagging bile into the waves.

Nothing I tried would keep the boat on course. We bucked in circles all night until the captain woke to take my place, shoved me across the wheelhouse for not holding our bearing, then let me go to bed.

I woke when the captain climbed into his bunk above me after his turn on watch.

In the first gray smudges of light through the portholes, I saw the bunkboards sag down over me with the captain's weight.

If they broke, the man would kill me when he fell. I was sure about that.

At mealtime, we ate olives and sweet bread and fish boiled in salty water. The engineer named Tony also worked as the cook. He poked me in the chest every couple of minutes to ask me if I liked the food.

I nodded and smiled and threw up off the bow while they played cards at the galley table.

After dinner, we'd go back to work. Often the wind blew hard and broke waves across the deck. Spray gusted in and soaked us.

Captain Tony had built two shelters out of plywood. He set them around the scallop pens, metal tubs where we cut the meat out of the shellfish.

One of the shelters fell off while we were still in the harbor. The other channeled rain down my back and Tough's back until he couldn't stand it anymore and shoved the whole contraption overboard.

Waves sometimes washed us across the deck. In the daytime, at least, I could see them coming, but at night the only warning was a gasp as our hull left the water before a blast of water smacked us off our feet.

Sometimes Captain Tony stood at the wheelhouse door, making fun of Tough because he had nothing better to do and because Tough couldn't ignore it.

After a while, Tough would throw down his scallop knife and tell me he was going to kick the captain's ass. He stamped away into the wheelhouse and shut the door.

Captain Tony would turn on the intercom without Tough having noticed, and I'd stand with the engineer, hearing Tough shout. But not kicking ass. "Leave me alone!" he'd be saying. "For God's sake, leave me alone!"

*

On the third day, sometime in the night, our running lights went out.

I had stopped being sick by then and found myself more hungry than I'd ever been before. I hid whole jars of olives under my mattress and ate them at night, flipping pits out the porthole.

Captain Tony climbed down into the engine room. The engineer followed.

I sat with Tough, playing dominoes by the red light of a storm lantern.

At dawn, the engine failed.

The sound of waves became suddenly loud, each thud on our bow like the blow from an ax.

The two men climbed up from the engine room and sat next to me at the table. Captain Tony said our engine would be fine if the damn engineer didn't keep pissing in the bilge.

He did do that. I saw him.

Engineer Tony said it didn't have a damn thing to do with him and told the captain the whole boat ought to be scrapped and used for firewood.

I agreed with him too.

Captain Tony shoved me and Tough off the table, sending our dominoes rattling across the galley. Then he leaned forward to where the engineer was sitting and punched him in the head.

Engineer Tony touched his nose, saw blood on the tips of his fingers, then reached down fast for something under the table.

I was backed up against the wheelhouse door with Tough. I held on to his arm and he held on to mine. Here we go, I was thinking. Here we fucking go.

Captain Tony saw that the engineer was probably going for a knife. So he took a Phillips screwdriver from a shelf next to the window and nailed the engineer's hand to the table.

Now Tough and I were behind the wheelhouse door and staring through the plastic window from the other side.

The engineer only gasped when the spike of the screwdriver came down. After a couple of seconds, he unstuck the screwdriver, held his hand to his chest and walked slowly over to the storage cabinets looking for a bandage.

The captain picked at his nails for a while, muttering to himself. Then he apologized and helped dress the wound. He talked while he wrapped the clean white strip across the engineer's palm and over the web of his thumb. Blood soaked through each layer, struggling to reach the surface.

The engineer nodded as Captain Tony spoke. When the hand was bound, he lay on his bunk with his back to us.

I watched all this in the light of the storm lantern and the glow of sunrise through the clouds.

Captain Tony gave me the job of calling the Coast Guard, since he didn't think they'd understand the way he spoke.

I stood at the wheel, trying to keep our bow into the wind, and called into the microphone that we were Fishing Vessel *Ocean Horse* and required assistance.

The others crawled around on their hands and knees looking for the dominoes.

For three hours, no one answered. Once we did reach the Coast Guard, it was another five hours before we saw the little speedboat they sent to tow us in. It was white with blue and orange stripes across the front.

It rained and the sea picked up.

Several times, I walked to the engine room door and peered down at our huge, beetle-shaped engine to see if it was on fire or if the hull was leaking. The sound of waves breaking on timbers seemed to me more than the boat could take.

The Coast Guard towed us with a nylon rope. Heavy and white, it chafed a groove in the *Ocean Horse*'s bow.

The three people on the Coast Guard boat wore blue uniforms and signal-orange life jackets. They moved across their deck like hunchbacks.

Captain Tony walked into the wheelhouse, where I stood at the wheel, and shut the door. He sat down in the wheelman's chair, the foam stuffing held in with strips of silver duct tape. For a while he said nothing. Then he leaned over to me, until I could smell how close he was. "You're a liar." He sat back and rubbed his hands together.

I stayed looking straight ahead, holding the wheel, concentrating on the white towing cord. It sagged down into the waves, then snapped taut and sprayed water across our windows.

I'd been thinking he might not have noticed that I had no experience. Or if he had, he would forgive me because I worked hard. But now, with him calling me a liar, I knew it was just something he'd been saving to stick me with when the time came.

He slouched in his chair and nudged my back with the toe of his rubber boot. "You told me you could fish. Alls you are is a liar."

"I worked hard for you. You know it was the only way I could get a job. You know that. I worked as hard as anybody else on this boat."

"I'm going to pay you what you're worth." Then he made a zero sign with his thumb and index finger.

I smiled at him. I smiled, and a couple of seconds later I laughed and turned back to face the wheel, concentrating again on the pale strip of the tow cable. It felt as if little hands were squeezing at my ribs and my lungs and my heart. I closed my eyes and held on to the greasy wheel and tried not to fall apart.

As we passed the Brenton Reef Light, the storm became a yellow stain in the clouds.

Wind gusted out of the north, tipping waves onto our deck, and then suddenly quit, leaving us cold in an ugly calm before the next gust.

The Coast Guard captain, a short man with a blond crew cut,

said there was a hurricane coming. He told us he wanted to lash his boat against the side of ours so he could guide us to the dock.

We looked around for material to use as buffers, but found nothing that would work.

The Coast Guard crew shook their heads and said shit, they had just finished repainting their boat.

I watched shavings of new paint scraped off their bow by the tattered hull of the *Ocean Horse*.

I suddenly wanted to jump overboard, swim to shore, walk up on the beach and go home. Only to be on land. To get home and be safe.

Rain made the harbor like stucco.

The place was jammed with boats seeking shelter from the storm. People in rain gear sat on their yachts. I could make out steam rising from their cups of coffee.

Tough and I stood on the bow with the wrist-thick mooring ropes, waiting as the dock pilings came close.

Sabatini said he was doing us a favor keeping his dock open late so we could unload our fish and scallops.

It took only ten minutes to unload the whole catch. The dockboys were laughing about it.

I stood with them at the end of a conveyor belt, sorting the yellowtail and fluke as they slid, clumped in ice, along a tray toward the weighing scale.

Captain Tony stood by the scales, making sure the dockboys didn't cheat on the weights. And even with him standing there, I saw a fishhouse boy set his thumb under the weighing plate.

It didn't bother me that they ripped off Captain Tony.

"How's it going?" I asked the fishhouse boys. "What happened while I was gone?"

Bright clusters of people moved in the streets. They crowded under umbrellas, wearing khaki and green or blue as if it were part of a uniform.

Men stood under awnings at a bar on the dock next to Sabatini's, one hand holding a drink and the other shoved into a pocket, pelvises jutting out for balance.

Women in loose dresses with pretty, wet hair sat at the bar tables. Sometimes they reached their arms out into rain water that trickled down from the awnings.

Waitresses weaved between them, black skirts on their hips. The skirts were so tight, I knew they had to lie on their stomachs just to do up the zip.

I watched them from under the big hood of my rain slicker and licked at the fuzz on my teeth.

Captain Tony and Sabatini settled up in Sabatini's office.

When Tony came back to the boat, he smelled of vodka and cigars.

He walked straight over to where I sat, on a pile of old fishing net, no longer bothered to stay out of the rain. He handed me a fifty-dollar bill and told me to fuck off forever.

"You remember what I told you?"

I folded the new bill and pressed it between my hands as if I were praying. I nodded.

"I asked if you remember what I said about you lying to me."

"I remember."

"So you know I'm being generous now, don't you?"

I looked up and squinted at his face. "Are you done?"

"You're the one who's done. You better find another job."

I looked around for the engineer or Tough. Someone to put a word in for me. But the engineer had gone to the police station to press assault charges against the captain. He walked off the dock with his hand held out, as if it no longer belonged to him and was only a piece of evidence.

And I knew Tough would be lying in his bunk, where he lived even when the boat was in port. He'd be looking at the porno pictures taped on the ceiling, eating black olives from a jar.

*

I took a bus home, over the Newport and Jamestown bridges, to Narragansett.

Old ladies crowded the front seats. I knew all of them by sight. They came to Newport in the mornings and stayed all day, rummaging for bargains in second-hand shops. Then they sat around at the Newport Creamery, gumming the plastic spoons that came with their coffee until it was time to go home again.

Captain Tony's only a poor old fisherman, I was thinking. A poor man working on a shitty boat with a half-ass crew, who probably takes no pleasure in being cruel. He didn't mean what he said, I told myself, the fifty-dollar bill crushed in my fist. He didn't really pay you what you're worth.

"Sit down." My mother pointed to a chair in the living room.

I sat.

"Do you know what happened while you were gone?"

"What happened where?"

"Out on the ocean. While you were gone." She stood with her hands folded on her head like a person who's just been arrested. Her lips were pressed tight together. She wetted them with a swipe of her tongue as she spoke.

My father stood next to her. He smelled of gasoline.

They had been fighting earlier. Arguing about what they would say to me.

I saw them at the bottom of the garden, through my bedroom window. They sat in the white metal yard furniture, too far away for me to hear what they were saying. Father set his palm down on the table to make a point. Then Mother turned away with one hand on her chin, showing that she disagreed. Father stood up and set his hands on his hips. He leaned over her and barked, keeping Mother in her seat because she had no room to stand. Then he held up his hands to show they shouldn't argue anymore. He stepped back and she got to her feet. They walked across the dry grass to the back door.

I lay on my bed and stared at the ceiling, in the last few seconds before the call. I knew it would be my mother and not my father. Knew the pitch her voice would have, starting off low but rising. Knew the way the word "James" would break from her throat.

"No. I don't know what happened while I was gone." I put my hands between my legs and pressed them together with my knees.

"Tell him, Russell." She sat down on the couch and stared at me.

My father scratched at his face for a moment as if he couldn't remember. Then he heaved it all out in a couple of breaths. "We read in the papers about some boy the same age as you who went to Yale. He flew out to Alaska to find a job on a boat. Only one he could get a spot on was some junk trawler made around nineteen twenty." He sat down next to my mother. It seemed he couldn't make up his mind whether to be angry or not. "Boat goes out and two weeks later this boy's body washes up in some cove. The only way they could identify him was from a letter to his girlfriend he had in his back pocket."

"Where's the rest of the boat?" I wanted to be someplace that didn't belong to them. Someplace where I didn't feel they grudged me my bed. My jeans were stiff with fish scales and grease.

"Gone. Whole boat vanished." My father took off his baseball cap and set it on his knee.

"Just like your grandfather's boat!" Mother slapped the arm of the sofa. "That boy could have been you! You could have asked us, at least! You could have asked your father for some advice. He knows what he's doing, you know."

And so do you, I thought. He's not as mad as you want him to be, so you're putting words in my mouth to make him pissed off.

"Boat you went out on is a wreck, James. I heard it broke

down three days out of port. Am I right?" Father raised his eyebrows. "Am I?"

"Yes, sir. It broke down."

"Boat you went out on just lost a crewman. Is that right?"

"I took his place." I could see it coming. The methodical buildup of questions. I saw it a mile off.

"They probably didn't pay you jack-shit either. Am I right?"

"Fifty dollars."

"Little fool." My mother slumped back in the chair. "You must think your father's some kind of idiot with his good advice."

"Let him speak for himself, Erika."

"I am. He is speaking for himself." She folded her arms.

"He hasn't called me a fool."

"He may as well have." She nodded at me.

I sat back and sighed loud enough for them to hear.

"Well." Mother stalked off to the kitchen and came back with a chair from the breakfast table. She sat on it, hooking her skirt under her. "Well, at least we're all agreed that James's trip was not a success."

My father laughed. "You could have made fifty dollars flipping burgers."

"I know it. They ripped me off." I pressed the blood from my hands with my knees.

My mother pointed at my father. "I don't think it's anything to laugh about."

He ignored her and kept looking at me. "You should have known they would rip you off."

"I didn't know anything! That's why I went on the boat. I heard a lot from you, from both of you, but it was mostly the same thing over and over again. I took that job because I wanted to work off-shore, and even after all your talk I still didn't know how it would be." I felt myself seal up. A sense of airtight hatches closing and their locks clunking shut. And I seemed then to be sitting in a tiny room far away inside myself, away from anything that could happen. How much can they hurt you? I said to myself in the little faraway room. What damage can they do?

My father took his hat off and whipped it at the floor. "Have you any idea what I've been trying to accomplish these last ten years?" Then he stepped forward and screamed. "Have you?" He stood over me.

I looked at the dirty socks on my feet.

"Do you have any goddamn idea why I still go out fishing and give all my damn money to schools and let the people on the dock make fun of me and why I wade through those parents on Parents' Day who think I'm the janitor come to wipe up their spilled drinks? Any clues? Look up! Stand up!"

I stood and looked at his forehead. I didn't want to see his eyes. Joseph taught me the trick. A person who's bellowing at you face to face is trying to beat you down with his eyes, but you don't look at him and he can't make you. That way you can keep from falling apart the way he wants you to.

"I'm asking if you know why I still do all that. Do you think I like it? I'm asking you if you think I like it, James."

"How can I know?"

"You'll know because I'll tell you. I hate it. Ever since I floated around like a dead man off Martha's Vineyard waiting for a boat to pick me up I've hated it. I'm doing it so you won't have to. So you can have a halfways decent life making decent money. Now" — he pointed at Mother without looking at her — "we have made a life for ourselves. But we see where it falls short. We're making it so your life and Joseph's life doesn't fall short. Do you understand what I'm saying to you?"

"Understand."

"Good. I got nothing more to say. If you want to go out and drown yourself, go do it at the beach so's we can get to the body before the fish do. So's we'll have something to bury. Am I still understood?"

"Yes, sir."

Mother held my shoulder and guided me down into my seat again. "We only want for you to be able to spend time with your family when you have one," she said. "To come home at the end of the day. That's what a family is. A family is coming home at the end of the day. And a family is not having to worry if a storm blows down from Canada. Please try and understand. Your father and I decided a long time ago that we would change the way our family was living. You know what happened to my father. Don't you see how that frightens us when we think of you out working on a boat? Why did you go out?" Her eyebrows were crooked with worry.

I felt sweat across my ribs and between my toes. My mouth tasted like steel wool. "If you were so worried about me working on a boat, why did you make me go out with Gunther in the first place?"

Father's face still twitched with disgust, but he had spent it now. Only the nerves still carried jolts of anger through his skin. "I sent you to work with Gunther because I knew he wouldn't go out if it was stormy. His equipment is good. I know that Gunther only works close in to the beaches. That's a big difference from forty miles out to sea. All the difference in the world. It's why we let you keep working for him. Can you honestly tell me you'd sooner work on a dock for the rest of your life instead of being a lawyer?"

Mother squeezed my knee. "A lawyer," she whispered and smiled, opening her eyes wide. "What kind of a life does Gunther have to give you? You know the kind of people who work for him. Lowlifes. Burnouts." She messed up my hair and said in a kind voice, "We won't let you end up like them."

"I wanted to see for myself. I can choose."

"You can." Father nodded, chewing the inside of his mouth. "But if you choose to be a fisherman for the rest of your life, you can do it without my help. You start from scratch." He

walked into the kitchen and fed some bones to the garbage disposal.

"Case closed." Mother nodded, smiling and searching for my eyes.

"I'll work for Gunther until I go back to school. He'll give me my old job again. I'll start tomorrow." I could feel myself falling asleep. The clammy touch of sweat drying on my stomach and back. Sound reaching me as if through a long pipe. Words making sense seconds after they were spoken.

Mother smoothed back my hair. "Take some time off instead. Take a little rest."

"A rest would be nice."

"I'll call Gunther in the morning, then. Tell him you quit." Father yelled over the sound of splintering bones.

"I'm taking a rest. Don't tell him I quit."

"Sounds like you're quitting to me." He stopped the disposal and turned on the tap. He held his head under the bolt of water.

My mother pressed on my knees and got to her feet. "It's just a word."

"Don't tell him I quit."

My father blinked at me. Water coursed down his cheeks and bare chest. "Gunther will know."

"Then I'll start work again tomorrow."

My father shrugged.

"For Christ's sake! Will the two of you ever let up?" My mother raked her fingers down her face.

The next day, Joseph drove home early from work to have a word with me.

He wore his blue plaid suit and yellow tie.

At twenty-six, he was already starting to lose his hair.

Sometimes strangers came up to him in bars and said he looked like a used-car dealer, and they were right. For a year now, he'd been a test-drive salesman at a car dealership in Providence. Most of what he earned went toward paying off his debts.

We walked down to Narragansett Beach and sat on the breakwater.

I hadn't cried at all since being kicked out of school, but now, at the time when I wanted most not to cry, I did.

I put my face in my hands. My breathing shuddered out of me in quiet gasps.

"Take it easy." He slapped my shoulder and looked off down the beach. "Dad told me to give you a lecture while he figures out what to do next, but I figure you don't need that."

"I don't." I could barely speak.

"I suppose you'll just spend the rest of this summer working for Gunther and then go back to school in the fall. Right?"

"I guess."

"What do you mean 'I guess'?"

"I have bad grades. I'm almost on academic probation already. My last physics exam said 'Absurd.' "

"I had bad grades. I just didn't punch anybody out. Couldn't you have brought him down from behind? That way he wouldn't have seen who you were. I bet everybody in that Executive Committee room was thinking that. This way you'd have saved everyone the trouble of kicking you out."

"I didn't think about it at the time. And even if I had, I wouldn't have done it that way."

"Look, I'm working on getting my own dealership now. In a couple of years I'll have one. Then when you get out of school, if you want, you can come work for me. Just keep that in the back of your mind. No more of this going out and getting screwed by a bunch of Portagees."

"I want my own boat. To do that, I have to work on one first."

"You already did on that Portagee boat. Considering how that went, why are you still thinking about it?"

"This time I'll find a decent ship with a decent crew. Remember when we used to talk about running our own boat?"

"A long time ago."

"I still want to. I'm going to try, at least."

"Just work for Gunther, will you? Don't make a fuss."

"I will until I can get back out on a trawler."

"That's your business. That's betwen you and Dad and God." He took a foil packet from his pocket and handed it to me. "Here."

The packet contained a moist towelette. I carefully unfolded it and wiped my face, smelling perfume.

Joseph rolled up his sleeves. "There's plenty of ways to make a decent living that you're not even thinking about."

"I'm not just thinking about the money."

"I'll ignore that. Listen." He pressed his hands together. "Tell Dad I gave you a hard time about going on the Portagee boat. And next time" — he took off his suit jacket and scratched at the sweat stains on his chest — "next time, don't let them push you around."

4

IT WAS EARLY in the morning.

I opened the front door and breathed in the cool air.

"I know where you're going." Mother sat at the kitchen table. She held a steaming mug of coffee.

I turned to face her. "I'm leaving for Gunther's."

"You're going to look for work on another trawler. I know you are."

"How do you know?" I thought of Joseph, still asleep in his bed upstairs. I wanted to go up and tip him onto the floor.

"Is that where you're going? Tell me the truth." She sipped at her coffee. It looked as if her hands were smoldering.

"It is where I'm going. Yes. How did you know?"

"Your father said you would." She tapped a saccharin pill out of a blue box into her drink and then stirred it with her finger.

I put down my backpack. "I want my own boat. It's what I've always wanted. I need the experience. I need to know how things work out there. How things really work on a well-run boat." I opened my mouth to say more and she cut me off, holding up her hand for me to be quiet.

"I know your reasons already, James. At one point or another, I've heard them all from your father. I just want you to remember what we told you. Before you go out there again, think of the cost."

"What cost?"

"The cost of your family and maybe the cost of your life. What more costs do I have to tell you about? I've already said what I have to say. Maybe if your father was here and not out to sea, he might have something else to tell you, but I don't."

I swung the door slowly back and forth, hearing the hinges creak. "When did Dad tell you he thought I'd go out again?"

"Same day you came back from that first trip. He said you'd probably have to go see for yourself and you'd probably get yourself killed and that he would at least be able to fall asleep with a clear conscience at night, knowing that he did his best. But what I want to know" — she blinked through the steam from her coffee — "what I want to know is where does that leave me?" She looked down at the table, then picked at one of the buttons on her night dress.

With that movement, I knew she was going to cry.

She raised her head. "If you weren't so selfish, you'd see we only want the best for you. We thought this out when you were still pissing in your pants, young man. If you were more like Joseph, you wouldn't be so selfish."

"Joseph is the best reason I have for going out."

"When your father said he wouldn't help you, he meant it. I want you to know that. I'll hold him to it." Her face was dirty with tears.

Hot day coming.

Only the coffee shops were open on Severn Street.

Shop owners swept the pavement in front of their stores. They sprayed water on the windows with green hoses and wrote new lists on menu boards.

I walked in the road on the fat cobblestones.

Jib lines of sailboats rattled against their masts in the harbor.

I carried my fishing gear, oilers, boots and knife in a bundle tied with orange twine, in case someone offered me a job right away.

*

Sabatini had his barrels up early. Two fifty-gallon drums linked by a chain and a sign hanging from the middle that said "No Parking. Violators Will Be Toad." If he didn't set the barrels out, tourists took all his parking space. Some slotted their cars in next to the loading ramp so his refrigeration trucks couldn't pull up.

People at Gunther's said that Sabatini sometimes fired all his dockboys in a single breath if one of them forgot the barrels. We used to watch Sabatini stamping across his dock, waving his arms up and down like a man trying to save himself from drowning.

Kelley once told me that Sabatini ate Alka-Seltzer tablets. He ate them without dissolving the tablets in water and his cheeks puffed up with the foam.

A woman with a food truck had parked on the loading ramp. She moved from one dock to the other, up and down Severn Street all day selling coffee and doughnuts.

A line of dockboys and trawlermen stood next to the truck. The dockboys wore aprons and rubber sleeve protectors. The fishermen wore rusty jeans and leather vests. Some had long hair tied in a ponytail. Their arms were maps of tattoos.

When the dockboys had what they wanted, they walked back into Sabatini's fishhouse and turned on the radio, which played through loudspeakers bolted on girders in the roof, same as at Gunther's. It made you deaf if you stayed in the fishhouse all day. When they turned the radio off at night, the speakers still hissed like a seashell held against your ear.

The trawlermen went back to their spot on the edge of the wharf, legs dangling down over the harbor. They were waiting for their captains to arrive, so they could get to the work of repairing scallop dredges or twining ripped nets before heading out to sea again.

I walked through the fishhouse, floor toe-deep in water from melted ice and hoses. Barrels of fish swung on ropes up from the decks of trawlers to the sorting tables and scales. Dockboys punched the slimy ice down through gratings on the tables and threw away fish too small or gone rotten.

One dockboy told me a scallop dragger called *Gray Ghost* was looking for a crewman.

The boat was maybe a hundred feet long, painted white with a dark gray stripe running the length of its hull.

Nobody on board. Engine off.

I sat on a pile of old fishnet, waiting to see if anyone would show and thinking about what my mother had said when I left the house that morning.

I wondered if things were ruined at home. A heaviness rested in my guts. I wondered if my father would refuse to pay for any more school if I decided to go back. I wondered what they said when I was gone.

Light broke off the water and stabbed at my eyes. It flickered up between the boards of Sabatini's dock.

I took a pocket whetstone from my bundle of clothes and spat on it. I began to sharpen the blade of my fish knife.

Kelley had said that sometimes a captain would ask to see a new man's fish knife, and if it was blunt, he'd know the man didn't take care of his gear and wouldn't give him the job.

Carefully I moved the blade along the whetstone, then turned the handle and sharpened the other side. A bright sliver of sharpness appeared on the edge. I wiped the gray paste of stone grit onto my jeans.

By ten o'clock, it looked as if the whole crew had arrived.

I didn't raise my head as they walked past me. I pretended to mind my own business and hunted for something in my pack, but really I was counting them. I strained my eyes to watch their work boots thumping across the dock and jumping down onto the rusted deck of the *Gray Ghost*.

The captain stood on the bow eating a hamburger for breakfast. His crew replaced the scallop dredges' bags by joining iron rings together with links. They used a big clamp for squeezing the links shut. Already they were sweating, and their shirts lay draped over loose cables that hung above the deck.

Now and then one of them walked to a space at the stern, a U-shaped cut in the back of the boat, and pissed into the bay. The space was there on most large trawlers, used to drag the net through when a boat was rigged for fishing instead of scalloping.

I hadn't moved from my place on the dock, because I needed to see why they had a full crew now. The dockboy told me they were running a man short. I waited for the best time to approach the captain, when instinct said to move in.

If a new man without experience had found the captain last night up at Mary's bar and asked for work, then I'd still have a chance of getting a job if the new man didn't pull his weight.

But if it was one of the captain's old friends, or a friend of a crewman who knew his business, then I'd only be making a fool of myself by asking for work.

I'd have to take the bus home again, eyes to the floor and with no strength left in me. It would be just like all the other times I'd come home from Sabatini's with no job. When that happened, it took all the will I had left just to hold the hand grip above the seat in front, as if even a gust of air would blow me out the window.

In the days when Joseph had his Rolomatic suggestion board on the basement door, he used to talk about a rule of his, that it didn't matter what you did as long as you got what you wanted and kept it. He drove to the chain stores each day with that in his head. Going to war in his VW bug.

I had left myself no choice but to think the same way. I refused to sit in my room again with a blanket over my head, trying to make myself empty, to turn off the energy I had stockpiled for use on the sea, and not let it rip me inside out like a piece of ripe fruit.

I would not go home on the bus.

I would not leave the dock until I had a job.

There was a new man on the boat. Easy to tell.

He sat on the hatch of the lazarette, a storage compartment at the stern, and he sharpened knives.

Every couple of minutes, he set the knife and the sharpening stone down on the deck and walked over to stare at the other crewmen, trying to figure out what they were doing.

Then one of the regulars would shove him out of the way or ask him what his problem was, and he'd go back to work.

"I already got me a man." The captain sat on a coil of rope at the bow. A pigmeat roll of gut hung from under his shirt. He licked ketchup off the hamburger wrapper. "Full crew."

"Maybe you could put me to work and if you thought I was better, you could let me take his place."

"I don't pay by the hour."

"I know. Just put me to work. If you don't want me, don't pay me."

"You say you been fishing before."

"Yes, sir."

"No need for calling me that."

"I fished on the *Ocean Horse*. Before that, I worked the trap boats over at Gunther's."

"Usually if I find a man who worked the *Ocean Horse*, I make a point of *not* giving him a job."

"I understand."

"*Ocean Horse* is a goddamned raft."

"I know it."

"So you want me to put you to work and if I think you're better than him, I take you on?"

"It's just that I need a job." I stood still on the hot whiteness of the bow, head tucked into my chest to dodge the glare. I waited for the fat man's word.

He balled his hamburger wrapper and flipped it into the harbor. He tapped the soles of his deck shoes together, mumbled to himself and sighed. Then he looked up suddenly, as if surprised to see me still there. "Why don't you take that other boy and go clean out the lazarette? Clean it and tidy it real good. What are you named?" He said it the same way a man would ask, What does your master call you?

"James Pfeiffer."

He nodded, turned away and coughed something out of his throat.

I dumped my gear in the wheelhouse and didn't look at the crew as I walked across to the lazarette.

I waited for the new boy to raise his head. He moved the knife back and forth along the stone that he had balanced on his knee.

When my shadow crossed his legs, he looked up. "Something the matter?" He blinked, eyes crushed tight together from the sun. His hair was dark and curly. Thin body, small bubbles of pec muscle behind his nipples. "Aren't I doing this right again?"

"Captain says we have to clean the lazarette. So get up."

The lazarette on a boat is a junkyard. Things are put in there that should have been thrown overboard or taken to the dump. Chains. Nets. Cogs from machines. Lumps of whalebone that came up in the dredge and were forgotten by the man who hid them. Rope. Beer cans. All of it pasted with dirt.

I pulled the steel hatch off the cover hole and stood back. Hot air rode up, carrying red dust with it.

"My name's Marco." He wiped his palms on his trousers so as to give me a clean hand to shake.

I climbed down the hole.

Crouching in the waist-high place, I tried to make out where the walls began and the chain and rope ended. My wrists dangled from my knees. The place looked like a giant bird's nest.

Dust drifted into my lungs and clogged them.

I tried to breathe through my teeth.

Marco jumped down beside me and moved on his haunches into the dark. "Let's get this done fast so we can go back in the sun." He dragged some chain down off the pile and it unraveled at his feet. "Let's go, buddy. What do you say?"

I turned to the other corner and peered into three milk crates filled with bolts and loose dredge links. I began to move the bolts and links a couple at a time, sorting them into separate crates.

"Get this done real quick and get out of here." Marco dragged the chain around behind my back. "Put this right here. This over here. Get this mother untangled."

I breathed very softly in the red air and tried not to think.

A block of blue sky showed above the cover hole, crossed now and then by the crooked chevron of a seagull. I dug my fingers into the grit of bolts and links and no longer bothered which pieces went where.

"Hey, buddy. Give me a hand, will you?" The grinding of chains stopped and I heard him sit down.

"Busy." I rattled the bolts.

"Jesus, it's hot in here. What did you say your name was?"

Heat. Making its way up through the iron plates of the hull. Dribbling down from the sky. Faraway crying of gulls.

My nose began to bleed. My skull seemed to expand and contract, putting pressure on my eyes.

Marco crawled past me up the ladder. "Hell with this. I need some fresh air."

I waited, then heard the captain shouting at him to get back in the lazarette and finish his job.

Marco tried to reason with the man. His voice was calm and quiet.

The noise of the captain's yelling faded as a shadow passed over the cover hole and someone leaned down to look at me.

I picked a handful of bolts and began sorting them.

"Want me to get you out of here, Pfeif?"

I looked up and saw it was Kelley from Gunther's dock. He gripped the metal rim of the hatch hole, the thumb missing from his left hand. He had cut it off with a chain saw, working as a lumberjack in Maine.

"Where'd you come from, Kelley? You looking for a job too?"

"I already got one. I been on this crew a couple of months. You'd have seen me if you weren't so much in a hurry to get down here and bake like a potato."

"I heard Gunther fired you." I wiped the blood on my shirtsleeve.

"It had to happen sooner or later."

"Who's this Marco man?" Rust trickled down into my eyes.

"He says he knows how to fish. Captain was going to take him out half share." Above Kelley's voice, I could still hear the captain yelling. A pendant on a chain around Kelley's neck dangled down into the lazarette. "You got a nosebleed, Pfeif."

"It's stopping."

"Want me to get you out of here?"

"Is the captain going to send Marco down again?"

Kelley looked up, then down at me. "Believe so."

"Then I'd better stay. At least until Marco passes out."

"Good enough." Blue sky slid back over the hole when Kelley moved away.

Marco climbed into the lazarette and waddled across to the chains. He began dragging them back and forth. "He just wasn't listening to me. I explained how it is down here but he wasn't listening. How long you been on this boat anyway?"

"First day." I picked another handful of bolts and sorted them.

"Yeah? Mine too."

Somewhere in the corner of my sight I noticed his hand, which he held out for me to shake.

*

For a while after the captain let us up on deck I couldn't see.

I walked across to Sabatini's fishhouse, holding my hands in front of me like slats of wood, and washed them in water from the hoses. I pressed my palms to the wet floor and then held them to my face.

The captain said his name was Gil.

He said he'd heard from Kelley that I could fish, so he was going to give me a break and put me on half share for the first trip. If I was worth more, I'd get more. He told me the only reason I could come along was in case this Marco boy messed up.

"We're leaving tonight. On the night tide. You got your gear?" He sat in the galley under a clock with a beer logo on its face and little beer cans at the ends of the hands. He drank iced tea from a blue plastic mug. The galley smelled of bleach and fried eggs.

"My gear's up on the bow."

"You got gloves and a scallop knife?"

"I'll buy them from the army-navy if you give me a couple of minutes."

"Go at lunchtime. Find yourself a bunk in the forward room."

I nodded, feeling the water dry on my face. "Do you have any employment forms for me to fill out?"

Gil squinted down at the table. Then he stuck a finger in his ear and twisted it around. "I don't think I'd know an employment form if it hit me on the head. Listen, Pfeiffer. If I say you can work for me, you can work for me. I don't need anyone else's permission." He nodded, pleased with himself. "Kelley said he wanted you in his bunk room more than the other guy." He sucked at the ice cubes in his mug. "Good friends, you and Kelley?"

"Not the way you're thinking."

"I hope not. I can't deal with that stuff. Least of all out to sea. You hear me?"

"It's nothing like that, Gil."

The beer clock hummed in the quiet.

He narrowed his eyes and fished an ice cube from the mug. He crushed it with his teeth. Then he walked out on deck and left me alone in the stale air of the galley.

The bunk room was like a family crypt. No windows. Each bed in the shape of a coffin with one side torn away.

I picked a bunk that didn't look owned. It was at floor level and had a slab of foam for a mattress. I lay on it, giving myself a minute to rest before going out on deck to help the crew.

Next to my head, wedged between the mattress and the wall, was an old mayonnaise jar filled with cigarette butts. Someone had played tic-tac-toe about a dozen times in charcoal pencil on the ceiling of the bunk.

I worked next to Kelley all day.

From him I learned the names of the others and how they were likely to treat me.

Kelley sat on a bucket and held out two pinky-thick steel rings. When these were linked together, they formed a large bag attached to the end of the dredge. This bag collected scallops as the dredge moved along the seabed. I fitted metal links around both rings and squeezed them shut with heavy pliers.

Sometimes I raised my head from the web of metal and watched yachts move past the dock. Men in white shorts and bare feet catwalked the decks, shouting orders at each other.

Kelley followed my gaze to the yachts, then turned back to his bucket full of rings. "Don't let Gil see you slacking off. He won't get mad if he sees you working slow, but he'll rail on you for staring at the rich men's boats." Then he smiled, fat cheeks almost closing his eyes. "We're going to have fun with this Marco."

A black man sat on the bridge peeling potatoes.

Gray hair grew like mold on his head.

I watched how evenly and slowly he carved the skin from the potatoes. He was far off in daydreams, I could tell.

Kelley nudged me. "That's Franklin. He's the cook. He's been on the boat as long as Gil." Then he looked across at Marco and grinned. Suddenly he snapped his fingers. "Boy!"

Marco pointed to his own chest. He mouthed the word "me?"

"Yes, you! Go into town and bring us back some scallop powder."

Marco checked his wallet, a polished block of leather that had left permanent creases in his back pocket. "Does it cost much?"

"No, they're having a sale. Don't come back until you have some. You hear?"

"I won't come back until I have some." Marco jogged into town.

The other crewmen watched blank-faced until he was out of sight.

Franklin dropped a potato and the knife in his bucket of water. He shook the drops off his fingers. "Every time."

The crew snickered into their armpits.

I kept my mouth shut, concentrated only on squeezing links and tried not to catch anyone's eye. I thought they were laughing at me.

A while later Kelley whispered, "No such thing as scallop powder."

At two o'clock, the crew knocked off for lunch. They bought a case of beer and drank it in half an hour. Then they fell asleep in a pile on the dock.

Gil jumped down from the wheelhouse and swore at them.

When he saw it was no use, he walked up to Mary's bar at the end of Sabatini's parking lot.

I watched this from the door of Sabatini's fishhouse, where I sat in the damp and shade of an empty ice cart, eating a bag of cookies I'd taken from the galley.

*

"Does Mom know about this?" My brother sighed into the telephone receiver.

I heard him pacing back and forth. "I told her this morning."

"Does she know you found a job?"

"That's what I'm calling to say." I leaned against a phone booth bolted to the corrugated metal of the fishhouse.

The sun went down in a row of silent explosions through the girders of the Newport Bridge.

"Is it a good boat this time?"

"Good enough."

"I'll tell her it's a very good boat if you don't mind."

"Fine."

"How do you expect things to be when you get home, James?" His voice was tired and angry. "I don't think Dad's going to go for being dumped on twice. You can only stretch things so far."

I stayed quiet.

"You still there?"

"Still here." I set my back against the fishhouse and slid down into a crouch. Across from me on the other dock, a woman in a bathing suit and white bathrobe walked across from one cabin cruiser to another. Her legs looked very long. The wharf was a tangle of lights.

"Mom's out sitting in the yard."

"What's she doing out there?"

"Just sitting. She has her hands on her lap and she's just sitting there. You want me to get her to the phone?"

"No. No need. Just tell her I got a job and I'll be back in a week or so."

He sighed again. "I can probably get you a job at the car place when you get back. Think about it. I sold five Rolomatics today."

"Five boxloads?"

"No. Five Rolomatics."

"Is that good?"

"No, actually."

Gil and Franklin walked past me and down to the boat.

"My boat's leaving, Joseph."

After I'd hung up, someone trotted across the dockyard and shone a light in my face. "Private dock! Mr. Sabatini don't like punks hanging around his property. So fuck away!"

When I heard "fuck away," I knew the man was Lester. Sabatini let him hang around as a human watchdog. He lived in a little gray boat, permanently moored near the land side of the dock.

Lester was bones spray-painted pink, with some eyeballs stuck on for effect.

"What do you need a flashlight for, Lester? It isn't even dark yet." I shielded my eyes from the glare.

"Eh?" The light wavered and came closer. "How'd you know my name? I don't know you."

"Everyone knows you, Lester."

"Eh? That's for damn sure."

"I bet even the President knows you." I pushed the light away from my face.

"Don't be wisebutting me! Now, fuck away!" He held the flashlight down at his side, shaking it slightly in the way Joseph and I used to swing a light quickly back and forth in the dark to pretend we were in old movies.

"Watch your mouth, Lester, or I'll sink your boat."

"You better not!"

"It's too late now, Lester. Your boat's as good as at the bottom of the bay."

"Quit kidding around."

"Wait and see if I'm kidding, Lester."

He turned off the flashlight. "You're just joking, right? Boat's all I got. I don't got a house. You're just making fun, right?"

I turned once as I walked through the quiet, hissing canopy of the fishhouse. Lester still stood where I left him, mumbling at me and wanting to know if I was only kidding about his boat.

Leaving the harbor, Kelley and I watched the lights of Newport growing small.

Yachts with their sails down and running on inboard motors passed us going home, bobbing in our wake. The noise of our engines was loud. The yacht people called and waved to us. I couldn't hear what they said.

One crewman stood in the middle of our deck. He wore a blue shirt buttoned up to the throat. Now and then, he jerked his head to one side, as if he heard a noise but couldn't tell where it came from. He caught me looking at him and glared back. A line of teardrops was tattooed down his cheeks.

I spoke to Kelley through clenched teeth. "Don't turn around. Just tell me who that guy is who's wearing a blue shirt. He looks mad as hell about something."

Kelley turned around. "Hey, Pittsley. What are you pissed off about?"

"Jesus, Kelley." I sighed and let my head fall forward.

Pittsley shook his head. "I'm not pissed off. Who says I'm pissed off?" He faced the other way, arms folded and singing to himself.

We rounded the point at Fort Adams.

"So who is he, Kelley?"

"That's Pittsley. He's a psycho left over from Vietnam. He doesn't mean any harm."

Gil aimed his boat at open water and hammered up the engines. I saw the cliffs of Jamestown and sometimes the lights of a car on one of the beach roads. The lawns of Newport's mansions were crowded, always crowded with parties in the summer.

The crew prepared to set down outriggers, which stabilized the boat in rough weather.

"I wondered what they were for." Marco peered into the rigging. He wore a down vest with the collar turned up.

"You've never been fishing before, have you?" I watched to see if the outriggers went down evenly. My job was to stand in the center of the deck with arms raised at the same angle as each outrigger and to call out if one moved more quickly than the other.

"I been fishing. I went out with my uncle. He has a twenty-foot dory."

"Starboard rigger coming down too fast! Hear me?"

"Slow down starboard rigger!" the mate called to the crew.

Kelley hadn't told me much about the mate, except to say his name was Reynolds. Several times that day, Reynolds had walked across the deck to us and asked if we needed any help. Always, Kelley lowered his head and mumbled no. Then Reynolds would stay for a moment, his long arms hugging his ribs. It was as if he wanted Kelley to say something else, something to start a conversation. But Kelley told him nothing, and Reynolds walked back into the galley.

I turned to Marco. "Have you ever been on a trawler?"

"No, I never been fishing like this. Alls the captain asked me was if I been fishing and I have. Want a cigarette?"

"You told Gil you could work the dredge, didn't you? How can you do that if you've never been out on a trawler?"

"I pull the winch handle one way, it goes up. I pull it the other way and it goes down. How much more do I have to know?"

"You're kidding me."

"Hey, don't tell Gil."

"You should tell him yourself or someone could get hurt."

"If I can't do it, I'll tell him."

I looked back at the lights of Newport Bridge. Strips of beach glowed in the dark.

After the last lights had tipped into the sea, I realized I was the only one on deck.

The wind picked up and the work lights closed me in. Beyond our boat I could make out only the gray of ocean and a paler gray of sky.

The first waves broke on our bow and sprayed across the deck.

I walked around removing the scupper plates so water could drain out. When I had finished, I saw a movement on the bridge.

It was Reynolds. He wore only a pair of shorts. His stomach was dappled with puncture scars. "I was just going to pull out the scupper plates."

"I saved you the sweat." I hurt my eyes in the dazzle of work lights.

Reynolds drummed his fingers on the rail of the bridge. "You better put on a coat. You'll catch cold."

When he had gone, Kelley appeared from the galley. "I was wondering where you got to." He sat on the deck between the two dredges, took off his shoes and picked between his toes. "How come you're out on the water again?"

He didn't know I'd been to college. He didn't know I went to school at all.

"So how come, Pfeif?"

"I'm poor."

"Stay with us and you won't be poor long. This captain, all he thinks about is bringing in the scallops. We're always making the best catch at the dock. He likes everything clockwork on his boat. He won't screw you. At least he hasn't screwed me yet." He stopped picking his toes and put his shoes back on. "I been making good money this last couple of months. But I'll be getting a new job soon enough."

I nodded and tried not to laugh. Almost every day at Gunther's he had talked about quitting. He often lost his temper at the dock. He'd take his ice shovel and beat it on the floor until it broke and then stamp off the wharf, yelling that he was finished. Gunther's dockboys would start clapping and shout, "See you tomorrow, Kelley." And they were right. He always came back, until Gunther fired him. He'd been fishing ever since he sawed his thumb off. At Gunther's, they'd heard it was the same up there. Always about to quit. Every tree his last.

How Kelley managed to stay on at Gunther's as long as he did without getting caught stealing I couldn't figure out. He tried so hard to look innocent and harmless in front of Gunther that everyone else knew he was thieving. Kelley would walk off the dock at the end of each day with ten pounds of bass stuffed down his pants. He put such a lot of energy into looking casual that Gunther must only have felt sorry for the man not to have busted him any earlier.

"So this is your last trip, eh Kelley?"

He slapped at his gut with both hands. "I'll be calling it quits soon enough." Then he wandered back inside.

I stayed sitting on the ice hatch. In each moment of quiet a picture shifted into my head of my mother sitting by herself in the garden. It spread and distorted and worried me.

"You all right?"

I opened my eyes.

Nelson, the only black on the crew besides Franklin, was shaking my arm. "You all right?"

"I was asleep." I sat up and rubbed at my face.

"Are you a friend of Kelley's?"

"I guess."

"Because of him, I just lost all my damn money." He stood with his hands on his hips. "Him and Gil ganged up on me in the card game and took all my money. They didn't take it exactly, but they pretty much did. I'm going to get it back. No question about that."

He sat next to me on the hatch. "Kelley doesn't even know

how to play cards. He just pays attention to Gil and Gil tells him what to do. I saw them. Winking and kicking each other under the table. How the hell do they think I didn't see them?"

"I didn't know there was a card game." I wished Kelley had asked me to play.

"You're safer out here."

I took the fish knife out of my boot and began to sharpen it with my pocket stone. I thought he was going to ask if he could borrow some money.

Instead, after tapping a cigarette out of a packet and lighting it, he told me the police had a warrant for him and he'd probably be arrested when he got back to port.

He said he had a friend named Marty. Marty dated a girl who used to go out with a Navy man from the Newport Academy.

The Navy man caught up with Marty and the girl in a bar called The Griffon. He sat down with them in their booth, Marty in jeans and a headband and the Navy man in his white academy suit. The Navy man said there had to be some mistake, his girl-friend sitting with a nigger. Definitely some mistake. Why don't you take your black ass away from this place, nigger?

Marty made a few calls and later that night the Navy man got jumped in a parking lot.

Marty's friends spread the man's left hand on the pavement and broke each of his fingers with a hammer. Between smashing the fingers, they said to the man that there had to be some mistake. Surely he wasn't the one talking about niggers and black asses. No, there was some mistake, they told him as they crushed his knuckle joints.

The week before Nelson started working on the boat, he and Marty and the girl were driving through town in Marty's jeep. Up and down Severn Street, all drunk on a Monday night.

Marty pulled up to a light in front of the post office, and while they were waiting for the green, Nelson heard a bang, which ruined his ears for a couple of days.

The girl began screaming.

When Nelson looked over, he saw Marty shot through the forehead with the Navy man's .45. The Navy man was in the next car over.

Nelson got out of the car and ran away. He left the girl screaming and Marty dead and took a flight down to Alabama for a few days, to be with his brother. When he came back, he heard the police were looking for him.

Nelson set his hands on his knees and rocked slightly on the hatch. "As yet, I have not informed Captain Gil of my situation." He cleared his throat. "I didn't know it was a damn federal offensive to be running the hell away. I didn't do nothing. Wasn't me with the gun. Didn't anybody tell me about a two-to-five for not reporting the crime and leaving the scene."

"You could talk your way out of it."

"I'm fixing to. I'm practicing. But I can't talk my way out of a federal offensive. May as well jump over and splain it to the fish."

*

I lay half asleep in my bunk, hearing waves like cannon fire on the hull. They raised my head from the mattress and threw it back again.

Kelley swung his leg down from the bunk above me. He stuck his foot in my ribs.

I didn't hear him speak or see his face, but I knew it was him because he had his name written in marker pen on the toe of each sock.

I looked at my watch. It was the middle of the night.

Kelley said we'd be taking first shift.

I sat on the floor, rubbing my eyes to wake up. "How much time do we have?" When there was no answer, I looked up.

He'd already gone out on deck.

In the last few seconds before I crawled from my bed, I thought of my mother and Joseph asleep at home. Then I thought of my father, who never seemed to sleep, out here in the dark someplace and riding the sea in his boat.

5

WE SENT the dredges down. They disappeared into the choppy sea and their cables shuddered through the waves.

I walked the deck, tossing over beer cans that had gathered in corners, the stems of welding rods, a tube of lipstick left behind by someone who spent a night on the boat.

When I looked up, a crewman named Howard was staring me in the face.

He smiled and showed his teeth.

It looked to me as if he'd been a rat in another life.

He and Kelley and I made up the first watch, with Gil in the wheelhouse.

While Howard swept a pile of cigarette butts out through a scupper, Kelley put his hand on my shoulder and talked in my ear. "You see how thin he is?"

I nodded.

"His wife is so fat she has to go to a special store to buy her clothes. You see them together and it's like looking at your own reflection in two funhouse mirrors. I figure she lives in their car. I never once seen her get out of the thing." He straightened up and shouted at Howard. "Quit sweeping the deck, Stick Man! It'll be dirty again soon enough."

Howard stopped swishing the stub of broom. "It's for luck!" He had dentures, which he could dislodge and jerk out from his lips. He did this absent-mindedly as he swept, as if it helped him think.

Kelley slapped his knees. "There's no luck in sweeping. Only bad luck things you can do on a boat."

"It's good luck to sweep the deck clean before you start work. I know it is." Howard set the broom aside and sat next to us on the ice hatch.

"Sweeping's just going to wear you away more than you already are."

Howard showed us his biceps. "I got muscles from sweeping like that."

"Alls you got is bones and hair. And some fake teeth."

"If you're so hung up on bad luck out at sea, Kelley, then what are you doing here?"

"Even more bad luck on land." Kelley held up the remains of his thumb, a purple-white ball of skin.

While we sat waiting for the signal from Gil to raise our dredges, Kelley explained all the bad luck that he said lived on the water.

You can't say "pig" on a boat. The reason is that a pig can't swim. Kelley told us he didn't know if there was another reason, but he knew for sure you couldn't say it.

Pig, I started thinking. Pig. Pig. Pig. The word flashed in my head.

You couldn't turn the hatch covers upside down, because it was like the motion of a boat capsizing.

You couldn't whistle. Whistling brought the wind.

If you ever pulled up human bones, you had to go straight home or the dead would walk your deck.

Never stick a knife into the woodwork of a boat. This would piss off the captain and amount to the same thing as bad luck.

If a land bird came on deck while you were out to sea, clean water and food should be set out for it, or you'd have bad luck when the boat got back to shore.

Kelley said he didn't know if he believed in all of it, but there was no sense going around mumbling "pig" just to see what would happen.

"And if you ever see a boat fishing nearby that you never seen before, look at its name and remember it. Then when you get into port, look it up in the log book at the Seamen's Mission." Kelley nodded and was quiet after that. He looked down at his rubber boots and kept nodding, wide-eyed, until Howard had to finish the story.

A few months earlier, when Kelley worked on a boat called the *Lobsta,* out of New Bedford, he saw a Galilee trawler named *Aggressor* fishing close by, and just happened to remember its name.

The next time in port, he was arrested for starting a fight in a bar and didn't make bail before the *Lobsta* left on another trip.

The *Lobsta* went down off Tuckernuck, Nantucket.

A cargo ship received the *Lobsta*'s last message. It said, "If we get one more wave on our deck, we're going down."

Kelley began searching for another job. None of the boats in Newport needed or wanted him as crew, so he took a bus to Galilee and asked in the bars and the Fishermen's Co-op if anyone would hire him.

One man he met offered to walk him down to the docks and ask a friend of his. He said it would give Kelley a better chance that way.

To make conversation, Kelley mentioned having seen the boat from Galilee named *Aggressor.*

The man stopped walking and asked him to say the name again. Then he pointed to a small patch of neatly cut grass next to the Co-op. Sunk in the grass was a gravestone:

In memory of the crew of F/V Aggressor. November 1968.
Save us when we cry to thee, for those in peril on the sea.
Placed here by Family and Friends.

The *Aggressor* had been gone almost a decade. Kelley promised himself that if he saw something like that again, he'd quit the boats and go back to lumberjacking forever.

"After he saw that stone" — Howard slapped Kelley on the arm and grinned — "he couldn't even light his own cigarettes, his hands were shaking so much."

The wind does come if you whistle.

It rides the flat water toward you. Dusty looking and hard. It hits, moves through you and keeps going.

Then you know who brought the wind. You start wishing there was something you could do to make it go away.

Kelley had no front teeth and most of his hair was gone. He combed the strands in strange patterns across his head to make it seem like he had more.

I heard it fell out after his divorce.

He had a wife and a baby in the days when he cut timber full time up near the Quebec border, in Jackman, Maine.

After a couple of good seasons, he had enough money to build a new house for himself. He wanted it constructed right next to his old house, which was beginning to fall apart.

He was away at a town planner's meeting, applying for final approval for sinking a new well on his land, while his wife carried boxes from one house to the other, back and forth, making a path through the snow.

She left the door open and the baby got down from its crib. It crawled outside.

She didn't check to see if the child was in its room when she returned. She fell asleep on the couch waiting for Kelley to come home.

Kelley arrived drunk and lay down next to her after putting a new log on the fire.

In the morning, they found the baby frozen up like a small

piece of sculpture. Its crawl prints circled their house, stopping at each window on the ground floor.

His marriage didn't last much longer after that.

Gunther told me this when I worked for him. He cornered me on the dock one day and hooked his thick arm around my neck. He pulled me to him so I had to breathe his breath and smell his hair, and he told me for no reason at all, except that by then Gunther must have known Kelley was a thief and didn't like me working alongside him. He told me I should never mention it to anyone, so I still didn't know if the story was true.

I hoped I could work the two dredges.

The *Ocean Horse* had only one, and a smaller one as well. The dredges on the *Gray Ghost* were twenty-one-footers.

I didn't ask Kelley for advice. I didn't want to owe him. As soon as things started, I told myself, it would all fall into place.

Resting my forearms on my knees, I looked at my boots, wondering if they would stay waterproof the whole trip.

Instead of buying a decent pair, I had the kind made in Korea that were shiny black with dull red trim. They rarely lasted a week when I worked on the trap boats, and then my feet would stay wet until I could afford another pair. After that, the only way I could keep my feet dry was to wear the plastic bags from loaves of bread over my socks. I scrounged them from the coffee-and-doughnut lady when she came by in her truck, and held them around my ankles with rubber bands.

And I thought of the impossibly long time it would take before I could run my own boat, with the chance always there of being cheated by the captain, or fired, or giving up and admitting I did not know what was best for me.

After the dredges had been down an hour, Gil called "Haul back" over the loudspeaker. The cable drums started turning. Gil worked them from up in the wheelhouse. The noise was loud enough to be painful for a while.

Howard and Kelley unlocked the drum brakes and the cables began rolling back, crackling as they threaded over the cylinder.

I leaned over the port side and watched cable stretch from the water.

Beyond the work lights I could see only black. Oily-looking waves barged from the dark and slapped at our hull.

After a few minutes, I made out the shape of a dredge.

It rose through curtains of green, broke from the water and crashed against the side. All along the base of the triangle, the brown metal had been rubbed shiny silver where it dragged across the ocean floor.

A few fish escaped from the dredge bag. Catfish, their guts burst from the change in pressure, floated upside down on the surface, slowly shaking the life out of themselves.

Sand filtered out in a white haze.

I set a winch hook in a ring at the top of the dredge. Kelley called it the bull ring. Then I ran to the other side of the deck, hooked up the starboard dredge and backed away.

Kelley and Howard locked the cable drums and worked the hydraulic winches, raising both dredges above the deck until the black sky on either side was gridded out by the chain mail of dredge bags.

The bags looked only a little filled. White-brown discs of scallop shells. Monkfish. Catfish. Crabs. Rocks. Sea sponge, the smell of it rotten and suffocating.

The dredges swung over and down on the deck.

I reattached the hook to a bar at the end of the dredge bag. The bar was lifted and the contents of the bag spilled out on deck.

The sound of scallops falling was like the clatter of dropped china.

Some shells and fish remained caught in the bag, so I raised my arms, hooked my fingers around the rings and rocked back and forth until the rest were dislodged.

As I swung, I looked at the huge bar and the finger-thick

cable holding it up. I wondered if there would be any chance of getting out of the way if the winch cable snapped.

Attached to either side of the deck was a chain with a large clip at the end. These clips had to be attached to the dredges before they were set over the side again. A pin held the clip shut. The pelican clip. When it was closed, it looked like the bill of a pelican.

Kelley and Howard raised each dredge until the only thing holding it over the side was the clip.

The boat idled and Gil appeared from the wheelhouse to see what had been brought up. He walked the deck with hands in pockets and toed the scallops and monkfish, which lay with their jaws locked open, a froth of fat teeth in their mouths.

A second after he disappeared back in the wheelhouse, the boat kicked out of neutral and swung around, engines deafening and diesel smoke billowing across the deck.

Stars cartwheeled past. We turned to plow another strip of ocean floor.

I stood between the dredges, holding a big hammer. My job was to knock out the pins in the pelican clips, sending the dredges down again.

Howard and Kelley held on to the brake wheels of the cable drums, like two race car drivers waiting to start.

When the boat had gathered speed, Gil shouted "Set them loose" over the loudspeaker.

I waited until we rolled deep in the trough of a wave. Then I struck the pin and jumped back. The clip thrashed out and down onto the deck.

I kept my eyes closed as I jumped, as if the skin of my eyelids would protect me.

When both dredges had gone, I stood for a minute catching my breath, then set the hammer down and felt my fingers still locked in a grip.

*

The cables paid out. Humming.

Kelley threw me a basket for collecting the scallops. It was gray plastic with orange handles.

I set the basket between my legs at one end of a pile and began flipping scallops into it. I rummaged through stones and fish, hauling the monk into the center of the deck for cutting.

Kelley and Howard rammed their fingers into the fish's eyes and used the sockets as holders.

With my rubber-gloved hand, I prodded a few times at the green eye of a monk but couldn't bring myself to do what the others were doing. I ended up kicking my fish over to the pile.

I learned to turn my head from the yellowtail and fluke as I reached for them. As soon as they felt my fingers, they exploded into flapping. The first few times I fell back with grit in my eyes. So I scooped them up fast or punched them dead, seeing their backs arch, fins spreading in a fish's scream.

When we had gathered the scallops and fish, we shoveled out what remained through the scuppers. The three of us paused for a second on the rail before getting back to work, heads down and no talk, watching the sea cut past in waves and white foam.

I dumped my scallops in a metal pen under the canopy of the bridge. It was loud under the canopy. The hammer of engines echoed off the gray iron plates, and diesel fumes seeped from the engine room.

Kelley worked at one end of the pen while I worked at the other. He busied himself with cutting and we didn't speak until it was over.

Howard worked by himself at a pen on the other side of the deck.

I held each scallop flat side up, stuck the tip of my knife into a joint where the two shells fused and drew the blade once under the top shell. This severed the muscle. Then I lipped my blade just under the gut on the bottom shell and flipped it, with the top shell, over the side. I scraped the milky white cylinder of muscle off the bottom shell and into a bucket set next to me.

A scallop knife was different from a fish knife. The scallop knife had a blade not more than a couple of inches long and thin in the middle. The handle was wrapped with black electrical tape that molded to the cutter's hand. After a while, I could tell knives apart by the different palm imprints of each crewman.

Over the first hours, I learned to cut scallops fast so I could rest before the next haul-back. When Howard and Kelley had finished what was in their baskets, they sat on the ice hatch, sharing cigarettes, while I continued cutting.

I didn't expect them to help. I'd have told them not to if they tried. This would have set me apart at a time when it seemed the most important thing to do was fit myself smoothly into the running of the boat.

In the mechanical motion of cutting out scallops, daydreams came to me. I snapped out of them only when I began to fall over, amazed to find myself on the boat and not just passing through another dream.

"I'm having the strangest thoughts, Kelley." I leaned against the rim of our scallop pen as a wave pitched onto the deck. It swirled at our feet before spilling out through the scuppers.

"Thoughts?" His head jerked up and he looked across at me. It was as if he'd been asleep. "What thoughts?"

"I'm having daydreams. I hardly know where I am." I watched the white cube of a muscle cringe as it slid off the shell into my bucket.

"It'll be that way for a couple of days. Always is. But then you get too tired to keep thinking up new things and you'll start running over the same dreams. Over and over. After a while you can't remember what day it is anymore. Can't remember how long you've been out here. After about a week, everything just fizzes out and you walk around like you're brain dead." He

didn't look at me as he spoke. As he picked each scallop from the pen, he was already checking for the next one.

We took turns cutting the monk.

People eat monk when they go to seafood restaurants. On the menu, they see a fish with some half-human smiley face and wearing a sailor's hat.

But the monk was the ugliest animal I'd ever seen. It made me ill just looking at it.

Some of them were the length of my leg. They lay on the deck with mouths open and clamped down on anything that got in the way. Sometimes their mouths were filled with other fish or sand, which made them almost impossible to lift.

They were all head and tail. Nothing in between.

I lifted each monk onto the rim of the boat for cutting. I held them by their eye sockets. There was no other way.

I made two diagonal slashes from the base of the fish's head to its gill openings. Then I punched the spine at the place where the slashes joined, breaking its back. Clear liquid splashed out from its spinal cord. One more cut under its belly to sever the intestines and I stepped back to let the guts fall out. Its tail, the only part we kept, slopped down onto the deck, and I sent the head spinning into the water.

Kelley used a Marine Corps Kabar knife, which was too short and messed up his hands on the belly cut. I used a British commando knife, bought years before at the Newport army-navy. It had a long stiletto blade, which made the job cleaner and stopped them thrashing the way Kelley's fish did. He twisted the knife in the wreckage of their bodies, mauling them to death with the fat blade.

Marco walked out on deck and was seasick.

He stood at the stern wearing only a T-shirt, rubber boots and his underwear. The boots didn't match. He didn't bring any with him for the trip and had to find some used ones down in the lazarette.

He stayed for a minute with his hands on his knees, spitting the taste of acid from his mouth.

Half an hour later, he came out again. This time he wore only one boot. He didn't speak to us. Perhaps he thought we were only part of a bad dream he was having.

Kelley nudged me and smiled as Marco hobbled back inside, wiping his mouth and swearing to himself.

While we rested between haul-backs, on the ice hatch or squatting on old milk crates from a dairy in Providence, Kelley and Howard told me about Gil. They took turns shouting above the rumble of engines.

All he cared about, they said, was the regular heartbeat hum of his machine. He weighed everything on a scale in his head, balanced the effective running of the *Gray Ghost* against any possible change and mistake.

The more I heard of this, the sorrier I felt for Tony, the captain of the *Ocean Horse*. He could never take any pride in the precision of his own boat. It was a piece of garbage and he knew that, but he'd probably sunk all his money into the trawler and had no other way to make a living.

I saw him once after he fired me, using a staple gun to nail down shreds of wood that had come loose from the hull while the *Ocean Horse* was out to sea.

He must have known how everybody made fun of him each time his boat dragged itself out of port, how people fell on their hands and knees laughing after the canopy for his scallop pen tipped into the bay.

I made up my mind not to let that happen to me. To follow precision and allow for no mistakes. As I made the promise, I realized how many other promises I'd heard from people on the docks that could not and would never be kept.

The first I saw of dawn was a blueness in the sky. It smudged to gray and then to yellow.

I watched the light change in puddles on the deck as I moved hunchbacked over piles of scallops.

The sun came up fast from the horizon. For a moment it stayed thin and rose-colored, the pale dome of sky overhead. Fragile. A slab of cracked turquoise.

The next time I looked, pausing with my basket of scallops at the metal pen, it burned at my eyes and stayed burning when I blinked.

Each time I set my hands on the rim of the boat to rest, Kelley rapped them with his knuckles.

I was too tired to tell him to stop.

It seemed to be a game he had invented, like a game he had from the year before on Gunther's boat. He'd sneak up on me as I slept next to the wheelhouse, with an oiler jacket pulled over me to keep out the chill. He took a crowbar from the engine room and slammed it into the metal next to my head. The noise was so loud I couldn't hear anything anybody said for half an hour afterward.

The one time I tried to pay him back, he was waiting for me. He grabbed my wrists and held them until I thought my bones would break.

After the fifth time of rapping my knuckles, Kelley shoved me. "You aren't getting it, are you?"

"Getting what? Getting any fun out of your game? Well, bust me up, Kelley, I guess I'm not."

"I'm not playing. I'm trying to teach you not to hold your hands over the rim. See, when the cable comes in like this" — he pointed to marks where cable had rubbed against the side and run a groove through the metal — "when it hits a rock down there, it jumps and swings right into the rim. Take your fingers clean off. Or worse, it just grinds them into garbage and there's nothing anyone can do to put them back together again. You keep your hands like this." He showed me how to keep my palms hooked on the inside of the rim.

Franklin came on deck and stood with his hands on the small of his back.

Then Reynolds, naked except for his boots.

I could see Kelley trying to think of something funny to say.

As the mate walked past and Kelley turned to speak, the mate said, "I know what you're thinking," which shut Kelley up.

Pittsley carried out a little shaving bag, sat on the lazarette and tried to shave, looking at himself in the mirror from a woman's compact. Then he cut himself and gave up, his face still half stubbly. He sat on the lazarette hatch and smiled so much I knew there must be something wrong with him.

I tried not to stare at Marco when he walked out from the galley. But everyone else was looking, so I gave up and watched as well.

Kelley had a bet with Howard that Marco would be ill again.

Marco tried to be sick, the muscles of his stomach slamming up into his rib cage, jaw locked open, but he had nothing left inside.

Howard walked over to our pen, wiping his forehead on his arm, blue rubber gloves like flippers on his hands. He held a flipper out to Kelley. "Pay me."

Kelley raised his eyebrows. "I won the bet."

"I didn't see him doing it. Pay me, Kelley."

"Course he was doing it. Wasn't he doing it, Pfeif?"

" 'Pends what you call doing it."

Howard put his fisted flippers against his waist. "I won that bet."

Kelley pursed his lips. "I don't think so, Bubba."

Marco watched us, squinting. His fuzzy-curly hair was squashed on one side and looked wind-blasted on the other. "What you talking about? You talking about me? Did I do something wrong?"

After the last haul-back on our watch, we dumped our scallop meats in the washer, a tub made of stainless steel with holes at the bottom to let water drain out.

I stuck the deck hose in the mass of white cubes and washed them while Kelley swished his hand back and forth through the scallops, looking for chips of shell and shreds of gut.

The meats gave off a musty smell.

Kelley picked one up and put it in his mouth.

The scallop bags each held forty pounds and were sealed with wire ties. I twisted them tight onto the bags, bruising my knuckles with the rusty, hooked twister.

When the scallops had been collected, Kelley and Howard climbed down into the ice hold to make a bed for the bags.

I walked the deck picking up yellowtail with a fish pick, a hammer handle with a nail driven through the end.

When I was out on the *Ocean Horse*, I swung at a fish with a pick, missed and drove the nail into my foot up to the wooden handle.

I eased over to Tough. "Help me get this out, can you?"

Tough wondered out loud whether he should pull the nail out fast so it wouldn't hurt as much, or slowly, to risk not tearing a bigger hole.

I set my good foot on the toe of my hurt foot and pulled the spike out myself.

Reynolds sat alone at the galley table, eating grits and bacon.

He wore some clothes now, white jeans and a T-shirt cut off at the navel.

I stared at the scars on his stomach.

Old wounds. Knots of white skin, crumpled and deep in his flesh.

He caught me staring as he sat mopping the last of his grits with a slab of brown bread. He turned his head sideways and peered at me, frowning. "Something I can do for you?" He polished his plate clean with the bread.

"I was just looking at the scars." My neck felt suddenly hot. "I didn't mean to be rude."

He made a small noise in his throat and went back to his meal. When he looked up again, I was still staring at the scars.

"What?" He narrowed his eyes.

I flinched. I opened my mouth to say something. Then I just shook my head.

He told me that three days after his nineteenth birthday he was running up a hill in Vietnam. A Cong jumped up out of a hole in the ground, not even ten paces away, and shot him seven times in the gut. The rounds went through his flak jacket. One of the bullets tore through his clothes, nicked his side and killed the man running behind him.

He was flown to Singapore and stayed there six months, going through one operation after another. He had a bag on his left side for piss and a bag on his right side for the rest. After Singapore, he was flown home and spent another year in a military hospital in Maryland.

Gil paid him cash, so he could still collect disability pay that the Army sent each month.

I leaned across the table. "Did you see the man who shot you?"

"Hell, yes. I got the fucker's ears on a piece of string in a shoebox back home."

I mouthed the word "oh." Then I looked down at my hands.

He cleared his throat. "What's your name?"

"James Pfeiffer."

He held out his hand. "Ernest Reynolds."

I'd never seen people do this on the docks before. My father never shook hands with anyone. Nobody at Gunther's did. I shook the mate's hand and felt the warmth of his palm and did not like it.

"How old are you?" He narrowed his eyes when he spoke.

"Twenty."

He breathed out slowly through his nose. "You like it out here?"

"I guess." I picked at my nails. I could feel his eyes, making me nervous.

"If you have any problems, you come and talk to me." He dabbed at his lips with a paper napkin. "All right?"

I looked up and met his blue eyes. "Sure."

Franklin set a plate of eggs, bacon and grits in front of me, then took a knife and fork wrapped in a napkin out of his pocket and set them next to my plate.

"Coffee or ice tea?"

"Coffee." I focused past the gray blur of Franklin's hair to the beer clock with beer can hands.

"Coffee every day?"

"Every day. Cream. No sugar. Please."

"I like people who say please. You say please to me and we'll get along fine." Franklin wrote down how I took my coffee on a notepad glued to the fridge.

He cleaned off the breakfast plates of the other watch and fried up another package of bacon for Howard, Kelley, Gil and me.

Up in the wheelhouse, Gil hawked and spat someplace. He yelled down for Franklin to bring him his food.

Franklin stood at the base of the ladder that led up to the wheelhouse. "If that was you spitting on the floor again, young man, I am not cleaning it up. Hear me?"

Franklin had been Gil's cook for years. Before that, he cooked for Gil's father, who also ran a boat.

Kelley told me that Franklin was always getting drunk and quitting the crew, then coming back when he ran out of money and begging for his old job. Each time, Gil made a fool of him, telling Franklin if he wanted his job again, he would have to stand on the table at Mary's bar and sing "Mr. Bojangles." And if Gil wasn't satisfied, he made Franklin pretend to be a washing machine. The bar would fill with people, who crowded around Franklin as he sat on a chair, rubbing his stomach in circles, making rumble and bubble noises.

Franklin had a girl in Newport, a pretty girl if you compared her to how ugly Franklin was. He brought her down to the docks and made people jealous, since fishermen had a hard time finding and keeping friends who were girls and who were not whores.

Kelley said the only reason she stayed with Franklin was because he paid her a hundred dollars a day to go with him, not including food and a place to stay.

It could have been a lie. Kelley was more jealous than anyone, and he always made up lies. He repeated them so often he no longer remembered where the stories came from, and convinced himself they were true.

The mate took a piece of bacon off my plate and ate it. He smiled at me as he chewed.

Outside I could hear the whine and clank of dredges coming up on deck. The next watch's first haul-back.

Kelley and Howard burst into the galley. Both had ice chips in their hair.

They grabbed their plates of food from Franklin and came to the table. Kelley wore a napkin tucked into his collar.

"Excuse us." They looked at the mate.

The mate swung out from the galley table. He climbed up to the wheelhouse.

Kelley aimed his fork at me. "You stay out on deck until all of us are ready to go in. You don't quit work until we do. That's fair. That's the way it is. Understand?"

I nodded, my mouth full of food.

Then Kelley tapped my leg under the table. "What did Reynolds say to you?"

I shrugged. "He told me he was in Vietnam."

"What else did he say?"

"He told me his name." I looked across at Franklin and then at Howard. "What does it matter?"

Kelley spoke quietly. "We don't like him."

Howard shook his head. "Don't like him at all."

"Why not?" I stirred the grits on my plate with a knife.

Franklin sipped at a mug of coffee. "He just gives us a funny feeling is all."

I kept quiet, expecting them to burst out laughing and let me know I had fallen into the trap of one of their jokes.

After a while, Kelley looked up from his plate. "You waiting for more reasons why we don't like him? Well maybe we don't have any more reasons." He gave me a serious look.

While he was busy looking serious, Howard leaned across and stole his bacon.

I lay in my bunk, right arm hooked over my eyes, hearing a slight hiss as the bow of our boat cleared the water, then a thud as it struck the next wave.

A pot hit the floor in the galley.

Kelley laughed.

As I fell away into sleep, I listened to our engines, the constant storming of the huge Cats down below.

6

I STOOD in the galley doorway watching a muddle of people who screamed at each other on deck.

Franklin leaned on my shoulder, explaining what happened. He said that Marco had tried to use the winch to raise a dredge on deck.

Pittsley smacked the fist of one hand into the palm of his other. His face was twisted with anger and he sucked his breath in through clenched teeth.

Gil stood between him and Marco, shaking his finger and yelling.

Reynolds shouted for everyone to calm down. He shifted from one foot to the other, waving his hands in front of him.

Gil barked at the mate. "Get the fuck up in the wheelhouse and drive this boat like I'm paying you to do!"

Reynolds let his hands fall to his sides. Slowly his feet stopped shifting. He turned on his heels and climbed up to the wheelhouse.

I felt a nudge against my shoulder as Kelley ran out half asleep from the bunk room, blinking in the light. "Are we sinking? Are we going down?"

"Sinking fast." Franklin grabbed Kelley by the shoulders and shouted, "Hurry! Hurry!"

"Oh my God! Oh my God!" Kelley ran back into the bunk room.

Franklin and I sat under the deck canopy with our backs to the galley wall.

Kelley reappeared at the doorway. "We're not really sinking, are we?"

"Marco said he knew how to work the winch." Franklin pointed to the winch hook. It swung loose across the deck in the motion of the waves. "Bringing his dredge up over the side I guess Marco did O.K., but setting it on the deck he brought it down too fast. The hook popped out of the bull ring. Pittsley was right underneath it. Dredge come down right over him, hit the deck so hard it left a dent. Only reason Pittsley isn't dead is because he was standing inside the triangle part of the dredge. By the time I get on deck, he's still standing there. Just standing there trying to figure out what happened. Then he goes over and nails Marco right on the nose."

"Broke it?" Warm salt air blew in my face.

"Well, it doesn't look like it used to."

Marco stood back from the tangle of Gil and Pittsley's arguing.

I led him over to the lazarette. I sat him down on the hatch, resting my hands on his shoulders and pressing until his legs gave.

He held his hands in front of his face.

I pulled them away, gently at first but then having to use force because he tried to keep them there.

His nose was swollen and pointing in the wrong direction.

"I got to ask you something." He wiped tears from his eyes. Not from crying but from pain.

"If you're going to ask me if it's broken, I'd have to tell you I think it is, Marco." I rocked back on my heels with the next wave.

"No. I know it's bust. What I want to know is if I let Gil take some money from my pay, will he go back into port and let me get off?"

"If you ask him something like that, he may lock you down in the lazarette for the rest of the trip. Or maybe he'll just tell you to go to hell. But he won't go in. You ask him, and he might not even pay you when we do reach port. Did you tell him you'd never worked a dredge?"

"I was watching Pittsley from before and figured I could do it."

"And now you have a broken nose."

"I know it."

"Just go back to work. Best you can do is lie low. Then go home and pretend it never happened. After something like this, I wouldn't be too sure you'll keep the job."

Kelley stood over us. His shadow blocked out the sun.

Marco looked up to see who it was. "If I see land, I'm going to jump over and swim for it."

Kelley sucked at something caught between his teeth. "You do that, chump, and you better know some things. There's sharks out here, for one thing. And for another thing, you better make damn sure what you see is land. Sometimes you look at the horizon and think you see an island or the coast but it's just your eyes playing tricks. And even if you're right, you have to make it by dark, or else know how to read the stars. Because once you're out there, some wave could pick you up and slap you down facing the opposite direction. Then you'll swim straight back out to sea."

"So what am I going to do? Pittsley said he was going to kill me."

Kelley shrugged and wandered over to see what Gil was still yelling about.

A wave sprayed across the deck. I tasted the salt. "Pittsley's a glass-head. If he'd wanted to kill you, he'd already have finished the job. He wouldn't be standing around talking about it."

Marco looked at me. "We got to stick together."

"You find someone else with a broken nose and stick with

them." Then I walked away and wished I hadn't talked to him at all.

Marco's face swelled up so much I almost couldn't see his nose.

Pittsley kept threatening to kill him. Or not threatening. He aimed a finger at Marco and said nothing, only stared.

Once, Gil told us at the table, Pittsley walked up behind where Marco stood cutting scallops at his pen, and Pittsley whispered, "I'm going to rip you in pieces and let God put you together again."

"And you know what Marco said?" Gil let his head fall back against the wood paneling of the galley wall and laughed so the fat on his chest jiggled in two mounds around his nipples. "Marco said, 'Please don't.' Ah-ha-ha-ha."

Marco stayed by himself at the scallop pen.

He worked too slowly with the scallops.

No one had the energy to help him because we were pulling six baskets of scallops a haul-back. It was hard enough for Nelson and Pittsley to keep up.

Marco stood cutting long after the others were taking a break on the ice hatch, sharing smokes with their eyes crunched up from the dazzle of sun on the water.

Sometimes he was still cutting when Kelley and Howard and I came out to start the next watch. Usually, by that time, he'd only be getting in the way, and Kelley would tell him to stop.

Gil said he didn't like the way Marco cut the scallop meats. Said he was wasteful, which was true, since Marco left half the muscle in the shell.

We tried being kind to Marco. Even Kelley asked him if he felt all right. But Marco looked so ridiculous, with his noseless face and black eyes, his voice a plugged nasal hum, that Kelley burst out laughing as soon as Marco opened his mouth.

Marco would walk over to me as I washed and bagged the

scallops. After a while of stirring his hand in the meats, pretending to help, head hung low over the wash tank, he'd ask, "How's it going, buddy?"

"Good enough," I'd mumble, and walk over to the ice hatch as if I had another job to do.

I didn't forget I was new. I tried to take nothing for granted. Tried to please. But I kept away from Marco as if he was diseased, before his mistakes became my mistakes and before the bad feelings of the crew toward him became bad feelings toward me.

Reynolds sat with Marco on the ice hatch. Reynolds talked and Marco nodded, listening.

Kelley and I watched them from the bridge, where we'd gone to sit in the sun.

"See?" Kelley whispered in my ear. "They're meant for each other."

"They're only talking." I closed my eyes and felt the sun warm on my face.

"So how come he doesn't talk to us? How come he tries so hard to keep out of our way and then sits there talking to Marco as if they're pals or something?"

"Maybe you didn't give him a chance."

Kelley slumped back and sighed hard with annoyance. "Everybody gets a chance."

It was true that Reynolds stayed away from us. He had a stash of food which he kept to himself and wouldn't share. Chocolates and cheese puffs and gum.

I would have killed for a mouthful of cheese puffs.

Reynolds never told stories the way the rest of us did, giving each other something to think about when our daydreams began to repeat.

Maybe he was just another fisherman who swore to God he'd be out only another month or so to make the mortgage payments. And when those months were over, perhaps he told himself, he was going back to land for good. In the meantime, the farther he kept himself from us the better.

Reynolds must have worked hard to earn his captain's license and learn the skills it took to run a trawler. Otherwise, Gil wouldn't have hired him as mate. But even with these skills, Reynolds left me with the feeling of a man who was just passing through. Out here by mistake. Who had no time for talk or stories or us.

Six hours on. Six hours off.
   Six hours on. Six hours off.
   I no longer remembered how many days we had been gone.
   I worked from midnight until six A.M. and then from midday until six P.M. For each day that passed, I felt as if I'd been through two.

In the night on the moon-bright water, I saw a whale breach and go down.

If I stared long enough at the horizon in the afternoons, I could make out a thin strip of brown in the distance, which I thought might be an island or beaches near Montauk.
   Even if the boat went down, I told myself, I could still make it to shore. I didn't like being out of sight of land.
   But the brown was only an image of the horizon, a hard line where it touched the sea, which my eyes had shifted and retained and made to look like solid ground.

At night I saw the lights of other boats, built up like Christmas trees on the water.
   When another trawler passed close by, I saw men shuffling

under deck lights in orange and yellow rain gear, the rest of their boat hidden in the dark. The men seemed to be in a capsule, a big busy bubble drifting past.

Sometimes the horizon glowed pink. I thought it might be the glow of a city's lights. The glimmer of Manhattan in the sky.

If the dawn was clear, we often made out submarines on the surface.

Once Gil brought down a pair of binoculars and we took turns looking at men on the conning tower of a sub. They wore black and smoked cigarettes and watched us through their own binoculars.

I stood on deck between both dredges, swinging the hammer from one hand to the other. I waited for the signal to send the dredges down.

The *Gray Ghost* shuddered under me, gathering speed.

Two chains that held the pelican clips to the deck began to creak.

I listened for a click when Gil turned on the loudspeaker. By the time I heard his voice, I was already next to the starboard dredge, legs braced as the *Gray Ghost* slid into the trough of a wave, ready to smack out the pin and jump back.

Kelley and Howard waited at the cable brakes, ready to set them loose, necks hunched down into their shoulders.

The starboard dredge chain creaked again.

I caught sight of the pin bending, heard a groaning sound and then fell back as the pelican clip sprang open. The chain flailed close to my head and down onto the deck.

The dredge disappeared and then crashed against our side. The cable brake was still on.

By now I was down on my knees, cowering from the other dredge, waiting for its chain to pop. Already I felt sick in my guts from the blame I knew would fall on me.

Kelley climbed the ladder fast up to the wheelhouse.

A moment later the engines slowed and then idled.

I stood, still gripping the hammer, not daring to raise my head as Gil's shadow appeared on the deck.

For a while there was no sound except the idled engines.

I stood watching the deck plates, studying rust and trickles of sand gathered in dents and cracks.

Then Gil's shadow went away.

I looked up. Only Kelley remained on the bridge. He shook his head at me and climbed down. "You didn't have the pin set right. It wasn't in all the way." Kelley knelt on the deck and showed me what I already knew. "Gil's pissed off, all right. But I guess you know that already."

"I set the pin the way I always set it."

Kelley nodded, and held out his hand for me to help him up. "That's why Gil didn't come down here and rough you up. He's giving you the benefit of the doubt. Next time you won't have an excuse. Even if it isn't your fault."

Each time Gil walked out on the bridge, as Kelley and Howard and I stooped over the rubble of scallop shells and sand and monks, I saw his shadow.

I never looked up.

Instead I began shoveling scallops quickly into the basket.

When he climbed down to inspect, I worked even faster. When he stood behind me, I was shoveling so fast that I began to make mistakes.

"You're missing some." He picked a few scallops out of the pile I'd already been through. "You're throwing away good money, Pfeiffer."

I didn't answer. I went back to the beginning of the pile and started again.

When we prepared to set the dredges down, I couldn't take my eyes off the pins in the pelican clips. I shifted my head mechanically from port to starboard, panicking each time the chains creaked.

At the end of our watch I went to my bunk without food. I lay in the dark, my stomach turning over.

The boat was Gil's house and I no longer felt welcome in it.

The air, cold from air conditioning, smelled of dirty socks and deodorant spray from the last watch getting dressed.

I pulled a blanket from the cupboard, rough olive-colored wool with US stamped in black on one side. I pulled it over me.

The door opened, letting in light from the galley.

Gil filled the doorway with his bulk. "You aren't going to eat?"

"Not hungry." I held the blanket to my throat.

"I put a new pin on the dredge. The old one was bent."

I sat up and banged my head on the roof of the bunk. "It *was* the pin! I knew it was!"

"Maybe."

"Oh, it was, Gil! That old pin was bent and no good." I crawled out of the bunk and stood in front of him in my underwear.

"Food's there if you want it. Creamed chipped beef."

Kelley yelled from the galley, "Shit on a shingle."

I poked my head out of the bunk room and smelled the food. Then I pulled on my jeans, sat in my place at the table and stuffed my face.

As Kelley said would happen, my daydreams began to go stale. I followed the same paths of thought until I couldn't stand them anymore.

A blackness welled up in my head as I moved from the dredge to the pile to the pen and back to the dredge. I no longer thought about what I did.

It was a comfortable blackness. I used it carefully, molding its numbness inside my skull to keep bad dreams away.

Franklin never came out on deck except to peel potatoes or choose some fish for dinner.

He stood in the galley doorway and rolled his trousers up over his knees. Then he walked very carefully in his bare feet over the junk of shells and rocks. If he saw a fish he wanted, he snapped his fingers at whoever was nearest and said, "Get me this one here. This one's for supper."

The rest of the time he spent cooking in the galley, asleep or up in the wheelhouse watching soap operas with Gil on a little television.

At five o'clock every morning, Gil called over the loudspeaker and told me to wake Franklin.

I walked to the galley doorway, pulled my oiler trousers down over my boots and stepped into the galley in my socks.

There was a hundred-dollar fine if Gil caught any member of the crew wearing boots or oilers inside.

The first couple of times, I woke Franklin by rapping on his head as if it were an old coconut. After that he ordered me to whisper him awake.

"Franklin," I whispered over the murmur of air conditioners, "get up. Time to make breakfast. Get the fuck up, old man." If he wasn't awake after that, I knocked on his coconut head again.

His food tasted greasy. The portions were big, like a Sunday dinner every day, and I overate on purpose at the end of a watch to help myself fall asleep. I became used to eating grits in the morning, stirring the white porridge paste into my bacon and eggs.

Franklin let us know when Gil was in a bad mood, so we could keep out of his way.

Franklin didn't know any life other than doing what Gil or

Gil's father told him to do. He had no self-respect. Only the pride of a well-treated slave.

I wore out my rubber gloves at the rate of a pair a day. They tore around the base of my thumb, where I gripped the scallop shell as I cut out its meat. I brought ten pairs with me for the trip.

Marco had only one pair.

They shredded after a couple of days, and then he borrowed a pair from Nelson. When those were finished, no one had spares to give him. So he used ruined ones until the skin of his palm between the thumb and index finger was spider-webbed with cuts from the sharp edges of shells.

This made him work even more slowly, and often his meals were cold by the time he got to eat them.

I saw his hands as he stirred them in the scallop meats. The cuts looked deep and bled in slivers across his egg-white palm.

I took a pair of new gloves from my locker, telling myself I could stretch out a pair over another couple of days without ruining my hands.

When Marco had gone to sleep, I rolled the gloves in a ball and put them in the pocket of his rain gear. I didn't want him to think I was doing him any favors. Didn't want to make the gesture. I hoped he'd just shut up and wear them, because I couldn't bear to see his hands in such a mess.

Every day around four in the afternoon we heard a bang in the sky.

We saw nothing. The sound punched our ears and shuddered away across the water.

Gil said it was the Concorde coming down from the sound barrier on its way in from London or Paris.

While we sat at the galley table after dinner, eating a whole bag of cookies, I told Kelley what I had read in a magazine article, that the shock of a plane crossing the sound barrier was strong enough to break all the windows in a town, which was why the Concorde slowed before it reached the coast.

Kelley pointed half a cookie at me and said I didn't know what I was talking about.

"No, I believe that's true." Gil arranged his cookies in little piles. We had divided them out equally from the package. Gil ate two in each mouthful.

"Then how come the portholes aren't busted?" Kelley squinted across the table at us, hurt that we were ganging up on him.

I tried to remember exactly what I'd read. "It's still too far away to break the windows. It has to be right overhead."

"Gil, I can't believe you're agreeing with Pfeif when you know plain as day he's lying."

"Calm down, Kelley." Gil nibbled on his last cookie and then looked around to see which of us might give him some of ours. "I read it in an article. That's probably where Pfeif read it too."

"That's right." I slapped Kelley on the arm. "It's common knowledge about the sonic boom." Gil's agreeing with me even on this small thing let me think for the first time that my job on the crew might be safe.

We all turned our heads to the door.

Shouting on deck.

Gil ran outside, his hands balled into fists.

I stood with Kelley in the doorway, peering through the glare of sunlight on the water.

Nelson was trying to hold Pittsley back from attacking Marco. He pressed his palms against Pittsley's chest and yelled, "Gennuhmen, pleez!"

"He's a thief! He's wearing my gloves and he stole them from my locker. This time it's for sure. This time I really will kill him!"

Pittsley's only a coward, I thought. If he wanted to, he could push past Nelson in a second and be at Marco's throat. But there he is making threats and letting himself be held back by someone nearly half his size.

I walked to the area where we put our boots and oilers when we knocked off duty, and saw the neat blue ball of new gloves that I'd left for Marco lying under a fire extinguisher. It seemed he hadn't noticed them when he put on his rain gear, and didn't see the gloves fall out. So whatever gloves he wore now belonged to someone else.

"Did you steal them, Marco?" Gil sat down on the ice hatch and sighed, ready to judge.

"No. I didn't steal nothing. I bought these myself." Marco stepped forward and stuck out his chest. He wiggled his fingers in the gloves.

"Oh, you did?" Pittsley scratched at his chin, scheming. "You bought those yourself?"

"Muh-huh." Marco nodded, eyes narrowed, trying to read Pittsley's mind. The gloves looked enormous on his hands. The shiny, unreal blue of a postcard sky.

"Well, if you're right, then I'm sorry. I will apologize. I will apologize to everyone and you won't get any more trouble from me." Pittsley folded his arms.

Marco's eyes opened a little as he thought of the chance that Pittsley might leave him alone for the rest of the trip.

I caught sight of Reynolds. He had come out of the wheelhouse and stood on the bridge looking down. I could see the worry on his face.

The sudden quiet on deck made me nervous. I didn't trust it, and stepped back behind Kelley, who had stepped back a second before. I felt the sweat slide in my boots.

Pittlsey touched the tips of Marco's fingers. Then he pulled the gloves off in one movement and handed them to Gil. "Look under the wristband there, Gil."

Gil took the gloves, rolled back the wristband and read out,

"D. P. Now I'm going to ask you one more time again if you stole these gloves, boy." Gil handed the gloves to Pittsley, looking all the time at Marco.

Pittsley held the gloves carefully, as if they were something alive that had to be cared for.

"I got to have gloves! My hands are all cut up." Marco raised his palms and showed us the scars.

Gil held his face close to Marco's and said quietly, "It doesn't matter what you need. You don't steal on my boat." Gil climbed the ladder to the bridge.

Reynolds waited for Gil to reach the top of the ladder, then approached him and opened his mouth to speak.

Gil didn't wait for him to talk. He aimed a finger over the mate's shoulder. "Get in the fucking wheelhouse!" Then he turned and yelled down at Marco, "What happens to you now is none of my business!"

I followed Kelley back into the galley, feeling the sun on my neck and smelling diesel blown down on us by gusts of wind. I had the same acid taste in my mouth as when I once saw a policeman shoot a horse that had run out of a field into traffic and been hit by a truck.

"Pittsley's a coward." I sat with Kelley at the galley table. My legs were braced against the table legs to stop myself from sliding with the pitch of the boat.

Kelley looked up from his magazine. "What are you talking about?"

"He's a coward."

"He used to be a Green Beret. He spent six months in Laos and another six months blowing up and down the Mekong Delta on a Hovercraft. Don't try telling me he's a coward. He's a hell of a guy."

I already knew Pittsley had been in Vietnam. He wore a green T-shirt with "Special Forces" written in yellow on one side. On the other side was "Live Brave. Die Strong." I stared at Kelley. I couldn't understand why he stuck up for Pittsley when it seemed obvious to me the man was out of his mind. "If he's such a hell of a guy, Kelley, why does he stand around muttering to himself?"

Kelley slapped down the magazine. On its cover was a picture of a woman tied to a chair with a gag on her mouth, and above her, in bright yellow letters, *True Detective*.

"You know what I'm talking about, Kelley. The man has whole conversations with himself."

Pittsley liked to stand on the lazarette hatch and stare out across the water.

Sometimes he stayed there long after the others on his watch had gone to bed, rolling his hips to keep steady in the motion of the waves.

He just stood there and talked. It looked as if bubbles were rising from his lungs and pushing their way out through his mouth. His lips curled around the bubbles as they escaped.

Once, as I stood waiting with the hammer to knock out the pins, I edged over to hear what he was saying. I sidestepped closer and closer, ready to turn when he turned, to make it look as if I were minding my own business.

There were no words I could make out. Only a constant muttering, like the drone of a bee.

Kelley sat back and sighed. "It isn't his fault."

I realized then that for the crew to treat Pittsley as well as they did, there must have been some bad time he went through in the past, something they all went through together, and now they cared for him only out of pity.

Kelley was angry with me for what I said. Of all the crew, Kelley liked Pittsley the best. He stood and began to pace across the swaying floor.

I watched his broad back underneath the blurred red and black squares of his lumberjack shirt. "Well, he *isn't* a hell of a guy!" I swung my legs and let my heels fall back hard against the floor. When there was no reply, I repeated more quietly, "He isn't."

Kelley spun around. "If you knew what Pittsley's been through, you wouldn't talk that way!"

I wished I hadn't opened my mouth. I stared down at the table and picked at the wood with my fingernails.

Kelley said that Pittsley had been hanging around the docks and fishing before I was even out of first grade. He worked the *Mary Louise Q* before she went down off Nantucket. He worked the *Halifax*. Sometimes he went on board as mate, sometimes as cook and sometimes just as crew.

"He could have had his own boat if he wanted it." Kelley still paced the floor. Now and then he turned quickly, as if afraid I would sneak out of the room and leave him talking to the wall. When he saw me watching him, he turned away again.

"I'm going to have my own boat." I yawned in the stale galley air.

"Everybody says that. Everybody I ever met fishing has told me that. And the boats get bigger and bigger in their heads while they get poorer and worse into being alcoholics and then they end up at Gunther's. So don't tell me about your boat until you have it."

"I have a plan."

"Keep it to yourself."

For a while we didn't talk. Then Kelley started to tell me how Pittsley's problems began.

He had always been paranoid about his wife when he was away from home. Thirty miles off shore in the middle of the night, he'd yell at the men on his watch that he knew she was sleeping with someone else. Right then.

For a joke, sometimes, the captain would let on that he'd received a message from land, from a friend who said Mrs. Pittsley had been seen with another man late at night. The crew would all nod and keep a straight face, say they thought maybe they'd seen her with someone else and even throw in a realistic location to make the story believable.

Pittsley almost collapsed from the worry in his guts.

The crew had to stop teasing him, because there was no humor in it anymore.

When the boat reached port, he would get in his car and drive straight home, sure that he could catch her in the act. He'd pay one of the dockboys a hundred dollars to take his place unloading the fish or scallops. People called that "lumping." It was the sign of someone who needed a drink or a dose of drugs too badly to wait an extra couple of hours before the captain dismissed his crew.

Usually Pittsley's wife would be down at the Laundromat or working with retarded kids at a health center.

If she ever stayed out late while he was on land, he rode through town trying to find her. Or he called motels, claiming to be a police officer looking for a suspect, and had they by any chance seen a tall woman with frosted blond hair and green eyes.

He sat by the phone, waiting for a caller who might hang up when Pittsley was the one who said hello.

In the times when people knew he had begun to lose his mind, Pittsley sat in the dark on a sofa in his house. He wore the shreds of his uniform from Vietnam, a tiger-stripe camouflage jumpsuit with "Sin Loi" in red ink on the back. He set a gun on the table in front of him and waited for the sound of his wife walking up the gravel path with another man.

"I seen it all for myself." Kelley sat down, tired of pacing. "One time I went by his house to see if he wanted to go out for a drink. I rang the bell a couple of times and nobody answered so I turned to leave. And there he was right behind me, pointing a gun in my face." Kelley set his index finger against his forehead. "Right in my damn face."

Kelley stayed quiet for a minute.

"Of course he said he was sorry afterwards. And I forgave him. But by then he'd already done too much wrong ever to set right again. All his friends gone. Sitting in the dark in his house, wearing camouflage. I told him if he was so worried about being away from her he should just work at Gunther's instead. Be on the water first thing in the morning and be done by noon. I told him everybody knows affairs don't happen in the morning."

Pittsley's job at Gunther's was to stand at a conveyor belt that ran from the boat up onto the dock. He sorted the fish. This job was only for the regulars, because it could be done one-handed and half asleep and drunk, while others lugged shovels full of ice across the fishhouse floor or carried splintery wood crates loaded with the day's catch to refrigeration trucks.

Pittsley had been working a shorter time than many of Gunther's men, but the regulars gave him status because they all knew him. He'd been around Gunther's before.

Pittsley's wife started taking aerobics classes in the studio above Leon's Dry Cleaning shop.

It wasn't long before Pittsley could be found standing under Leon's neon sign: humm blink LEON'S blink DRY blink CLEANING blink darkness twisted gray glass tubes humm blink LEON'S.

He always had some excuse to be out at night. Kelley said that when it was over, his wife had almost no idea how paranoid he'd been. He kept it a secret from her and rarely asked where she went, thinking that she'd lie if she wanted to. He tried to keep everything level and calm in their house while he went quietly out of his mind.

Pittsley watched the heads of the aerobics dancers bouncing in and out of view.

He didn't wait there so he could walk her home. He waited so he could follow her. And it was bad news for Pittsley that one night she didn't just walk home. It was bad news, and then again it was what he'd waited for all this time.

She stood in a bus shelter until a man in a white Mustang picked her up.

This happened every other night.

The worry in his guts drained all the color out of him and made his hands shake.

He hired a private detective. Her name was DeMico and he hired her because once he knew a man with the same name.

The DeMico woman sat at her desk, clenching and unclenching a wrist strengthener, and asked Pittsley if he had ever considered the fact that his wife might be taking driving lessons. Had he thought of that? She wanted to know. Did he ever hit his wife? She wanted some facts and she wanted them now.

Pittsley told the detective that he had a fairly good marriage.

"If you did, you wouldn't be here sniveling the way you are," the detective told him.

Kelley knew all the details because they appeared in the paper afterward.

The detective asked Pittsley what he did for a living, and when he told her he was a fisherman, she said he ought to think twice before hiring a detective. She didn't want to take his money if it was a false alarm. And besides, if Mrs. Pittsley ever found out she was being tailed, she'd be pissed and it would take a long time to set right. The DeMico woman guaranteed him that. So did he know for sure what he wanted to do?

"I know what I know," Pittsley told her.

"Well, do you know two hundred dollars a day plus expenses?"

Then Pittsley leaned down, breathed in her face and told her, "I know ugliness the rest of the world has never seen."

Kelley said he had the paper clippings at home. He cut them out and stuck them in a scrapbook.

"I remember at the time, when he hired the detective" — Kelley twisted his hands in the air, looking for words — "he acted different. He was moving in fast motion. You'd say hello to him and he'd answer back 'Fine' without waiting for you to ask him how he was."

For a while the DeMico woman couldn't find out what was going on. She knew the driver of the car was a man, but no more than that. She met Pittsley every night in a bar to tell him what she didn't know.

Mrs. Pittsley started asking where he was going in the evenings. He invented some excuses, and when she found out they weren't true, she slapped him.

But Pittsley didn't explode. He stayed calm the way he'd always stayed calm in his house, and he stored away the anger like barrels of explosives behind his ribs.

To keep up the payments to DeMico, Pittsley told Gunther he had a good tip on a horse race and needed an advance on his pay. Gunther decided to lend him the money only if Pittsley would let him in on the tip. So Pittsley gave him two bogus bets for the next week. Gunther made him promise there'd be no mistakes.

"I don't make mistakes," Pittsley told him.

"No. I don't believe you do," said Gunther.

His wife accused him of having an affair. She demanded to know where he went in the evenings.

But he still wouldn't tell her. He had begun to take pleasure in making her feel the way he'd felt all this time.

He received a call at the dock from the detective, telling him to meet her at a bar on a side road off Severn Street.

When he got there, the detective bought him a drink and slapped him on the back with her strong hands. His wife had been seeing a psychiatrist. One of her friends at the aerobics club had suggested it, and Mrs. Pittsley went.

"You've been so wrapped up in your own damn problems and thinking everything was fine at home that you didn't see she was hurting." The detective bought him another drink. "So you've got some mending to do. Some apologies and rethinking to do."

The worry in him slowly drained away. The barrels of explosives dissolved. "I'll make things better now," he said.

A while later, when he and the woman were a little drunk, Pittsley looked up and saw his own car pull up on the pavement outside the bar. Then his wife barged in and walked toward his table.

Pittsley stood up and held out his arms to hug her.

Mrs. Pittsley smacked him in the head with the barrel of his own service pistol.

While her husband lay on the floor, she aimed the gun at the DeMico woman, fired and blew her backward off her chair. She set the gun against Pittsley's chest and yelled, "I ought to!" She looked at the people in the bar and yelled again, "I ought to!"

Pittsley cowered on the floor with his arms covering his head.

Mrs. Pittsley threw the gun away across the bar and sat down at the table. She sat by herself, where Pittsley and the detective had sat, and screamed at the top of her voice, "I did it! I came here to do it and it's done! You can do what you want with me because I'm finished now!"

She had heard from friends that her husband was seeing a woman at a bar each night. She pieced together what she overheard in gossip and felt sure he was having an affair. And when Pittsley wouldn't tell her where he went at night, she became positive.

She was sent to a home for the criminally insane and ate a lot of lithium.

The whole thing hit the papers and stayed in them for weeks.

Pittsley got no peace. Journalists called him at all hours of the night and waited by his car to ask him questions and flashed cameras in his face when he left for work in the morning.

Some accidents scared trawlermen like my father away from fishing, but left them no other trade to practice. The way of life was already too deep-set in their minds. It forced them to return. It was the same with Pittsley. He had no place else to go. The death of the detective and the loss of his wife sent him out to sea for good.

Pittsley hated land the way my father said he hated the ocean.

While the *Gray Ghost* stayed in Newport, Pittsley lived on the boat. He stood on deck talking to himself among the dredges going rusty, or he drank himself stupid up at Mary's bar.

"I don't want you telling anybody what I said." Kelley jabbed a finger against my arm. His cheeks looked red from the sun. "You keep your mouth shut. Now you know why everybody's good to Pittsley. Because they're afraid if they don't treat him kindly, that the same thing could happen to them." Then Kelley stood and hammered the pins and needles out of his legs. "And don't you go nuts like him either, because people won't treat you well the way they treat Pittsley. You haven't earned their respect. They don't like you so much."

"Gil likes me." Hearing about Pittsley's wife being as messed up as Pittsley hadn't made me feel any respect for the man. It only made me sorry for him, to learn about his Mekong Delta days. I felt sorry for Kelley as well, who had built Pittsley up into his private hero.

"Gil likes you because you're still a little kid." The pins and needles in Kelley's legs were too strong for him and he had to sit down. "He thinks you need taking care of. The only friend you got on this boat is me."

Being friends with Kelley didn't amount to much.

Out to sea, I usually felt too tired to ask him the right questions or listen to his stories and pay attention all the time. And on land I didn't like getting drunk the way Kelley did, ending up with no money after three days of alcohol and cocaine.

Always in the back of my mind and in the back of his was the knowledge that he had been working longer. He would always be senior to me.

It seemed that no one stayed really close on a boat. The best a person could do was work alongside a friend on the water, and then get drunk with him at the dock.

People who stayed together as friends on a boat set themselves apart from the rest of the crew, which made for friction in a place where we didn't have the energy to waste on arguing and fighting.

There was no middle ground where things were calm and un-hurried and in focus.

I would have been lonely on the boat without Kelley, but I never told him that.

"I told you about Pittsley so you won't think he's just an idiot for no reason." Kelley moved a strand of hair to the other side of his head, then smoothed it down with his palm.

I could tell he wished he'd never mentioned Pittsley. The story didn't come out the way he wanted it to. After a few minutes of breathing in and sighing, he walked into the bunk room. I heard him singing softly to himself.

I went up on the bow and watched the sunset. I was always calm then, in the marmalade light, and always calm at dawn, when the sun stayed weak and pretty and new.

This feeling never lasted long, as the heat of day arrived or the sky turned purple with the closing in of night.

Kelley rolled a sinsemilla joint.

He shared it with Howard and me. The three of us lay in our bunk room. The light was still on. None of us had the energy to get up and turn it off.

Kelley's hand swung down from the bunk above mine, the white stick billowing smoke between his fingers.

"Nobody talk. I don't want to hear anybody talking." Howard hadn't taken his clothes off all trip. His shirt looked molded to his body like another layer of skin.

None of us had showered. Sometimes we combed our hair

before going in to eat, and we washed our hands and some of us brushed our teeth, but otherwise we didn't have enough time between eating and sleeping to stay clean.

I had lost track of time on the boat. It was all I could do to remember how many hours we had left on each watch, from the bleeding of sunset and the colors of dawn splattered on the sky.

For a while the sinsemilla didn't hit me. I talked with Kelley about our time at Gunther's, my voice choked from holding down the smoke and trying to speak at the same time.

Then the drug pushed through my head and blew my brains out through my ears, leaving behind an empty, vibrating space.

I concentrated on the knots of wood in the ceiling of my bunk. As I watched, the knots became stars. I felt myself racing toward them, vertigo shuddering against my nerves. As I neared these stars, they stretched into the long bars of hyperspace and turned into the strands of a spider web. I dodged past the strands, which changed color and became the hair on a person's head. My own head. Then I felt myself step back, leaving my body and seeing what appeared to be me riding a horse across a field. The horse jumped hedges and fences that sprang up in the way. Through all this I was not afraid. The horse moved so fast that gradually the skin began to peel from its body. After a while, I was riding on bones, which fell away and left me spiraling toward the same knots of wood I had seen in the beginning.

I had to go out and get some air.

I walked into the galley. It was empty and dark except for the stove's blue flame under the always-brewing coffee pot. I made myself an enormous sandwich out of bologna and lettuce, and ate it sitting at the galley table.

Then I climbed the ladder to the wheelhouse and stood behind Gil, who hadn't noticed me come up.

He sat in his chair, feet against the wheel, watching a game show on his television.

People on the show were guessing the prices of items on display. Whoever came closest to guessing the price won the item and a chance to spin a big roulette wheel to win more money.

Gil pointed to a set of screwdrivers on the screen and yelled, "Twenty-five dollars!"

To his left, a gauge that mapped our course over the sea had run black lines back and forth over the same place until it seemed the page had worn through. Beyond him, our gray bow snubbed the horizon.

"Sure is a lot of water out there."

Gil turned around fast in his chair. "What? Something wrong? Did the air conditioning fritz out again?"

I stared at him, feeling my eyes dried out. "Hello there, Mr. Gil."

"Get out of my house."

I stood on the bridge, watching fog roll by the boat. The sun was a weak ball the color of cantaloupe. Suddenly a huge sailing ship cut past the stern. Its sails bowed out in the breeze. The ship made no sound, and I saw no one on its deck. The hair bristled at the back of my neck. The ship appeared transparent, the mist a grainy filter surrounding it.

"That's the Coast Guard training ship out of New London." Gil was standing behind me. "See the blue and orange slash on the bow? That means Coast Guard. Are you feeling all right, Pfeif?"

I nodded, climbed down to my bunk and fell asleep with my eyes open.

7

"THEY'VE KILLED HIM." I stood on deck with my hands over my face, slowly letting in the light. "They've killed Marco." I peered around again, but saw only Pittsley and Nelson cutting scallops at their pen.

Kelley pointed to a padlock that had been run through the lazarette hatch to a cleat on the deck. "I don't think they bothered."

When Marco crawled out of the dust and heat of the lazarette, his lips were fused with spit.

Nelson handed him a can of soda, which Marco drank after spending five minutes trying to pull the tab. His skin was peppered with rust. No expression showed on his face.

Pittsley ignored Marco completely. He bagged the scallops by himself and then ordered Nelson down into the ice room.

Marco slowly handed the fat bags down to Nelson and waited until both Pittsley and Nelson had gone in to eat before taking off his boots and following them.

I looked down into the lazarette and felt the heat still rising, saw coils of chain and rope like the opened belly of a whale.

While we waited for the next haul-back, Kelley, Howard and I sat on the ice hatch. We stared blank-faced and calm at the horizon.

Bottles often came up in the dredge. Old medicine bottles with a marble inside, which allowed for the correct dose to be poured out when the bottle was turned upside down. Three-cent milk bottles with wide mouths and crabs living in them. Sometimes the crabs had grown so big they could no longer get out. Once I found a hermit crab that had made a house out of a small jar. His fragile innards were visible through the glass.

We pulled up the skull of a dog miles and miles from any land.

A popped balloon came up among the scallops. Attached to it was a card written in indelible ink from a Hebrew kindergarten in Far Rockaway, New York.

Mounted on the wheelhouse wall was a plate that had been pulled off the bottom two years before. The center of the plate showed a beehive. Around the beehive, in dark red letters, was "British-American Steam Packets." The other side had a Staffordshire maker's mark. Gil said it dated from a time when the Americans and British used to deliver mail across the Atlantic by steamship.

On his mantelpiece at home, Gil said he had the rusted remains of a whaling harpoon, pulled up off Shinnecock in the winter of 1979. The metal stem of the harpoon was twisted like a corkscrew. Gil brought it to the Nantucket Whaling Museum, and they told him the harpoon was twisted that way because the whale thrashed in the water after it had been struck. They showed him other harpoons bent and curled the same way. Gil said he had never seen anything that told him more about pain than the ruined harpoon that came up in the dredge.

We pulled in old fishermen's boots, full of mud and with sprigs of weeds growing from the soles. Even after so much time on the seabed, some of them were still in better condition than the ones Marco wore.

Howard collected the boots, claiming they were good luck, which brought back the argument that a person could only do bad luck things on a boat.

This ended with Howard and Kelley throwing monkfish at each other across the deck.

I sat on the ice hatch, shouting out the score of who hit who. Then a monkfish bounced off my shoulder with a rubbery slap.

Gil had thrown it. He climbed down from the bridge and joined the game of monk throwing until all the fish had either sailed overboard or slid under the winches, out of reach.

Gil said he'd had enough fishing for now. Tomorrow we'd be going in.

I was happy to be going home, and grinned like an idiot as I chopped ice with a heavy iron pick down in the hold.

No one else seemed to care, so I hid the smile and flailed harder at the ice, sending white chips up over my shoulders and across the floor.

Howard gently laid the scallop bags side by side on a fresh bed of ice.

I noticed he was giggling. "What are you laughing about?" I stopped work. Steam rose off my sweaty arms.

He shook his head and kept giggling. After a minute, he was laughing so hard that he had to sit down. "I always get this way when we're going in. I feel like such a fool but I can't help it."

I nodded, then sat down next to him and felt the grin spread on my face.

The moon looked yellow and diseased.

It burned through black clouds and wallowed on the horizon.

We passed the Brenton Reef Light at two in the morning.

The light stood on heavy metal stilts. Iron buoys floated nearby. Bells attached to the buoys clanged as each wave beat against them.

Newport looked dark, except for street lamps and the necklace of the Newport Bridge.

I watched car headlights swing past on Ocean Drive, like animals that came to spy on us and ran away again.

Gil slowed the *Gray Ghost* just outside the harbor and we brought our outriggers down. I did my job of standing on deck, arms raised at the angle of each rigger, calling out if they lowered unevenly.

Marco's face had deflated a little, but his nose was still a bubble. He walked on deck when we came in sight of land.

Nobody pushed him to work after he crawled out of the lazarette. No one had to, since there was no more work to do.

We passed a couple of small lobster boats heading out to their pot lines in the coves and off the local beaches. Each boat had one- or two-man crews. They waved to us as they sped by, strong motors pressing their open sterns close to the water.

They'd be back with their loads before the markets opened.

I thought of the lobstermen, close to shore and running their own businesses without the worry of being caught in storms or handling large crews. I thought of them walking through empty streets down to the docks in the early morning and coming home to their houses at the end of the day.

The times I had watched boats from the beach and wondered how it was to be a fisherman, it was lobster boats I saw. When Joseph and I talked about running a boat, it was a lobster boat we had in mind.

I decided to stay with Gil until I had the money to buy a small boat for myself. Then I'd set down lobster pots and start a business of my own. If I was wrong, I could turn around, sell the boat and go back to college.

It was the first time I had thought of school in ages. My memory of the place and the classes and the people seemed old now. Already they were vague and yellowed, packaged away and unimportant. I realized then that I wouldn't be going back in the fall. It came to me so calmly and clearly that I felt as if I had always known.

The heavy smell of land reached me from across the water. A heavier smell than the sea. Sitting thicker in my lungs, as if I didn't need to breathe as much of it to keep myself alive.

We tied up at Sabatini's, and Gil said for everyone to be back on the boat by seven A.M.

Howard left for home and Franklin went to find his girl. The rest of us sat at the galley table, eating whatever we could find in the food lockers.

Kelley made a sandwich out of white bread and cake frosting.

The sight of him putting it away made me feel ill, so I walked out on deck.

"Where you going to, Pfeif?" Gil stood on the bridge with a six-pack of beer dangling from his hand.

"I guess I'll sleep here if it's O.K." I squinted up into the work lights.

A can of beer sailed out of the dazzle and I caught it.

"You can stay here if you want. You can live on the boat like the others if you need to."

"Do I get to keep my job, then?" I had been worried about losing my spot on the crew, and was waiting for the right time to ask.

"Do you want to keep it?" He switched off the deck lights. The huge bulbs died.

"I'll keep the job as long as I can." I pulled the tab and beer shot up in my face.

"Are you just a summer kid? I've been meaning to ask. Are you planning on just a couple of trips and then blowing away and I don't see you until school gets out next year? I like things to run smoother than that."

"I know."

"I like a smooth-running machine. If I keep switching crews, things'll never settle down. Enough things go wrong when I think I'm doing them right. So do me a favor and let me know if I can count on you for more than a couple of trips."

"I'm saving up for my own boat."

"What kind of boat?" He crumpled an empty can in his fist.

"I'm thinking about a lobster boat. Small one. A boat I can run by myself."

Gil nodded, chewing at his lower lip. "I'll put you on full share. Then you can earn your boat."

I opened my mouth to say thank you.

Before I could speak, Gil walked into the wheelhouse and shut the door. The light in his cabin blinked on and then off.

Marco appeared from the galley and climbed onto the dock. He turned and looked at me without speaking.

Beer dripped from my eyebrows. "Are you coming back?"

He picked at the tar on top of a piling. "Gil gave me a hundred dollars and said he was being fair." He looked up suddenly. "Do you think he was being fair?"

I drank from the can and shrugged. If he had given Marco nothing, I wouldn't have been surprised. "You have to take what he gives. Are you pissed off about it?"

"I don't know yet. My nose hurts and I can't think straight." He walked off the dock and up toward Severn Street.

A flashlight beam shone from Lester's boat. Lester shouted, "Private dock! Fuck away!"

Marco reached Severn Street.

I bet myself a dollar he'd turn right.

He turned left and disappeared.

I took a dollar bill from my wallet and dropped it into the water.

I didn't think Marco would come around again. I knew it. I was sure.

Steam rose from the concrete ice room floor.

Muffled sounds filtering down from the deck.

I used a hammer to chop ice from around the bags of scallops.

Nelson lifted the bloated white sacks and handed them to Kelley. Kelley brought them to the scales, where Howard hovered over the dockboys, making sure there was no cheating.

Suddenly Gil yelled, "Damn you!"

When I looked up, he was staring down at us. His face had puffed up red with anger.

I couldn't tell whether he was yelling at Nelson or at me. I shifted my eyes over to Nelson, as if to guide Gil's stare toward him.

Gil's body blocked out the light as he swung down the ladder.

In the couple of seconds it took him to reach us, Nelson and I looked at each other.

Nelson stood with his arms by his side, mouth half open, snorting small bolts of steam. He seemed to be hiding himself in his own fog cloud.

Gil's feet slapped on the floor as he touched down. Then he spun around and shoved me in the chest.

I fell over onto a pile of ice, feeling my hands sink into the sharp frozen crumbs.

"You son of a bitch! Don't be using a hammer to take out the scallops!"

"I'm sorry. I'm sorry." I didn't dare raise my head. You won't fire me now, will you? I thought. Not after you said I could keep the job. You can't fire me now, Gil.

"When you take the bags out" — he bent over me and twisted my shoulder so I faced the scallop pen — "you use your hands." He made his hands into rakes and dug them into the ice, clearing it away.

Over and over, I rammed my fingers into the ice. I uncovered the pale bags and handed them to Nelson. As if Gil wasn't there anymore. As if he had never been there and I'd never thought of using a hammer.

Gil watched for a while.

I saw the hair smoothed flat on his arms as I twisted my body to hand the next bag to Nelson.

When Gil finally left, I looked at my fingers. From all of them except my thumbs, fat trickles of blood ran down onto my palms.

"How long you been fishing, Nelson?" I tried to make talk now that Gil had gone away.

Nelson shuffled his feet in the ice and rolled his eyes, thinking. "Five years."

When he arrived at Sabatini's that morning, he was driving a red Trans Am.

Kelley caught me staring at it and said not to be so impressed. To meet payments on that car, he told me, Nelson would be fishing and living with his parents and eating macaroni until his bones grew old and cracked. It wasn't even a little bit paid for.

"Have you fished all the time with the *Gray Ghost*?" I handed over another bag, cold and heavy.

"Always."

After a few more questions, I gave up talking to Nelson. He never answered with more than one or two words.

Pittsley poked his head down into the ice room and grinned at us upside down.

During the night, he'd gotten drunk on grain alcohol called Ever Klear. While he was drunk, he decided to shave his head. Now his scalp looked blue next to the red sunburn on his face and neck.

"Any relation to Russ Pfeiffer?" He smacked his lips at me.

I nodded. "My father."

"I worked on his boat. The *Glory B.*" He made fun of the name by the way he said it. "That was about two years ago. I quit."

"Why did you stop working with my dad?" I looked up at him through shreds of steam.

"It was an O.K. boat but he didn't ever catch any fish. We used to stay out a week and come back with less than other boats made in three days. I swear, he had the worst luck of any fisherman I ever knew."

I couldn't tell if he was trying to be mean or just telling me because maybe it was the truth.

"He put my brother through college and he'd put me through too, if I wanted to go. He does all right, Pittsley. Maybe you just hexed the boat."

"Put your brother through college? He was always talking about how his sons would never fish. I remember now." He grinned. "And there you are down in the ice room of a trawler."

"I fish because I want to, Pittsley." I thought about saying something to him about his wife and the detective. Something that might end in a fight. Something to hurt him deep. But it didn't seem he was laughing at me. He had only told the truth and found it funny. "My father catches enough fish to put my brother through college. That and keep a house and a wife. That sounds like plenty of fish to me, Pitts."

Then he smiled with his whole face. "He makes his money. He does that all right. But I still quit his boat." He went away and Gil yelled down to hurry with the scallops.

It was a bright day outside. The streets were full of Gatsby boys and girls, clean and sharp-featured and hiding their eyes behind aviator sunglasses. They drove up and down on the cobblestones of Severn Street in their Jeeps, stopping traffic to talk when they met a friend coming the other way.

Punks on skateboards did tricks in front of the ice cream shops.

I didn't want to call home yet.

I practiced the blank stare I would need when my mother and father made up their minds what to say to me. I wondered if they'd figured it out already. Perhaps they had even rehearsed, sat facing the couch where they would sit me down, sharpening their words and making up replies for anything I could answer back.

I remembered the place far inside where I could go and hear their voices only as echoes, hear myself saying, "How much can they hurt you now? What damage can they do?"

We sat on the dock waiting for our pay.

Kelley said a crew could never tell what the amount might be, because only the captain knew how much fuel had been burned, whether new parts for the boat had to be bought and whether the price of scallops and monkfish had risen or fallen since the last time in port.

Crewmen who'd been fishing long enough would know if they were being cheated.

But the captain could pay his people whatever he wanted. He could fine them for some made-up offense or lie about the cost of fuel. He could be a pirate to his crew. There would always be new people ready to take the places of the ones who quit. But he ran the risk of having his boat burned at the dock. Or his house torched. Or seeing his car in flames.

It seemed to me that a thieving captain was always paid back with fire. All the stories I had heard of crookedness and cheating ended with gallon cans of gasoline.

When Gil appeared from Sabatini's office, he walked quickly across the hot tar of the dockyard to our boat. He carried a black trash bag knotted at the top.

He ordered the galley door shut and the wheelhouse locked. Then he sat us all down at the galley table.

He handed out stacks of bills to each of us and said we all were getting the same. Nineteen hundred dollars with no social security numbers taken down, no job forms filled out and no questions asked about where we lived or next of kin. The bills were bound with yellow rubber bands.

Gil told us to be back on the boat at noon in three days' time.

Kelley asked me if I wanted to drink with him at Mary's.

I said I had to go home.

He held my face in his hands and squeezed. "Well, you know where to find me."

I didn't know where to find him and I didn't ask. I was thinking too much about going home.

Swaying slightly, I walked across the asphalt toward Severn Street, the motion of the boat still inside and making me move like a drunk.

I recognized the thin shape perched on one of Sabatini's barrels long before it came in focus.

My father sat with one leg hooked over the other, blinking in the dust and trickling heat that separated me from him.

When I came close, he took off his hat and smiled. Then he scratched at his face and stopped smiling. "Hundred forty bags of scallops isn't bad." He waited for me to speak but I stood looking at his boots, the tan leather chafed into suede and the toes pointing in at each other. He cleared his throat. "Not bad at all."

"It was a good boat so I took the job." My pack felt heavy so I set it down.

"*Gray Ghost* is a fine boat." He uncrossed his legs and rocked forward slightly on his hips. "Need a ride home or are you going up to Mary's?"

I thought, You're showing me that wherever I try to go you'll be there. Everything that happens you'll know about. How big the catch. How much money. How good the boat. You want me to think you'll know what I'm going to do before I've even thought of it, and maybe you will.

I sat in the truck, hugging my pack to my chest as we drove up the Newport Bridge. Waves on the bay became threads of white two hundred feet below.

"I'm not angry." He looked ahead, hat turned backward on his head like a baseball catcher, the way it always was when he drove. "What I want to know is, are you going back to school in the fall?"

"I want to buy my own boat."

He nodded and didn't speak until we were off the bridge. Then he stopped his truck by the side of the road and turned his whole body to face me. "You go out for one trip and you come back wanting your own boat. You expect me to say nothing about that? You expect me not to call you a fucking idiot?"

"I want a small boat. A lobster boat. Something that stays in close to shore that I can run with one other person or by myself. I thought about all the things you told me, about all the dangers of storms and having no family life, and I thought about you drifting out at sea that time you fell overboard. And none of that's going to happen if I just run a small boat close to shore." I sat back and stared at the hood of the truck. It seemed to be dissolving in the heat. "I've been wanting my own boat since the first week you sent me to work at Gunther's."

He stayed quiet for a while. "What kind of a future is that? What kind of prospects does that give you?"

I thought then, without speaking, of the way it would be, heading out into the glitter of sunrise each morning, water skimming past the hull, then the ride back, holding tanks weighed down with lobster. I looked at him. "I'd start today if I could."

"What if it doesn't work out?"

"Then I could go back to school. I don't see what you can have against me running a small boat close to shore, not after all you've said."

"It's true you'd be home at the end of the day. And maybe you wouldn't get yourself killed. Maybe." He tapped me on the shoulder. "We can talk about this." He smiled and tapped me again. "At least this is something we can talk about."

He started the truck engine and just as suddenly he switched it off again. "I can't help you with paying for the boat. The money's a little tight now. I haven't told your mother this, but even if you were going back to school, I don't know if I could make the payments. I've been looking into guaranteed student loans. The fishing is poor right now."

"I met a man who used to work with you on the *Glory B*. He said the fishing's always poor with you. Man's a fool."

"What's he called?"

"Pittsley. I don't know his first name."

"Tall? Black hair and blue eyes? Lost his mind in the Nam?"

"Him. Yes."

"I fired that man."

"He said he quit. He's about the only one on the crew I don't get along with."

"I fired him." He turned the key and gassed the engine but it wouldn't start. He turned it again and it still didn't start. Then he screamed something that didn't sound like words and punched the rearview mirror, which broke and fell at my feet.

I felt my stomach muscles cramp when he screamed. I had thought he was calm and didn't know what it was that made him explode.

To break the silence as we drove home, I asked him if it was really true that he had bad luck with fishing. He turned to me, lips pulled back over his teeth. "What do you care, as long as the money comes in?"

At dinner, I told my mother about my idea to run a small boat.

"And if it doesn't work, he'll go back to school. It sounds safe enough to me." My father nodded.

She didn't seem to be listening. She gnawed at a piece of corn on the cob and said nothing. Then suddenly she dropped the cob on her plate and stared hard at my father. "You're an old fool!" She turned to me. "And you're another fool! Make your father tell you about Henry van Gerbig! Tell him, Russ!"

"I never heard of anyone by that —"

"Oh, yes you have, Russell! Henry van Gerbig. Used to live on Jamestown."

"Oh, I remember." He nodded and stood up with his plate, making for the kitchen.

"You tell James about van Gerbig, or I will."

He set down his plate and sighed. "Man named van Gerbig

used to run a small boat out of Jamestown. He sold his lobsters in Newport about twice a week. He worked by himself, had one of those boats with an open back so the pots could slide off easily. Well, one day he must have just fallen overboard and nobody found him. His boat washed up on the south end of Jamestown. We took you to see it. Remember?"

I remembered the boat. It had sunk just short of the beach, and only its mast showed above the water. It looked like a dead tree in a flooded field. We reached the place at twilight and stayed until the mast from van Gerbig's boat had folded away into the dark. Then we rode home. Joseph and I stood in the back of the truck, our faces whipped by the wind.

Father told the story of van Gerbig and made another move for the kitchen.

"No! Finish it!" Mother slammed her hand flat on the table. Our glasses jumped. The milk in them swayed back and forth. "Tell James now what you didn't tell them then!"

Father sighed and scratched at the back of his neck. "You know how the lobstermen around here set five or six pots on one line and pull them up on deck with little winches? Well, they set those pots down again by putting the boat in gear. They push over one pot and the other ones get pulled in after it. You have to watch the line between the pots because it pays out pretty fast." He caught his breath. "Well, van Gerbig must have caught his foot in one of the coils of rope and got pulled down."

"And what else?" Mother spoke softly now, seeing that it hurt him to recall the way the man had died.

"They know it happened that way because one of the cleats on the boat was torn out. He caught his foot in the rope and grabbed the cleat and tore it out on his way down. And there was blood all over the stern where he ripped up his face and his hands trying to hold on." Then Father walked into the kitchen.

I heard him set his dish in the sink.

Mother rested her hand on my arm. "You see? You see why I

made him tell you that? They never found van Gerbig. He ended up as bait for his own traps."

"I still think James is on to a good idea, if it's what he wants to do." Father sat down at the table again. "There's a lesson from what happened to van Gerbig, but it's no reason to go screaming and hollering in the opposite direction."

"Are you forgetting all the talks we had when he and Joseph were little. Are you?"

"Van Gerbig was a drunk. Your father was a drunk. I bet they were both drunk when they died. I bet it was why they died. You're living in fear of the wrong things."

I sat through this with my neck hunched down into my shoulders, feeling the air hot with old anger rising to the surface.

My mother dabbed at her mouth with a napkin and then said very softly, "Don't you talk to me about living in fear, Russell."

He sat back in his chair, the wood creaking with his weight. "I'm glad he's found something he wants to do."

"So do it." She smiled and clapped her hands. Her face was ugly with sarcasm. "Do it today." She walked out the back door and I heard her feet crunch on the gravel of the driveway.

I sat for a moment picking at the loose kernels of corn on my plate. "I would if I had the money."

Father looked up and sniffed. "I know it."

I had no idea how long I would be working on the *Gray Ghost* before I'd have enough to buy my own boat. And then I'd have to work as an apprentice for someone, to learn the ropes. I'd have to buy pots. Find out where to set them down. Buy a license. Insurance. Rent a spot on a pier.

It all plowed around in my head and I couldn't sleep. I blinked dry-eyed out the window at the orange street lamps, feeling my bed too large after the cramped bunk, and strangely naked after days of sleeping in my clothes. My hair was like fluff after the hour-long shower. The only dirt that remained was rubbed into the calluses on my palms.

Joseph had a new plan.

He heard from a friend about people who sold surplus factory items on a television program called *Shopping at Home*. Models walked back and forth in front of the camera wearing clothes or jewelry that hadn't sold in stores, while the announcer worked up his audience by saying that the item's retail value was a hundred dollars, but anyone who called in the next ten minutes could have it for thirty. Then *$30* would flash on the screen while the model smoothed her hands up and down her dress and smiled, and the announcer said he couldn't believe what a bargain it was.

Joseph bought five hundred copies of a record from a warehouse in Massachusetts. The records cost two dollars apiece and he hoped to sell them for fifteen.

The record was called *National Anthems of the World*. The cover drawing showed dozens of people in national costumes. They all had their mouths open. Out of their mouths came words in different languages. On each record was a red sticker that said "Jumbo LP."

"You want in?" He stood in the bathroom while I showered. He had to shout over the noise of rushing water.

"What's 'in'?" It was my second shower of the day and my third since coming home. I couldn't stay out of the water.

"On the deal. You want a cut of the profits? The records are all set to go on the air tomorrow night. The TV station gets fifteen percent. It's all been taken care of. So the hard part's done. I'm just offering you a cut is all."

I switched off the shower and groped past the curtain for my towel.

He shoved it into my hand.

I wrapped the towel around my waist and stepped out. "You want me to buy some records?"

Joseph measured a space in front of him. "You buy them wholesale and take the profit when they sell on TV. Minus the fifteen percent, of course. I'm only" — he measured another space, blocking out his deal — "only doing this to give you an introduction to business. Maybe talk some sense into you, when you see you don't have to float around Narragansett Bay for a living."

"I'm saving up for a boat."

"You'll get your boat a lot faster my way."

"I'm going to think about it."

"Come on, James! Seize the day!"

"I'll seize it when I have some time to think." Then I went to my room and sat very still. The whole Atlantic Ocean thundered through my head.

Joseph brought home a girl named Rachel.

He met her when she asked to test-drive a car. He liked her so much he told her where to get a better deal. He came home with a sack of lobsters and the girl, and we cooked his lobsters in a big black pot on the stove.

She was a dental assistant. She talked about fluoride and asked to see our teeth. She'd just been down to the Bahamas. Her legs were smooth and red-brown from the sun.

We ate the lobsters with melted butter, breaking the claws with nutcrackers. The pink armor of their shells piled up in a bowl my mother had set out in the middle of the table.

Rachel talked fast and smiled when she ate.

Joseph glared at us in the moments of quiet, ordering us with his eyes to make conversation.

"Can we go out on your boat sometime, Mr. Pfeiffer?" She held up a piece of rubbery claw meat and waited for his answer, butter running down her fingers.

"It's not —" My father talked into his milk mug, voice bouncing back in his face. He set the mug down and cleared his throat, touching the knuckles of his fist against his mouth. "It's not really the kind of boat you go out on unless you're working."

"Why is that?" She set the lobster meat on her tongue and seemed to swallow it without chewing.

He blinked once at Joseph, knowing then that Joseph had not told her the *Glory B* was a trawler. "It's a fishing boat." He nodded, agreeing with himself. "I'm a fisherman."

"What is it you fish for?" She picked a roll from the basket and pulled little bits off it, letting them fall on the wreckage of her lobster.

"Anything we can get!" He laughed and sat back in his chair.

Joseph fiddled with the nutcracker, crunching loose pieces of lobster shell.

"I like to fish." Rachel sprinkled salt on the roll and nibbled at it. "But I don't like taking the hooks out."

"What kind of boat did Joseph tell you I had?" My father started gathering the plates.

Joseph stood and began to collect the remaining things on the table, as if he were in a competition with Father to see who could carry the most. "What's for dessert?"

"Well, I don't know, Joseph." Mother was pleased the topic had changed. "You said you were taking care of everything."

Through all this, I sat wondering why it was that I always felt awkward when Joseph brought girls home. I had stayed quiet during the meal. A last slight pitching of the boat still ran through my head, back and forth the way the mackerel used to rush in Gunther's nets, dark silver-green shadows under the iron-gray water.

I made inventory lists in my head, checking off things I would need when the time came to run my boat. Rope and buoys and anti-fouling paint.

"No. Really." Father stacked the plates and held on to them, as if Joseph might try to take them away. "What kind of boat?"

"Oh." Rachel twisted a silver bangle on her wrist, still smiling. "The little rascal had me thinking it was a cruise ship."

"I didn't call it a cruise ship," Joseph said very quietly.

"Well, that's what it sounded like." Rachel turned her head to speak as he walked past into the kitchen.

"A cruise ship." Father's face stayed blank for a second. Then he grinned. "Cruise ship!" He looked at Joseph in the kitchen and smiled and was miserable.

I put all my money except a hundred dollars in a savings account at a bank near Sabatini's.

Then I walked across the street to Mary's, where I knew the crew would be. I peered through a fishing net strung across the window and decorated with lobsters. The door was open. I listened to the talk inside.

Franklin and Gil were trying to buy a pinball machine from the bartender, who had long and greasy gray hair. The barman said it wasn't his to sell.

"I want it! I want it and I'm going to get it!" Gil stamped and sat down at a little table with a red and white checked cover. He ordered a dozen raw oysters with hot sauce.

Franklin fussed around after Gil, pulling the chair out for him to sit down. "He means it!" Franklin cut the air with his palm in the direction of the barman. "Gil gets what he wants and it's a fact!"

Pittsley was talking to a crewman from the *Halifax*, which pulled up the remains of a small plane off New Bedford the week before. It was a Cessna, and all that remained of the pilot were some bones and bits of rotten clothing in the cockpit.

The *Halifax* crewman showed Pittsley some Polaroids he had taken.

Gil raised his hand, like a pupil in class, and asked to see. A big smile of hot sauce was smeared across his face.

Howard stood on the bar in front of a television bolted up

near the ceiling. He turned from channel to channel. He was wearing a new leather jacket zipped to the throat.

I looked up at him. "What are you doing?"

"A New Bedford trawler got caught last night running drugs off the New Jersey shore. I heard about it this morning from one of the Newport police, and now I'm waiting for it to hit the news." He gave up turning channels and switched the TV off. "What you drinking, Pfeif?"

"Maybe some mescal."

He ordered me some. "What do you think of my jacket, Pfeif? Cost me damn near two hundred dollars!" He stood and waved his arms, like a bird with tar on its wings.

"It makes your legs look thinner than they are."

The bartender handed me a shot glass full of mescal.

I sniffed at the honey-colored liquid and drank it fast. As it burned in my throat, I began wishing I'd drunk water or something with no kick.

"I was thinking that too!" Pittsley tried to fit quarters into the jukebox but kept dropping them on the floor. "Your legs look even more twiggy than before!"

Eventually the barman had to help Pittsley with the jukebox, inserting the quarters and asking in a soft voice, "Which song do you want?"

Pittsley bent down over the clear screen and pointed to the titles.

The mescal reached me, like being hit over the head with a pillow. "Where's Kelley?"

"Now tell me the truth!" Gil rested his forearms on the little table. "Did you ever kiss Kelley on the lips?"

I snorted and turned back to the bar and ordered more mescal.

"He bought himself a new camera and went to take pictures. That was a while ago." Gil pulled a plastic lobster from the window net and bit off its tail.

*

142

I walked down Severn Street to the bus stop.

Someone called to me as I cut across the grass by the old court-house, a brick building with white stone steps left over from Colonial times.

I looked around but couldn't see anyone.

The call came again, and then I saw it was Kelley. He stood locked in a set of punishment stocks outside the courthouse.

In Colonial times, criminals were put in them for minor offenses and left there overnight for people to throw tomatoes at.

Kelley said he'd been walking around with his new camera and saw some tourists having their picture taken in the stocks. When they were finished, he ordered some kids playing on the grass to take his picture in the stocks.

While one kid stood back with the camera, another kid came up from behind and stuck a branch through the iron loops that locked the stocks together.

Then they used up the rest of the film, taking pictures of Kelley going insane and trying to escape.

When the film ran out, they put the camera around his neck and ran away.

"At least they gave your camera back." I set him loose.

"I just hope no one I know saw me in there." He looked around for signs of anybody staring, but saw only the taxi men, who kept their yellow cars in the shade of trees that grew on the courthouse lawn. They sat on the hoods of their cars, wearing jeans and T-shirts with suspenders. People said they all went and had vasectomies together.

"I used to have a camera, Kelley."

We sat at the bus stop, hogging a bench.

"Camera like this?" He held up his purchase. It was cheap, with a plastic lens.

"Different."

Kelley handed me the camera. "Help me get the film out."

I rewound his film, opened the back and took out the canister.

143

"So what happened to your camera?"

"Someone stole it."

"This one only cost me twenty dollars. Get one of these."

I opened my mouth to tell him about how I was kicked out of school, then said nothing, feeling the familiar anger rise up in me when I thought about it.

A bus swung around the corner and stopped in front of the YMCA. Old ladies clattered out onto the street. They huddled for a few seconds, trying to get their bearings, before heading off in different directions.

"Going home?" He stuffed the roll of film into his shirt pocket.

I nodded, thinking that he would forget to have the film developed and I should see to it for him. "Where are you staying?"

He pointed upward. "I got a room at the Y. It's clean, at least."

I climbed on the bus and poured a handful of change into the fare box. As my bus pulled away, I looked out the window and saw Kelley still sitting on the bench, taking pictures with no film in his camera.

I took my camera bag from the closet and rummaged through the filters, each one in its own plastic case. I checked the dates on my spare rolls of film, saw they were expired and threw them away. I put my hand in the empty space where the camera should have gone and brushed out crumbs of dirt.

Over and over in my head I saw Bartlett sliding off the hood of his car.

Then I saw myself through the eyes of the Executive Committee. Saw myself fiddling with my top button, feeling choked by the tie. And I saw how I took a handkerchief from my pocket and pressed it against my face to soak up the sweat.

In the final picture, which returned and returned to me at night before I fell asleep, I saw my room at college. My bed stripped and only a mattress on the bed frame. Torn poster corners from where I had glued pictures to the wall. The drawers of my desk open and empty.

I put the camera bag away and sat on my bed, wondering if I should have done what Joseph said and brought the boy down from behind. And even if I did that, I wondered how much longer I'd have stayed before finding some other reason to leave college. I thought about writing Bartlett a letter and thanking him for stealing my camera. Then I laughed to myself in the empty room. My voice bounced back off the walls.

"What's wrong? What happened?" Joseph sat forward in his chair and slapped the television.

"The sound is broken again." Mother knelt in front of the screen and played with the controls. "It's been doing this for a while." She turned to Joseph. "And it doesn't help one bit you punching the set."

"But it's my night! They're selling my record tonight! How am I supposed to know if they're doing it right if there's no sound?" He was red in the face and kept smoothing back his hair.

"We'll just have to watch it with no sound." She sat in her chair and folded her arms. "The picture's worse since you hit the set. That solved everything when you laid into the panel there. Did a lot of good, didn't it?"

We had been watching the *Shopping at Home* channel for half an hour, waiting for Joseph's record to be displayed. They sold a luggage set, then switched to a gold-plated necklace and after that a sweater with a picture of a parrot sewn on the back.

The announcer stood holding a microphone in front of the camera. He wore a jacket and tie. He moved his mouth.

"Goddamn you to hell!" Joseph stamped on the carpeted floor.

Then the picture showed the cover of Joseph's record. The little people with strange black words seeming to pour into their mouths rather than out.

The announcer again. Talking. Not talking.

Now they must have been playing one of the anthems.

The camera showed two models saluting and smiling. One of them still wore the sweater with a parrot on the back.

Announcer. He pointed at the camera. $25 flashed on the screen, on and off while the announcer kept talking.

The two models again. They both held on to the record cover and smiled. The screen still flashed $25.

Then a red X appeared in front of the $25, and at the other end of the screen $10 appeared and began flashing.

"No! Fifteen!" Joseph stamped both his feet on the floor. "I told them fifteen!"

"You did say the records were going to cost fifteen dollars." Mother nodded and bit her lip. "That's what you told me, anyway."

"No!" Joseph ran into the kitchen and phoned the television station.

Mother and I sat watching the screen. We didn't speak.

"This is Joseph Pfeiffer. Mr. Carrera? Yes, this is Joseph Pfeiffer. The one with the records. Look, I told you to sell it for fifteen dollars, not ten. Yes, you have ten dollars up on the screen. Yes, please, I would like it changed immediately. To fifteen! I don't care. I want it done now! Thank you, Mr. Carrera. Yes. Goodbye."

A few seconds later, a red X appeared over the $10 and the price went up to fifteen.

The announcer smiled and pointed at the camera, his shoulder hidden by the blinking $15 sign.

Joseph sat down next to me.

I kept my eyes on the screen.

I dreamed I was lying in a box and couldn't move.

My hands were crossed on my chest and I smelled of chemicals.

Then someone I could not see put a lid on the box.

I realized it was a coffin and felt myself being carried down a flight of steps.

The box shuddered as the people set me down.

I waited for the lid to open.

Something hit the lid of the coffin, and something else, and then more thuds, which I knew were earth, and I was being buried.

I called for help but no sound came out. I yelled until it felt as if my throat would rip but made only the faintest murmur.

I yelled and yelled and felt the air becoming thick and unbreathable in the coffin.

Then I sat up in bed and filled my lungs with damp breeze blowing in off the salt marshes and through my open window.

Suddenly I heard a cry from my parents' room. Then another. I realized that the sound from the other room had become my own crying in the dream. It had worked its way into my sleep.

It was my father. He kept saying "Please," dragging the word out. Pleeease. Pleeheease.

I left my bed fast and opened my bedroom door.

Joseph stood in the way, having left his bedroom and crept on bare feet across to my room. He held up his hand for me to be quiet.

Father's voice was cracked with tears and he breathed heavily between each call for help.

"Russ, it's only a dream." My mother's voice was hushed and sad. "Russ, it's not there."

"The fish. The fish is coming. He's under me. I can see him. He's coming around. He's coming right at me!"

"Russ! You're going to wake everyone. Russ, honey."

I heard his cries muffled as she held his head to her chest.

"He's there! I can see him. He goes away but he always comes back. Oh, please somebody come get me. Please somebody come. I'm so tired. I can't stay floating much longer. Pleeeese."

"You're on land now, Russ. You want to take a walk in the

147

garden? Russ?" She whispered at him, and I heard the bed-springs squeak as she rocked him back and forth.

He screamed. "The fish!"

Joseph and I both flinched when he cried out. Joseph stood with his jaw clenched and eyes almost closed, still with his hand raised as if I might try to go forward to the white door of our parents' room at the end of the dark corridor.

"Russ, you can't keep having these dreams. You just can't, honey. It'll tear you up inside. Don't make me cover your mouth again. It hurts me to do that. You're home now and you're safe. Safe. The fish isn't here."

"He's here." He was exhausted now. His voice became a murmur. "He goes away but only for a while."

I had never heard him calling out before in the night. Maybe it started only a short time ago, I thought, or maybe in the past my mother had been quicker to cover his mouth and hide his crying.

When the noise from their room had stopped, Joseph walked to his room and shut the door. He had not looked at me once.

I stayed for a moment, alone in the hallway, then moved silently back to my bed.

8

"JAMES!" It was Emily. She pressed her nose against the window of the café where I sat drinking tea and waiting for Mary's to open.

I had left on the bus for Newport early that morning, before my parents were awake.

I told Joseph to let them know I'd gone on another trip.

We didn't speak about the night before.

He only nodded and said he would tell them, as he fumbled with the coffee pot.

The boat wasn't due to leave until the next day, but I decided to stay at the Y. I didn't want to see my father's face worn out from the bad dream. I didn't want an explanation.

"So here you are being a Gatsby boy!" She sat at my table and set aside the newspaper I was reading.

"I'm not being a Gatsby boy. I'm only drinking tea."

"But that's how every good Gatsby boy begins his day. In some flashy café with the daily news." She wore white trousers and a blue sweatshirt with URI in faded letters on the front. She looked pretty. More pretty than I remembered.

"I ran after your car that day I saw you last. I tried to catch up with you."

"Why?" She opened her purse and pulled out a pack of cigarettes.

"I was going to tell you . . . I was going to say . . . say we shouldn't have left things the way we did." I glanced down at my cup. "That's what I was going to say."

"And how did we leave things?" She talked with the clean white stick of an unlit cigarette between her lips.

"You said it was a shame about us."

"It was. Maybe if you'd run a little faster, it wouldn't still be a shame."

"It doesn't have to be."

"Oh, it does, James. It absolutely does."

"All these years." I remembered the dozens and dozens of tiny fights she and I used to have. Never big fights. Never fights that decided something. Only little fights that stopped us speaking for days at a time.

"All these years." She repeated what I said, then lit her cigarette and waved the matchstick in front of her until the dot of flame collapsed into smoke.

I knew if we kept on talking like this, there would be yet another fight. I sat back and drained the last milky trickle of tea from my cup. Then I set the cup carefully back on its china saucer. "So how's living with your uncle?"

"Good. My uncle got me a great summer job."

"Which is?"

"I work up at the Tennis Hall of Fame. It's easy. It's better than working at the East Bay Plant." She reached across, took my teacup, then realized it was empty and set it back on the saucer. "I have to admit, you aren't dressed like a Gatsby boy. What are you doing in Newport?"

"Working on a boat."

"Off-shore?"

I nodded and pressed my lips together.

"Did your dad make you?"

"No, this time he didn't. I'm trying to earn enough money to buy my own boat. Just a small one to start with."

"I thought you were going to school."

"I was until recently." I caught the waitress's eye.

She held up a full pot of coffee and raised her eyebrows.

I nodded, and before I realized what she was doing, she had filled my teacup with coffee.

Emily frowned at the girl. "He was drinking tea."

"He was?" The waitress looked from her to me to my cup. "Oh, I'm sorry. Let me get you another."

"That's fine. Really." I took a packet of sugar and shook it.

"It's no trouble."

"Don't worry about it." I stirred the sugar into my coffee and opened two little tubs of cream that the waitress set in front of me.

"Were you waiting for someone?" Emily pulled her ear lobe.

I shook my head and smiled. "Would you like some lunch?"

She sat back. "Yes. Let's go someplace nice for lunch."

"You name a restaurant and I'll take us there."

"I have a boyfriend."

"Excuse me?"

"I have a boyfriend, so you might not want to take me out to lunch. I mean, he and I are living together at the moment, and I thought I ought to tell you . . . that."

I should have run faster, I was thinking. If you had run a little faster, you stupid dockboy, this wouldn't have happened. Now there you are with no way to back down. "I just want to have lunch. I'll take your boyfriend out too if you want." I tried to look sincere.

"I just thought I ought to tell you. No offense." She laughed loudly, the way I remembered she did when she felt embarrassed.

We walked down to the Brick Market and did not hold hands.

Her earrings were tiny gold maple leaves.

"How's your father?" I watched her from the corner of my eye.

"I don't really know. My uncle said he's fine and still in the

Bahamas. But how he knew that he wouldn't tell me. My mother has probably tanned herself into a fritter by now."

"Do you miss them?"

"Sure. But he's a crook and I've known that for a long time and I'm not surprised things turned out this way."

A man walked up from behind. He stepped in front of us and blocked the way. "Where you going, Em?"

"Hi!" she yelled, embarrassed again. "Hi, Rex!" She lunged at his shoulders and squeezed his arms to his body.

The man raised his hands slowly to her back and I could tell he was confused.

Emily wheeled around and grabbed my hand. "This is Pfeif! He's a friend from high school. He works on a boat and we were just going out for some lunch."

The man named Rex snapped out of his confusion and shook my hand with a look on his face that said, "I didn't mind you walking down the street with my girlfriend just then." He had on blue trousers, a white shirt and a blue tie. Pinned to his chest was a plastic tag with REX stamped on it.

He managed a convenience store nearby. He had been crossing the street to find some lunch when he saw us walk past.

"I got lucky and they made me manager," said Rex.

"Well, listen." Emily took us both by the elbow and led us down the street. "James offered to take us out to lunch. We were just heading over to the Boathouse. Why don't you come along and listen to us talk about how boring it was at our high school?"

The Boathouse, I thought. That's about the most expensive place in town.

"Oh. I only . . ." Rex's chin edged back into his jaw.

"Come along. Really." I pressed my palms together to show it was already settled, wishing he would come up with an excuse not to join us.

"I only . . . You guys . . . I really appreciate . . ." Sometimes

152

Rex looked at us as he spoke and sometimes he stared off into space as if trying to read cue cards that kept changing in the distance. "Are you the guy who worked at the fishhouse?"

"That's me. Now I'm working on a trawler."

"Maybe we'll be eating some of your fish for lunch!"

"Actually I work on a scallop dragger."

"Well, I'll make sure I order scallops, then. Real nice of you to have us out like this."

The Boathouse was an old ship that had been permanently docked and turned into a restaurant. The floors lay at an angle because of the shape of the boat, and some of the chairs had one leg shorter than the other to balance out.

Rex was older than both of us. He asked questions about the trawlers and kept his eyes fixed on me when I answered.

He said there wasn't much to being a convenience store manager and I believed him and we left it at that.

I had become used to swearing on the *Gray Ghost,* and my sentences sounded empty without them. Brief, blurred scenes rattled through my head as I guessed at how Emily and Rex might have met.

Once during the meal, when Rex had been talking too long and was shoveling at his food to catch up with us, I looked Emily in the face and mouthed, "Remember me?" It happened very quickly.

She looked down at her plate for a second, but it was only a second and I couldn't be sure she had noticed at all.

Paying the bill, I tried not to think about the money I'd earned walking the deck, cutting scallops and butchering the monk, turned into the undersized portions slid in front of us at our restaurant table.

Rex said to stop by the convenience store any time.

Emily told me to call her when I next came into port.

I didn't want to walk all the way back to the dock with them, so I said I had to make a call. I stood at the phone booth outside the restaurant and told them to go ahead without me. I smiled and nodded goodbye and held the receiver to my ear.

They waved and walked away.

The receiver buzzed. I pressed a few numbers, hearing the different beep tones. Then a recorded woman's voice asked me to hang up and dial again.

Just as Emily and Rex turned the corner, I saw him bend down and whisper to her. She laughed and ran her fingers through his hair.

I booked a room at the Y. It was clean, with linoleum on the floor and khaki-yellow walls. My window looked out over the bus stop and the taxi men.

Sitting on the bed, I caught my vague reflection in the window pane. Spices from the lunch still burned at the back of my mouth. My bones felt heavy in my skin, ribs like rusty iron bars weighing on my lungs.

That was a pleasant lunch, I said to myself. Oh yes, James, that was a very pleasant lunch. Oh, fuck me, that was pleasant.

I sat on my bed watching the sun move across the dull walls until it died. I did not sleep, or blink, or move.

The desk attendant from downstairs knocked on door. He said a man named Kelley had seen my name on the check-in list and wanted me to meet him outside Gunther's at midnight.

I stood on Gunther's dock, smelling the dampness of fog in the harbor. Fish scales caught the light of street lamps and winked at me as I paced on the soggy dock boards.

Laughter sounded from the hulked boat moored at Gunther's where the wash-ups lived. A couple of seconds later, a man in jeans crawled out of a hatch and stood on the deck.

I stayed very still, knowing the shadows would hide me.

The man threw a bottle high above the water. It cartwheeled over the mast of a moored sailboat, the glass catching light, before it slapped into the black water.

Kelley showed up wearing a child's birthday party hat. He'd won it for being one of the first ten customers at a bar up the road. He asked if I wanted to go drinking with him.

A bouncer at the door of the bar carded me and I couldn't get in, being twenty, one year under the legal drinking age.

Kelley said for me to meet him around back by the washrooms and he'd get me in through a window.

"Why can't we just go to Mary's, Kelley? I know I could get a drink there."

He didn't listen and barged through the crowd.

I crept up a stinking alley between the bar building and the one next door. Mossy brick rose up around me, blotting out the sky. Garbage cans with lids chained to the bases were stacked on either side.

Kelley stuck his face up to a small rectangular window and lifted the glass, which was opaque with steel wire in a grid built into the pane.

"Think you can make it through this?"

"Don't be ridiculous."

His head went away for a moment, hands staying locked in the window frame. He was thinking. Then his eyes slid into view again. "Why don't you meet me at Mary's in an hour? I had to pay six bucks cover charge to get in here and I don't want to waste it."

I sat in the all-night Laundromat and washed my clothes. It was too bright and the air felt sticky. The whole time I thought about Mrs. Pittsley sitting in one of the orange plastic Laundromat chairs, reading gossip papers and being spied on by the detective.

I didn't go to Mary's. The minute hand on my watch eased up

to the hour, then past it, and my clothes were still in the dryer. I doubted if Kelley would show anyway.

At nine-thirty in the morning, the door to my room at the Y blew open and Kelley walked in.

First I thought I was back on the boat and that everyone had left the bunk room but me. I had missed my food time and would have to go straight out on deck. My stomach felt suddenly empty.

Then I realized where I was.

Kelley sat on the window sill. He opened the window and sniffed at the breeze. "Sorry I didn't make it to Mary's."

I didn't tell him I wasn't there either.

He told me he had found himself a girl.

It was probably a lie. I asked myself if he knew how unbelievable his stories were sometimes.

Every morning when I worked with him at Gunther's, I had to listen to the story of his night-before, hearing him swear he spent the time in a hotel even though a dozen others had seen him drunk and asleep on the dock.

I let him tell his story, laughing now and then as if disgusted, so as not to hurt his feelings.

It seemed to me that fishermen were always lying about girls.

I heard lies about most things on the docks.

Lies from people who said they were there only for a couple of weeks so they could make some extra money, but who had been fishing for years.

Lies from wash-ups who said they had just bought a boat and would be putting it in the water any day now. They'd talk to me as if I had a chance of being on their crew if I played my cards right. I fell for it several times at the beginning, doing their jobs while they snuck off to a bar. I was surprised they could keep it up, lying all the time and believing it and expecting others to believe it too.

156

Kelley explained to me at the time that it was all these people had. If they didn't keep up the lie to everyone and themselves, then they'd have to face the fact that they should have retired years before and be living on pensions. But they didn't have pensions. Probably they didn't have more than a couple of hundred in the bank, if they had a bank account at all. Most likely they were the same as Kelley, and kept their money stashed in Tupperware boxes.

"You try thinking how it would be," he told me, "with nothing to lean back on and your body all falling apart with old age. You'd be lying too."

I didn't care. Someone had to show them what thin-air talkers they were. I wanted to pull the plug on all those wash-ups and see them deflate onto the deck of Gunther's boat as they rode out at six each morning, the air filled with a smell of eucalyptus ointment, which they used to kill the pain of arthritis in their joints.

"You bear up," said Kelley. "Let the poor bastards say what they want."

So I let the wash-ups talk the same way I let Kelley talk.

Sometimes I wanted to pull the plug on him, too.

The Patriot Hotel served a buffet brunch. All a person could eat for twelve dollars.

It was cold in the lobby. Gold-painted marble pillars held up the ceiling. The marble itself seemed to be sending out the chill.

We walked up a flight of stairs to a banquet hall painted cream with blue trim.

Kelley came here as often as he could, amazed that it was possible to eat and keep eating with no one allowed to stop him or charge him extra. He pointed to a row of tables decked with food. "The way they do it is start you at the left and you file down the line and when your plate is full you go to your seat and start eating. They try to fill you up on pancakes and bread so you don't have room for the good stuff. See the way all the pancakes are at the front, and see the way they try and put some on your plate without you even asking? This is the way we do it." He walked to the wrong end of the line and shoved his plate in the face of a man who wore a chef's hat and white apron. "Let me have some of them trout amandine. And some for him, too." Kelley took my plate and stood with both arms extended while the server piled on food.

At the end of the meal, when our waitress asked if we wanted any more coffee and we said no, she wrote out a bill and stood waiting for us to pay.

I looked at the black bow tie knotted at her throat.

Kelley pulled a roll of money out of his pocket. He flipped through hundreds and twenties and tens.

The waitress watched the money. Her eyes were stuck to it.

Kelley gave her thirty dollars and told her to keep the rest. When she was gone, he leaned over to me. "First couple of times I came in here with my boat money and dressed the way I am, they thought I stole it. I remember seeing the manager holding up one of my bills. He was trying to see if it was real. They're used to me now, though. They think I own one of the mansions out on Ocean Drive."

I had been thinking about money.

Suddenly money was everything. Every gesture, every move, was not safe or possible without money. I was not a man unless I brought home a salary. I lacked promise unless somebody thought I'd be bringing in dollars farther down the road.

It seemed to me that all I had learned in school was how to make money. Any class that didn't tell me directly, told me indirectly. Teaching me the attitude. Giving me connections.

I got tired of that, the same way I became tired of working for Gunther and Vic. I wondered how long it would be before I was tired of working for Gil. I wanted to work for myself. It didn't seem too much to ask.

But the more I thought about it, the more I realized I was wrong. It was a lot to ask. I saw it was what everybody wanted. It would be years and years of working for Gil or for someone else before I could work for myself. The weight of it pressed on my skull. Money. It was all about money.

I thought of the television preachers who said it was possible to live without wealth. They made their sermons, and at the end of the show they asked for what little money I did have so they could go on saying how I could be happy without it.

But I never met or heard about people who could be happy for long without money or who were made happy by something that didn't cost.

If it wasn't the fact of holding the money in their hands, it was the idea of turning the dollars into something else. Land. Food. Possessions.

I guessed maybe the Buddhist monks I studied in school had no money, and I supposed there was something to what they preached about not needing wealth, about needing only the ability to bend in the wind like a willow tree. But nothing I was ever taught and ever saw put to use had anything to do with bending like a willow tree.

I should always have known what I wanted.

I was angry at my father for pushing me toward a way of life he did not understand. He only had a picture in his head.

And I was angry at my brother for trying to live in the picture, in his blue plaid suit that made him look blurry at the edges like a 3-D baseball card.

In the end I was only angry at myself for not having figured it out sooner.

All afternoon we worked on the *Gray Ghost,* repairing the dredge bags and welding parts that had come loose.

I watched Nelson welding, the way he fitted new welding rods into the grip of the welder and tapped them on the metal deck until they sparked. He worked with a heavy black mask over his face, lifting it now and then to see the work. The crackling flame of his welder was blue in the center and frothing magnesium-white at the edges.

I shouldn't have watched. In the evening, my eyes began to hurt as if salt had been rubbed into them. I washed them out, thinking it had to be some chemical, but the burning didn't go away.

Franklin saw me sitting at the galley table with my thumbs dug into my eye sockets, while everyone else was up at Mary's having a last drink before we left port. He told me the pain came from burning out some inside part of my eye with the brightness of the welding flame. He chopped up some raw potato and made me pack it onto my eyes. The starch in the potatoes would ease the hurt, he said.

I lay in my bunk with two eyefuls of mashed potato, hearing the crew return to the boat. The engines fired up. Then the *Gray Ghost* swung away from the pier.

When I woke later, the pain was gone.

Waves thudded on our bow.

I knew we were far out to sea.

"Where's the mate, Franklin?" I sat at the galley table, feeling a faint rustle of seasickness in my guts. "I didn't see him today."

"How come you want to know about Reynolds?" Franklin didn't face me when he spoke. He stayed hunched over the stove, stirring soup in a pot for Gil's supper. "Well, he's gone. That's where he is."

"Gone where?"

"Never you mind, boy." He tasted the soup, still facing away from me.

"What's wrong, Franklin? Is Reynolds dead or something? Should I just go ask somebody else or is this some kind of game you're playing?"

Now he turned. "No game at all. Now I'm going to tell you

something and then I want you to shut up about it. Understand?"

I shrugged. "I guess."

Franklin told me that the night before we left, he had seen Reynolds and another man walk out of a bar near the dock. Since Franklin had nothing else to do and since he was a nosy fart, he followed them to see where they'd go. He hadn't seen the other man before.

Reynolds and the other man walked up an alleyway between two cafés.

What Franklin saw when he walked past was Reynolds pushing the other man up against the wall and kissing him for a long time. The other man had his hands around the mate's neck, his thigh set against the mate's groin.

Franklin beetled over to Gil at Mary's bar and told him. Gil made Franklin promise not to tell anyone about it, then he left the little red and white table where he always sat and walked out into the dark.

Reynolds just disappeared.

Pittsley took his place in the wheelhouse. Franklin worked on deck with Nelson in addition to cooking the meals. Howard and Kelley and I often stayed out after our last haul-back, to help with the cutting. Gil didn't need to hire a new man.

No one talked about Reynolds. A nervousness sifted through us, which died only after a couple of days. It became an unmentionable thing.

9

A DREDGE came up filled with bones. I stared at the hard tangle of white in the dredge bag.

A second later, a smell blew across the deck that made me breathe through clenched teeth.

It was dark. The lights of Martha's Vineyard showed on the horizon.

Whale bones. They fell from the dredge, rattling across our deck. The stench cut into my windpipe and left it raw.

I shuffled through huge pieces of rib and finned blocks of the whale's spine.

The ribs were like curved oars with tatters of gristle at the ends. Their surface was not smooth but patched with the remains of flesh. Each joint of backbone was almost a foot across at the solid center. Fins stretched out at least a foot on either side.

I searched through the pile but found no other kind of bones.

Howard and Kelley didn't mind the smell. They picked up ribs and beat each other over the head. Then we piled the backbone sections one on top of the other. Kelley said the whale must have been as long as a school bus.

Kelley thought we could sell the bones to a scrimshaw man in Newport, but after a while the reek of bad meat got to us and we heaved most of them over the side.

I watched the great arcs of rib twisting over and down into the dark water.

We each kept a section of backbone to use as a seat on our rests between work.

Somewhere in the darkness of my daydreaming, I realized Howard was tugging at my arm.

"What do you think the skull of that whale looks like?"

For a while I only stared at him, still swallowed in thoughts, my hands constantly moving as they cut out the scallops.

Howard stood, hands on hips, chewing his upper lip with a worried look on his face. He passed his eyes from me to Kelley and back to me.

Kelley said that once when he worked a boat named the *Mirabelle*, out of New Bedford, they dredged up the jaw of a killer whale on Georges Bank.

"It was like the bow end of a rowboat, racked up with teeth the size of your hand." He set his fingers together at the tips and held out his hand in the shape of a killer whale tooth. "And I had a friend once who was long-lining for swordfish way up on the Grand Banks near Canada. They set out lines with hooks and bait on them, then reel the line in and pull the fish up on deck with a little crane. One day at the end of their line they see something big thrashing around. White and black and huge, and they knew it was a killer whale. They couldn't cut the line or they'd have lost all the swordfish past that point. So" — Kelley set down his scallop knife, his cramped palm returning, out of reflex, to the grip it had before — "they shoot the bastard half a dozen times with a shotgun and it's still kicking around same as before. They tried to winch it up on deck and it bent their little crane over into the water. They gave up after that. Cut their lines and went home." Kelley nodded and licked his teeth.

"But what do you figure its skull looks like?" Howard's legs swayed in rhythm with the waves, his feet remaining planted to the deck.

We sat on the ice hatch, damp with spray that cut bright silver clouds across the work lights and fell hissing across the work area.

Each of us in turn formed with our hands the shape we thought the whale's head might be, stripped of meat and skin, explaining each curve we drew in the air and trying to be the one who was right.

I moved quickly and without effort onto the treadmill of the boat.

The concentrated repetition no longer bothered me. A part of my head just shut down, keeping me in the trance of daydreams.

Gil smiled down on us from the bridge. He was pleased that we had joined the chorus of his machines and clockwork running of the *Gray Ghost*.

The air conditioning broke.

Our bunk rooms became trenches of sweat. Nobody could take it, so we lay up on the bow or in the galley. It stayed breezy on the bow but the sun burned our skin after an hour, sending us down into the gloom and heat of the galley.

Kelley said it was about time he had a tan. He stayed in the sun while Howard and I slept at the dinner table, faces resting in the crooks of our elbows.

Franklin didn't like us taking up his space and he sang while he prepared the meals. He told us he always sang when he readied the food and wasn't about to stop now. He warbled his voice into gravel to make the point.

That night, at a slow time on the watch when few scallops had come up in the dredges and Howard, Kelley and I sat on our whale-bone seats staring blank-faced into space, Kelley tugged at my arm and pulled me into the galley. The place was empty, since Franklin had gone to bed. The other watch was asleep on the bow, wrapped in blankets. Gil stayed in the wheelhouse with his portable fan.

Kelley took off his shirt, smelling like a tropical paradise from the lotion he'd smeared on himself before going to lie on the bow.

He had blisters on his back the size of plums.

"I feel like I'm dying, Pfeif. My head is going to explode. My back's all burned up. I don't think I've ever felt this bad."

I gave him some aspirin from the cupboard, then burned a needle with a cigarette lighter. I popped the blisters and slowly squeezed out the fluid, which ran down his back in clear trails. Then I poured rubbing alcohol on the raw places.

He made a noise in his throat when the alcohol touched his skin, but made no more sound than that. We had no bandages.

When it was done he said thank you and left without looking at me. He felt embarrassed having to ask for help and he didn't want to owe me.

I didn't want any favors from him either, and never mentioned it again.

Sometimes, leaning over the side to fit the winch hook in the dredge, I saw the gray sides of sharks slipping down into the green.

They followed both dredges to the surface and turned away when they reached our boat.

I saw them tear apart fish that had escaped from the dredge, and watched their dorsal fins trail our boat as we cut the monk. The fins disappeared as each bleeding, ugly monk head fell beneath the waves.

At a distance I could make out the fins of larger sharks, which usually kept their distance, leaving the pickings to smaller, six- and seven-foot makos or blues.

The larger fins belonged to great whites, Gil said. The area we fished was their northernmost feeding ground. They always appeared in mid-summer.

I stared without blinking at each dark half-moon fin, which seemed to me to be all the coldness and sharpness and effectiveness of the sea forced into one fifteen-foot barrel of muscle that would, if I ever fell overboard, rise up from below and bring me down dead.

I thought about my father and his nightmares, and later, in my bunk, the picture of the fins replayed in my head. The sea became for me then a black place, shuddering angry with dull eyes and scales and fins, warring across dark spaces. Silent, sharp-toothed war in total silence. Eyes always open. Constant vision war, and me with no way to fight. No tools for war in this place. Nothing to reason with.

It became a dead end thinking about the sharks, hearing again my father call "Please" as the nightmares raked through his brain.

Each time the pictures came to me they seemed as ugly as before. There wasn't even the hope of staleness that nightmares can take on when they have crashed through a hundred times.

I no longer cringed and went to my bunk feeling sick when Gil exploded at me. Most times, he ought to have been yelling at the engine or the winches, but it satisfied him more to be shouting at a person.

I wasn't afraid anymore, and hoped he thought I'd never been afraid.

Kelley and Howard, I noticed, took on the same look of indigestion when they were being yelled at.

Pittsley still mumbled to himself when he stood on the lazarette, gripping his Styrofoam cup of coffee.

At certain times he would seem sane and normal, and then he

would be a different person from the man who gaped off the stern, making speeches to the fish.

It was as if he had built himself into everything he ever heard said about him, while the rest of his mind stayed blank. As if each day he stood in front of the dirty mirror in the *Gray Ghost*'s bathroom and asked himself, Am I tough like they say? Do I live brave and die strong, like it says on my T-shirt? Am I the Mekong Delta man?

He probably couldn't remember. He had already lived brave and died strong and his heart was only beating out of spite.

A Coast Guard cutter broke out of the mist and circled us.

It looked bigger than the trawler, with a machine gun mounted on its deck. The hull was painted white. A blue and orange stripe cut diagonally across its bow.

Kelley went inside and flushed his bag of marijuana down the toilet.

Gil walked out of the wheelhouse, shook his fist at the cutter and yelled, "Oh, yeah? Well, fuck you!"

"He must be talking to them on the radio." Howard set down his scallop knife and we both stood watching. "If you have any pot with you, I suggest you flush it down the head ricky-tick."

"I don't have anything." I had promised myself not to smoke it anymore after I tried Kelley's sinsemilla.

Pittsley staggered out of the galley in his underpants, still bald but with patches of fluff growing back over his ears. He stood on the lazarette and beat his chest in the direction of the cutter. He cupped his hands to his mouth and shouted across the milk of fog, "You'll never take me alive!"

I edged over to Howard. "Are they after Pittsley?"

"Eh?"

"Do they want Pittsley?" I wanted to be the first one with my hands in the air if they started shooting on account of Pittsley.

Howard fed himself a raw scallop, sliding it off the shell into his mouth. He shook his head and swallowed. "Nobody wants Pittsley. I'm sure he wishes they were after him, but they're not."

I felt the engines slow to an idle under my feet.

Gil shouted down from the bridge that we were being boarded for an inspection.

The cutter swung around and backed up against us, stern to stern. Men in blue uniforms and flak jackets crowded the back of their boat.

As soon as they were close enough, men began jumping onto the *Ghost*. A megaphone calling from somewhere on the cutter ordered us up on our bow.

The Coast Guard men held their shotguns in front of them at some regulation distance. They kept telling us to "move it."

Up on the bow of the *Ghost*, two men guarded us and made way for a third, who looked to be an officer and carried a gun in a holster under his armpit. All of them wore baseball caps with bright yellow numbers on the crown. The flak jackets had USCG printed on both sides.

"All right, boys." The officer crouched down to be on eye level with us where we sat on the coil of bow line. He balanced himself with the spread fingers of one hand. "Anybody got anything to declare?"

"Like what?" I had raised my hand a little without meaning to as I spoke, realizing from the way the words caught in my throat that I was afraid.

Gil turned on me. "Now shut the fuck up."

"No, you shut the fuck up, Chubber." The officer barked at Gil, not taking his eyes off me. "I mean, do you have a little smoking grass on board? A little" — he sniffed and smiled — "coke?"

I shook my head. I was sweating even on my knees.

The officer stood up, without looking at me again, and pushed past the two guards. He climbed down the ladder onto our deck.

168

The two men held the shotgun butts against their hips, keeping their index fingers pointed straight along the trigger guards. They had high cheekbones, straight noses and suntans. They looked like brothers.

I saw nothing more of the search, hearing now and then an order shouted across the deck.

The cutter wallowed at our stern.

The sea was a calm blue field that moved around us and past us.

Kelley and Howard were called down on deck to open the ice hatch.

One guard handed a stick of chewing gun to the other. He balled the tin foil wrapper and bounced it off Pittsley's bowed head.

Pittsley didn't look up. He stayed looking at his shoes, picking at the laces.

I peered across at Nelson, who gaped at the guards, his mouth making chewing motions as if he also had a piece of gum.

When Kelley and Howard returned a while later, their trousers were wet from the knees down. Their faces looked pale.

Gil propped himself up on one elbow and stared.

Nobody spoke.

A few minutes afterward, the officer poked his head out of the wheelhouse and squinted at us. "Captain?"

Gil followed him inside.

I scooted over to Kelley. "What happened?"

"Nothing."

I scooted back to my place on the rope.

"Cut the talk." One of the guards lifted his gun from one hip to the other.

"We're not even allowed to talk?" I shielded my eyes in the glare and looked at his face.

"Not if I say you're not." He jerked his eyebrows up into the bill of his cap and brought them down again.

Quiet.

Sea rocking the bow and sending us a breeze.

Then the cutter blew its horn twice. The shotgun boys wheeled around and vanished. More orders. People shouting "Hustle! Hustle!" The cutter fired its engines and sped away, trailing a fat wake that rolled itself into the other waves and became nothing.

Kelley said the officer had made him and Howard climb down into the ice hold. Then the guards began rummaging through the monk and scallops, looking for drugs.

"You got it here, don't you?" the officer kept saying.

Kelley told him to cool his fucking jets.

The officer walked up to Kelley until their faces were only an inch apart. "I believe this man is going to make a run for it. Fuller, does this man appear to be making a run for it?"

"Believe so, sir," Fuller said.

The officer made Kelley and Howard kneel on the floor of the ice hold with their hands on their heads. This was how their trousers got wet, from melted ice washing back and forth across the concrete.

"Fuller, these men appear to be obstructing justice."

Kelley and Howard stayed kneeling on the floor, ice fog rising around them.

"Yes, sir!" Fuller slid back the cocking mechanism on his shotgun and popped out a new black cartridge, which bounced onto the chilled monk tails.

There were no brave words from Kelley, and Howard bit off the end of his tongue.

Then the officer and the shotgun boys laughed. They climbed up on deck and left Howard and Kelley behind.

Kelley stayed on our bow, screaming at the cutter as it moved away across the blue field.

Gil sent the dredges straight back down. He was angry beyond words. For him, it was as if someone had broken into his house and rifled his drawers and he'd had to sit there and take it.

"I just now thought of all the things I should have told them." Kelley climbed into the ice hold again and brought up the shotgun cartridge.

We took it apart on the galley table. It had six copper balls in it. After that, we poured out the tiny gray grains of gunpowder.

The Coast Guard had set things back tidily. The rooms were neater than they'd been before. Each of us went to his bunk and rearranged his gear the way it used to be.

Gil sat beneath the beer clock drinking iced tea from his blue plastic mug.

He said if the Coast Guard nailed a man with even a gram of pot or cocaine, they could impound the boat and catch, and send the crew to trial. "And if they nail you with a whole drug shipment, the Guard would just as soon shoot you and say you started it. Times like that, when you know they're going to find what they're looking for if they come aboard, you either give up without a fight or kill every single one of them, blow their boat full of holes and sink it fast before they call reinforcements, or soon enough you'll have some Air Force jet bearing down on you and you become eviscerated."

Pittsley laughed and repeated the word "eviscerated."

"Oh, Pittsley. Go someplace and grow your hair back on." Gil rattled the shotgun pellets in his hand and threw them, the way a person throws dice, all across the galley.

At dinner time, Gil set a jar of jalapeño peppers down on the table. He said he'd pickled them himself at his home in Virginia and he dared us to eat a whole one.

I nipped a little piece, then followed it down with a mouthful of mashed potato. I didn't want to spend the next watch with my tongue feeling as if it had been dragged down a cheese grater.

"That's no good!" Gil slapped the table with the flat of his hand.

I shrugged my shoulders. After swallowing the mouthful, I said they had a good taste to them.

Gil leaned over and patted me on the head. "That's what I wanted to hear!"

Howard ate one, bit the pepper off right at the stem and chewed. Then he put his hand over his mouth and said, "Fum uv uh bipf" and left the table.

Kelley ate a pepper and didn't flinch.

"Tough guy Kelley." Gil grinned and swallowed a pepper whole. Then he rubbed his stomach and made good-to-eat noises.

Kelley ate another and gurgled a little in his throat but smiled when it was over.

Then Kelley and Gil divided up the remaining peppers on their plates, leaving the jar half filled with cloudy green juice.

They stuck out their chins and leaned across the table toward each other, making fancy gestures with their fingers, like Italian chefs, as the peppers were crushed in their stubbly jaws.

Tears dripped down Kelley's cheeks.

Gil puffed and aired out his mouth.

When the peppers were gone, Franklin handed them each a glass of milk and said he hoped they could take the pain.

Howard and I applauded and they bowed. Howard's thin hands clapping looked like two dead branches coming together.

No sound. I woke and it was quiet. My ears pinged like a sonar.

No light. It seemed as if everyone had left the boat. I waved my hand around in the dark beyond my bunk and slapped Franklin on the head.

Franklin said the name of a girl and went back to sleep.

It was pitch-black in the passageway, with no light in the galley either.

Then I heard voices on deck. I stubbed my toe against the galley table trying to find the door.

All the crew except Franklin stood on deck. They didn't speak. As I watched, Gil and Nelson climbed down into the engine room. The bar of light from a flashlight waved out of the hole and then disappeared into the guts of the boat.

"Engine's out." Kelley looked spooked by the quiet. "Whole damn rig shut down. I never seen a Cat shut down this way. If you can't trust a Cat, what the hell else can you trust in the world?" He pointed to our dredge cables. They dangled straight down in the water.

This meant we could lose the dredges, since only the tension caused by the boat moving forward kept the hooks in the bull rings. Without our dredges, there was nothing to do but go home.

Kelley ordered me to follow him onto an outrigger.

I was too tired to argue.

I was annoyed at the thought of going home, since it meant being paid very little for the trip.

"Pretty out here." Kelley hooked his legs around the rigger and hunted in his pockets for a cigarette.

The moon made a mercury path on the water. It pooled at the horizon.

"So what are we doing out here?" I rubbed my eyes.

"We figure out if the dredge is gone." He leaned down until he had a grip on the cable, pulled at it, grunted, pulled again. "Still there. Sure enough."

"You're pulling on a couple of hundred pounds of steel cable even if the dredge is gone. You can't know one way or the other just tugging at it like that."

Kelley twisted himself around on the rigger and looked at me. "Sometimes you look like a girl, Pfeif."

I couldn't see his face, only the silhouette. The remains of his hair hung in dark threads around the block of his head.

"I've been out here seven days with no shower. I haven't brushed my hair. Haven't shaved. And you think I look like a girl? What does a girl look like to you, Kelley?" I spat.

"I didn't mean any harm."

Out by the path of the moon, I saw the black arc of a whale cut the surface. Black like India ink in the night. It had come up for air. Now it was pushing itself down again into deep water.

I'd heard they sometimes came up alongside boats because the squeaking of winches sounded like whalesong.

I thought that if my mother could see just once the way it looked out here, could have seen the whale breaching, then she wouldn't grudge my going out to sea.

I realized that for her not to know first-hand how it was on the boats must in a way be worse than anything my father had lived through, since she could only guess from his mumblings and his nightmares and the faraway memory of her own father washed up on a Block Island beach.

And the more I saw out here, the less I could understand why my father hated his job. I didn't see the possibility that someone could become tired of it for long.

I had heard all his stories and heard his nightmares and he seemed to me now little better than the wash-ups at Gunther's, pretending to hate what he did, making himself noble through sacrifice and running over old lies day after day like a stuck record.

Nelson lay on his back in the engine room, trying to unscrew something from the yellow casing of the starboard engine.

Gil shone the flashlight so he could see. Gil repeated over and over, "Fucking tit for ass engine."

I climbed down the ladder. "Need any help?"

Gil looked up, thought for a minute, then shook his head. "Fucking tit for ass engine. Wake Franklin up at four and tell him to cook us breakfast. If he tries to tell you he can't cook with no power, remind him we have a kerosene stove stored in the bow section. He can bring that out on deck and use it. I don't need you for anything else."

I sat at the galley table thinking this was what it must feel like to be blind. Not even the redness of light through my closed eyelids. Now and then, I struck a match to see the time on the beer clock.

At four, I shuffled into the bunk room, lit a match and knocked on Franklin's head. "Gil says it's time to make breakfast."

"I can't cook with no power."

"He told me to remind you —"

"About the kerosene stove." Franklin rolled out of bed and looked for his socks. He had been awake when I walked in and was hoping Gil would have forgotten about the spare stove so he could get more sleep.

A match flared in my face.

I had been dozing a while in my bunk. I swatted the fire out of the person's hand. "Don't wake me like that."

"Out on deck." It was Franklin. "Big trouble. Wake yourself."

"What the hell did I do wrong?" I asked him as we moved along the passageway and through the galley. "What am I in trouble for?" My stomach cramped. "It wasn't my idea to go on the outrigger. If anything's broken, you can't say it's my fault."

On deck, I figured out fast that the trouble wasn't with me. I sat down on my whale-bone seat and felt my stomach muscles loosen.

"That thing hits us, we are fucked and dead. And there's

sharks around. I've been seeing them all night." Gil fumbled in a metal box as he talked to us.

"When what thing hits us?" I turned from face to face, looking for an answer.

Pittsley pointed at a large ship moving toward us on the horizon. He said if it was a tanker, it would need several miles to slow down and at least half a mile to change course. If it was a barge being towed by a tug, and we drifted onto its towing cable, the *Gray Ghost* would be torn in half. If the tanker hit us, they might not even feel it and we would be broken apart by the impact.

We had no power, no running lights, and Gil couldn't raise the ship on our radio.

Gil found two flares in his metal box. He couldn't decide whether to light them now and risk not being seen, or light them later and risk having it be too late. He weighed the two flares, like sticks of dynamite, in his hands and muttered to himself.

Pittsley and I stood on the bow, holding the flares over our heads. Bright red light crumbled ash down onto my hair and burned it. The flare crackled with a sound like bacon cooking. I waited for the flame to reach my hands, but the flare was meant for hand holding and fizzled out before the fire touched my skin.

We could see now that it was a tanker. Pittsley and I stood with the dead, smoking flares in our hands. We watched the ship come closer, pushing the blueness of its wake.

I glanced at Pittsley and tried to think of something to say. He looked hollowed out and old in the half-light. I wished for a moment that I had known him before he went to Vietnam.

With the flares gone, we had nothing left to do but wait on deck with the survival rafts, named Givens Buoys, ready to go.

Kelley found himself an old life jacket in the lazarette and put it on. All the stuffing had come out of one side.

Gil edged over to me and whispered, "Go into my cabin and find my survival suit. It's under the bed. Get it and bring it down."

"Why don't you do it?" I whispered back.

"Because I'm telling you to is why!" Gil yelled and jabbed his finger at his cabin in the wheelhouse.

The bunk room smelled of concentrated Gil. His bed looked like a nest. A picture of his wife and kids hung on the wall, and an enameled plaque with a poem on it, which talked about true love and friendship. It was the kind that could be bought in any gift shop, for people who couldn't figure out how to say it themselves.

I pulled the survival suit from under his bed. It was tied with string, which I bit through. The rubber suit flopped out across the cabin.

It had the same feel as a diver's wet suit, the rubber signalorange with fluorescent silver stripes running down each side. It also had a whistle attached to the zipper. Flotation pads were built into the suit, one big one at the back and two smaller ones in front across the chest. It covered the whole body except the face.

Written on the front in bright yellow letters I read:

Wear Minimal Clothing Under Survival Suit.
Do Not Wear Shoes.
Put On Survival Suit Before Leaving Vessel.
Once In Water — Breathe Regularly.
Blow Whistle To Attract Attention.
Relax! Remember — You Cannot Sink.

I put on the suit.

All the time I pulled and stretched the rubber over me, leaving my clothes in a pile on the floor, I was mumbling, "See how you like this, Gil. If you're too much of a coward to get your own suit, then I'll just borrow it for a while. If that's all right with you, Gil. Of course it's all right. Just you try and get this thing off me once I'm wearing it. Teach you. Wasn't my engines that died on us."

I walked out onto the bridge and stood looking down at the crew. The suit made me walk duck-footed.

I could see the tanker closing in, the chisel of its bow high in the air. As if it had been specially built to sink us. Designed for the job. A hundred-foot-high shark fin bearing down on our boat. Close now. Close. The noise of its engines was loud.

"Get out of my suit!" Gil bellowed from the deck. "I didn't tell you to put it on. I told you to bring it here!"

Pittsley and Howard turned to look at me. They had a Givens Buoy ready to push over the side.

I wanted to tell them it was no use.

"Why'd you send the boy? You should have gone yourself!" Kelley slapped Gil in the belly with the back of his hand.

The tanker's engines howled. Louder than thunder. Bright cubes of light shone up on its tiny bridge, far behind the bow.

Gil grabbed a fish pick and started to climb the ladder.

"Do we abandon ship?" Pittsley braced his legs, ready to heave the Givens over.

But Gil wasn't listening. "You take that damn suit off! It's mine and I paid for it and you take it off right now!" He climbed the ladder like a pirate, the fish pick held in his teeth.

I duck-walked to the bow. "Oh, shit," I was yelling, barely able to hear myself over the drone of the tanker's engines. Its hull passed in front of the moon as if it was a cloud. "Oh, shit. Gil, please don't hit me with the pick!"

The *Gray Ghost* shuddered with the force of the tanker's approach.

I wobbled up to the bow, waving my arms to keep balance.

Gil followed.

I stood at the tip of the bow and had no place else to go.

The tanker had become the sky.

"It's too late, Gil! Don't hit me with the pick!" I held my rubber-gloved hands out in front of me, trying to make fists.

Gil threw himself down on the coiled bow line. Then he began hammering the deck with the fish pick and shouting, "Give me my *suit!*"

And the tanker that had become the sky moved past, its deck far above us speckled with lights and the faces of people looking down.

A cigarette butt sparked as it landed on top of our wheelhouse.

Gil covered his head with his hands, as if taking cover from artillery.

The engines grew louder as the ship swept past. When its stern came into view, I saw the word MAGNATE in letters bigger than me, and under that, LISBOA.

I stood watching, my arms sticking out a little to the sides from the way the rubber held me. Then I stepped over Gil, who was still flat on his face, and climbed as fast as I could down on deck. "Don't let him get me!" I tried to untangle myself from the suit, hopping on one leg until I fell over. It isn't so bad being locked up in the lazarette, I was thinking. It won't be bad at all.

When Gil walked onto the bridge, he no longer carried the fish pick.

The tanker's engines hummed in the distance.

"Last time I ever tell you to get something for me." He was embarrassed in front of his crew, to have sent me for something he should have fetched himself.

Kelley and Pittsley began making fun of Gil, saying he wouldn't have fit into the suit anyway.

Gil smiled and didn't answer. Instead, he pointed at the fading bulk of the tanker and shouted, "Lisboa! Lisbon! They were Portuguese! Probably the only reason they missed our boat was because they were aiming to hit us." Then he told Franklin to bring out the kerosene stove and cook us all bacon and eggs.

Franklin put the eggs and bacon in English muffins and called them McBoat.

Gil and Nelson fixed the engine by dawn.

We hauled in the cables and found both dredges still attached.

Gil gathered us on deck and said he didn't want to risk the engines breaking down again and maybe losing a dredge next time, so we'd be going in.

"But only" — he raised one finger and shook it at us — "only for as long as it takes to make sure the engine's running right. Then we'll be coming straight back out to make some money."

Then came the time I looked forward to, of sitting on the bow with my legs dangling over the side.

After several hours, small boats came into view.

We passed the khaki cliffs of Block Island. I saw white houses built up on the bluffs.

Kelley sat next to me, combing his hair first one way and then another, his armpits a froth of anti-perspirant. The smell of after-shave reached me in gusts from his face.

"Have you ever seen Gil's family?" I waited until he stopped combing and had patted his hair into the shape he wanted.

"Once they came up from Virginia. Only once I saw them."

"Why does he fish up here and have his family in the South?"

"Maybe the fishing's better here. Maybe he can only get a fishing license in Rhode Island. I don't know. He goes down to see his family around twice a month. Takes a plane from Providence. I hear he owns what used to be a tobacco plantation. A lot of land. Our captain is a wealthy man."

"But he doesn't want them living up here?"

"All he wants from up here is the scallops, which bring him the money to take down there. Nothing wrong with that. He hardly ever sees his family, but he wouldn't see them anyway, being out to sea all the time."

180

"My father doesn't spend much time home either."

"Can't have it both ways."

"He says he hates his job."

Kelley scratched at his chin. "I doubt he can hate it that much."

"He's had some bad times."

"If you want to live out here" — he waved his hand across the pale horizon — "then you can't live on land. Unless you fish close to shore and come home every day."

I looked at him and opened my mouth to tell about my plans for a lobster boat. Then I remembered what he said about the way wash-ups talked, and shut my mouth again.

I breathed in the smell of the land, surprised at the greenness of everything after days of gray and blue. I smiled at sailboats cutting by, spinnakers arched out in the wind. And I waved to little motorboats as they crossed and recrossed our wake on our way into the clutter of Newport Harbor.

10

~~~~~~
~~~~~~

A STRANGE man hung around the dock.

He always wore a raincoat and brown suit, the trousers of which were known as flood pants because they stopped just above his ankles.

He moved stiff-legged across the dockyard, lugging a plastic briefcase, his face shot red from drinking and the sun.

He told people he was an insurance agent, but I never once saw him sell any insurance. Never saw him sell anything to a fisherman or a dockboy or even open his briefcase. I thought perhaps he was only a bum who pretended to be an insurance agent, like a man in the courthouse park who wore an Army trench coat and smoked a corncob pipe, telling everyone he was General MacArthur and believing it himself.

The morning of my first day on the *Gray Ghost,* Kelley persuaded Marco to buy insurance from the man. Marco rushed straight to the bank and took out some money, but it seemed as if the man hobbled away every time Marco went looking for him.

Kelley said he was bad luck, said he was the Grim Reaper, who'd come into the world with clothes bought at the Salvation Army.

As we left port, less than a day after a mechanic from Fall River had repaired our engines, the insurance man stood on Sabatini's dock and waved to us.

"I don't like that one damn bit." Kelley leaned against the stern. Wind twisted his hair back and forth across his skull.

I'd been on land so short a time that the motion of the waves never stopped in my head. I was glad to be back in the rhythm of the boat, where I had a place and where I belonged.

A storm piled up on the horizon.

Gil put music on the loudspeaker, and we danced to it with short, hobbling steps, made clumsy by the pitching of the boat. We were far away from land, hedged in by a gray wave of thunder that stretched miles into the sky.

The sea changed color. With the bad wind coming, it took on a sheen like tin, heaving up through the scuppers and across our deck.

I saw the path of the storm, churning water as it approached. I felt the first warning dapples of rain.

Clouds with a strange brassy light in them crowded down to the water. They pushed forward a hedge of mist and clogged air, which sifted past us and blew high-pitched squeals through the rigging.

We dressed in our rain gear and lived in the rubbery clothes. The huge hood of my jacket blocked my view like blinkers on a horse.

Lightning flashed in the bellies of the clouds. Thunder reached my ears as if from under water.

I tasted salt from waves that broke in spray against the bow. When they struck, I staggered a few paces out of my way and then continued working.

As the dredges came over the side, they swung across our deck and smashed into each other like huge, ragged cymbals.

I crouched behind the lazarette until both dredges lay flat on the metal plates, then attached the pelican clips and waited for Gil's order to hammer out the pins.

Far down in the trough of a wave, I heard Gil yell over the loudspeaker to send the dredges down. I swung the hammer.

183

By the time I had my balance back, the dredges were gone and the clips lay like dead snakes on the deck.

Now and then, while Kelley and I cut out the scallops, strips of foam blasted under the canopy and left us soaked.

From where I stood leaning over the scallop pen, I could see nothing of the deck except ladders of water pouring down from the bridge and a grayness of rain along the stern.

During a pause in the work, when we sat on our whale-bone seats, legs braced to take the shock of waves, I asked Howard if he didn't ever worry about losing his wife to another man when he was out to sea.

I had been thinking of Gil and the faith he had to have in his wife, or whether he loved her at all. And I thought of my parents, wondering how it was that they had learned to trust in the time spent away from each other, without jealousy forcing things apart.

"Well, I know you're asking me a serious question." Howard sat with his hands on his knees, hidden in his storm gear so that the only parts of him I could see were the tips of his fingers and the tip of his nose. "But you'd laugh if I told you the truth. I don't think anybody else would have her."

I didn't laugh. I saw Howard's fingers tighten against the knobby cups of his kneecaps. He was waiting for one of us to make fun of him.

Kelley giggled, then snorted and shook all over.

Howard turned to us and I saw his face now, wet strands of hair in trails down his face. "I mean, she has such *habits*. I remember when she was pregnant, she used to drive round and round in circles past the McDonald's drive-through, ordering cheeseburgers." He looked at us as if that one habit would explain all the others she might have. "I been with her a long time. Unless I don't know her like I think I do, I could tell if she was seeing another man. I just could."

184

"So what was it like before you were married?" I raised my voice over the splatter of rain.

"What's the matter? Are you getting married?"

"No. I couldn't help but think about it is all. My father is a fisherman and he isn't home much. I've only just now started wondering how he and my mother work things out."

"You should ask them."

"It's easier for me to ask you."

"Well, I met my wife before I started fishing. I was running a bar down in Roanoke. Then somebody started breaking into the place two or three times a week. I had an alarm system installed but they got around it somehow. I asked the police for protection and they hung around for a few nights but nothing happened. So they went away and that same night somebody broke in. I couldn't stay in business. When it got to the point that I would either have to shut down or move someplace else, I bought a shotgun and hid behind the bar after closing time."

Kelley leaned closer to listen, the yellow of his rain gear smeared with oil and monk blood. His hands were knotted together in a big fist.

Howard spoke louder so we could hear. "The second night of waiting, around two in the morning, the light on my alarm system suddenly goes out. Then I hear a noise in the bathroom, and a minute later there's someone standing in the middle of the barroom. I stand up and point the shotgun at him" — Howard crooked his hands as if he were holding the gun again — "and I tell him to put his hands up. For a second he just stands there. Then he reaches into his jacket. So I kill him."

Waves broke in regular jolts against the bow. The deck seemed to melt with the force of rain coming down.

"I didn't know you killed anybody." Kelley's hands stayed knotted together.

"He didn't die right away. But he died. He had a gun in his jacket, so when the police came I pleaded self-defense and got away with it. But by the end of my trial I was poor. I was dirt poor and wouldn't have opened the bar again anyway. The trial went on for weeks. It was the most expensive thing I ever lived through."

"You'd think it would be more clear cut." Kelley touched the toes of his boots together. "A man breaks into your house or your business. He's trying to rob you. He has a gun. You kill him. He obviously expected to kill anybody who got in his way or he wouldn't be carrying a weapon. You'd think it would be more clear cut."

"After the trial it was clear cut. After I was poor. Gil was a customer in the bar. He offered me a job and I took it. That was maybe eight years ago. It was the best thing that ever happened to me and my wife. If we had to be together all the time, we wouldn't stay married. One time, just after Gil made me the offer and I was still looking for other jobs, she and I had a fight, and do you know what she did? When I left for a job interview, both of us yelling and screaming at each other, she went out and rented a wood chipper. You know, one of those machines you can feed a log to and it busts the log into little bits of sawdust. She took every piece of furniture in the house and fed it to the chipper. Even my record player. I got home and she was sitting on the front steps crying. 'Howard, I wish I hadn't done it! I didn't mean to do it, Howard!' The front lawn was covered with sawdust and shreds of plastic. The neighbors were all lined up on the street corner, pointing and whispering. I knew right then that if I didn't take Gil's offer, our marriage wouldn't last a week."

The storm hadn't quit by dinner time.

Sitting at the galley table, we had to keep our cups stuck between our legs so they wouldn't fall over.

The ketchup and Tabasco sauce swung in their wooden rack along with the pepper and salt. Back and forth, swaying like people at a football game.

186

Franklin arranged a plastic mat on our table to stop our plates from sliding. He showed us scars on his hands from times before when he'd been cooking in storms and the rocking of the boat threw grease out of frying pans onto his skin.

Kelley came in late and sat down, dripping at his place. His hair hung in dreadlocks over his eyes. He swept it back, and in that movement he was himself again.

He reached over, took my hand and spat something into it.

A pearl.

"Give it to your girl." He sat back, smiling.

It was a little, little pearl and not even round but still a pearl.

"It's a scallop pearl. I found it about halfway through the last watch and had it in my mouth all this time." He was very pleased with himself.

"So Pfeif has a girl?" Gil set down his knife and fork, which immediately tipped off the plate onto his lap.

"Sure enough." Kelley nodded and ate a mouthful of potato, filling his cheeks to bursting point.

"How do you know if I have a girl?" I squinted at Kelley.

He swallowed. "I saw you walking down Severn Street with a girl the last time we were in port. Well, the time before that. She was pretty." He turned to the others. "She had on jeans and a white shirt. She was pretty, all right."

"That was Emily." My cheeks felt hot.

"She's still a girl."

I was made to describe her and rate her and tell if I loved her.

Then Gil sighed and shook his head, said he'd never known a fisherman and a woman to stay together forever.

"Well, what about me?" Howard craned his neck up.

"You haven't been with her that long. You two keep breaking up and getting back together. You know what I'm talking about. You tell me honestly if I'm wrong."

Kelley said it was right, sure enough. You couldn't blame a woman for taking off when her husband hardly ever came home, and stayed mostly drunk when he did. "At the same time, you can't blame a fisherman for drinking himself into an idiot after two weeks of cutting up the monk and getting so he thinks the scallops are talking to him."

Howard looked around the table. "That happens to you too? Sometimes I could swear those scallops are whispering to each other."

"I know what I say is true. I've seen it all from up there" — Gil jerked his thumb at the wheelhouse — "and I know what I'm talking about."

At the end of our next watch, I sat in the ice room with Kelley and drank a beer that he had stashed there while we were still in port.

Gil had said he'd fine anyone he caught drinking alcohol on the boat four hundred dollars, so we stayed down with the monk and scallops in the musty air.

The storm still shrieked through the outriggers. Warm sea-water splashed down through the ice hatch.

We stayed a while longer in the hold, drinking the beer slowly because it was so cold it hurt our throats. When we decided to go up and have some food, the next watch was already bringing in the dredges from their first tow.

I climbed the ladder ahead of Kelley. As I came to the top, I looked up to see the sky and it was not there.

On my hands and knees.
    Pain.
    Gray. White. Brown.
    Pain.
    I spat crumbs from my mouth.
    Focus. Gray. Focus, you fucker.
    Why can't I see?
    Pain. Tight-veined, shuddering pain.

My body thundered. I was deaf from it. Clattering and thundering.

I saw the floor in front of me. I saw it and it popped back out of focus. I spat out more crumbs, closed my mouth to spit and pain like a spike rammed up through my jaw into my brain. I bowed my head down and screamed.

Eyes open now. Speckles of blood on the floor. The ice room floor. Back in the ice room. What am I doing in the ice room?

I touched my tongue around my mouth. My gums felt as if they were lined with broken glass. The crumbs I had been spitting out were my teeth.

I bit down again and the spike crushed up through my flesh and bone into the miserable softness of my brain.

Trying to sit up, I fell over and banged the back of my head.

Kelley stood over me. He spoke, but with the thunder going on inside me, I couldn't hear. He bent down and touched my shoulder. Cold water running across the floor splashed against my head and ran down my back.

Out of focus. Kelley's face blurred and far away. Very far away.

I was sitting at the back of the ice room.

Franklin dabbed a cloth against my face.

Gil stood behind Franklin, hands on hips.

Pittsley looked down from the ice hatch.

The cloth Franklin used was dirtied red.

Everything stayed in focus now. The thunder in my head continued.

I touched my face and touched it again. There was a hole in my jaw. Tatters of skin, warm and soft and bloody against my fingers. I pressed the hole and felt the bone of my chin through the wound.

Then I tried to stand, but Franklin pressed me down and said something that reached me only as a snuffling sound.

"I want to see." I bit down as I spoke and screamed in Franklin's face with the pain. Everyone jumped back. I bled quietly onto the chest of my oiler coat until they came back.

Franklin squinted at the wound, trying to measure the damage. "The dredge swung over the ice hatch and nailed your head as you were climbing out. How do you feel? Can you understand me?" Franklin's voice was out of sync with his lips, like a badly dubbed movie. "How many fingers am I holding up?" He held up his hand.

"What's the damage? What am I going to do? Can you fix me up again?" The shock of being hit forced a pressure on my chest, making it hard to breathe.

I tried to stand again, then remembered the bits of teeth and went down on my knees to look for them. "Help me find my teeth." I tried not to sound panicked as I crawled on the floor around their feet. I pawed through the meltwater washing back and forth across the ice room.

"It's no use, Pfeif." Franklin set his hand on my shoulder.

"Well, if you won't help me, I'll just have to do it myself." I couldn't see any teeth. I could barely see the floor. Then I sat back on my haunches. "All right." I spoke carefully so as not to bring back the pain. "All right, I can't do it by myself. Please help me." I tried to focus on the concrete, still bleeding from the wound on my chin.

Gil hooked his hands under my armpits and lifted me up. "It's no good crawling on the floor."

I blinked at him. "Why won't you help me? It won't take long to find them if we all pitch in." My eyes blurred and my lips pressed tight together.

Then Gil and Pittsley helped me up the ladder into the galley.

Franklin walked me to the bathroom so I could see the damage for myself.

In the polished steel mirror, I looked at the gash on my chin. The wound was swollen and puckered. I touched carefully along the length of my jaw, waiting to feel the raggedness of broken bone but there was none.

Some of my back teeth had been cracked from top to bottom. One had split in half and the piece was missing. My front teeth didn't even look chipped. I couldn't understand how it happened this way.

Franklin sat me down on the toilet seat and dabbed yellow-brown iodine on the gash. I yelled in his face again as the liquid pinched my nerves.

It was hot in the cramped space of the bathroom. I took the hand towel and pressed it to my face, the thunder now only a mutter far away inside my skull.

"I'll take good care of you." Franklin pushed sweat from my eyebrows with his thumb. "There's something you have to understand."

"What?" I let the word slip carefully from my mouth, afraid of the pain if my teeth touched together.

"You have to understand that Gil isn't going back to port just because you broke a few teeth. It wouldn't be fair to the crew and it would lose us a lot of money. The only time he'll even think about going in is if we're running out of fuel, or we have a full load of scallops, or if someone's dying. You understand me, or are your bells still ringing?"

"I understand." I hadn't thought about going in. In time it would have occurred to me. The only thing on my mind for now was how I would be able to eat.

"There's something else you have to understand, which is that you aren't officially registered as a member of the crew. That's why Gil's paying you cash. This means you're going to have to pay for the damage yourself."

"How much is it going to cost?" I lisped at him, only now feeling my hip and back hurt where I struck the concrete floor.

"Not much, I guess. They just fix your teeth and off you go again."

"Fifty dollars, maybe?"

"About that, I suppose."

I opened a drawer under the sink and fetched out a needle and thread. I held them out to Franklin, needle in one hand and thread in the other. "Stitch me up."

"I can't do that. Besides, it's not a big hole. Just keep it clean and it will close up fine."

I stood up, stooped in the tiny room. "I'll get Kelley to do it."

Franklin pushed me back down on the toilet seat. "Now don't be asking Kelley to do anything like that. He'll sew your face into a quilt. Now you just sit there and rest a bit. Kelley and Howard will take care of the work."

When he was gone, I cried, dabbing at the wound and watching my fingers come away red.

Then I felt suddenly tired, knowing I would have to work again in a couple of hours or risk losing my pay. I rested my head back against the wood-paneled wall and fell asleep.

Franklin fixed me porridge for every meal, making it sweet with brown sugar and cream.

I couldn't chew except with my front teeth, like a rabbit, and could drink liquids only at room temperature, since anything too hot or too cold rammed the hurt into my head again.

The boat carried no medical supplies. Nelson gave me a Band-Aid but it wouldn't stick to my chin because of the sweat. I washed the gash before and after every watch. The wound turned purple and began to fill in.

To avoid infection in my mouth, I gargled with the iodine, careful not to swallow. It stained my lips yellow and left behind a taste of steel.

Sometimes I bit down in my sleep and woke up fast and in pain.

It was the sharpest and the worst pain I had ever felt. As long as I didn't bite down, there was barely any discomfort. But I felt tired all the time, and was miserable whenever I ran my tongue over the wreckage of my teeth.

By the third haul-back on each watch, I was exhausted. Sometimes I fell over after knocking out the pelican clips. The force of the hammer swing carried me off my feet and set me down hard on the deck.

Then Kelley or Howard would move to help, but I always made sure I was standing before they reached me.

Once as I swung the hammer against a pin, the hammer sailed up over my head and into the water. I stood looking at my empty hands.

Kelley grabbed a spare hammer from the tool chest and gave it to me without a word.

We stayed out another seven days, and might have stayed out longer if the dredges hadn't started flipping. They turned upside down before reaching the sea floor and dragged along, catching nothing.

The first couple of times, Gil yelled at me. He climbed down on deck and shook his fist in my face, saying he didn't make allowances for the dredges flipping, no matter how bad I felt.

I watched bug-eyed and panicked as each dredge climbed from the water, trying to make out whether the dredge bag was empty.

Gil told me I didn't knock out the pins on time.

I became so tired from worry and the ache in my jaw that I could barely stand.

Gil stamped across the deck as another flipped dredge came on board. He snatched the hammer from me and knocked out the next set of pins by himself. Then he threw the hammer down and stamped away again.

When we hauled back an hour later, I was praying for the dredges to be flipped.

I cackled when a dredge bag rose empty from the water.

Now he couldn't say it was my fault. I shuffled over to my block of whale bone and sat down, grateful for the rest the flipped dredge would bring us. I had stopped caring about money. I only wanted to sleep and have my teeth fixed.

Gil decided it must be Kelley and Howard's fault for letting the cables pay out too fast. "I'll show you!" He jerked his head at each of us in turn. "Do I have to run this ship by myself?"

But the dredges flipped again.

Gil went purple in the face. He swung himself back and forth on the ladder that led up to the bridge. "Goddamn it to hell! Aaaaraafuck!"

It became impossible to sit at the galley table when Gil was there. If any of us said anything, he told us to shut up. If we stayed silent, he sighed and tapped his spoon on the table, then asked in a loud voice if we were keeping secrets from him.

The three of us hunched over our scallop pen, cutting out a few baskets of shells that came up in a dredge that somehow didn't flip.

Out of instinct I looked up.

Gil stood close by.

He raised his head from staring at his shoes. His face looked blotchy. "Did one of you jinx my boat?"

Kelley set down his scallop knife. "Excuse me?"

"Oh." Gil breathed out for a long time. "You know. Said something to jinx the boat. Did something, maybe. There's things a person can do. You got to tell me if you did. I won't be mad." He chopped the air with his hand, cutting down the thought of being angry that we might have jinxed his boat.

"We wouldn't do a thing like that, Gil." Howard looked over at his pile of old boots, stacked neatly by the stern.

I could tell Howard was wondering for a moment whether to believe what Kelley said about how a person could do only bad luck things on a boat.

"I just had to be sure." Gil looked down at his shoes again. "I had it on my mind." Then he shuffled back up to the wheelhouse. His head shuddered now and then, as if a strange electric charge was running through him.

I lay in my bunk trying to sleep. A picture of the dredge, like a photographic negative, swung out of the dark of my closed eyes.

It seemed only a matter of time before the thing nailed me again.

I moved more cautiously around the machinery now, unable to work as quickly as before.

Kelley and Howard were losing patience with me. Gil stayed in the wheelhouse sulking at his bad luck.

That afternoon, I moved like a drunk from one end of the deck to the other, hooking and unhooking the dredges.

A shadow appeared over my head. Kelley. He held me by the shoulders, an angry look on his face, and shoved me over toward the ice hatch. "I'll do it. You quit farting around and sit there for a while."

"I can work."

He turned his back and spoke facing away from me. "Well, then work decently. None of this pussying around like you never handled a dredge before." Then he called for Howard to run the winches and began hooking up both dredges by himself.

He set the port side working as fast as he could, and as he moved across to the starboard dredge, he glanced at me to see if I was watching how quickly he worked.

He fixed the winch hook in the bull ring and stepped back, slapping dirt off his hands.

Howard raised the dredge.

Then suddenly the hook popped out and swung back.

It struck Kelley in the head just as he reached the stern, ready to knock out the pins when Gil gave the word.

The hook wasn't sharp but it was big and heavy. Added to that was the weight of the cable.

Kelley cried out once and tripped back, arms raised, out through the gap at the back of our deck.

He disappeared into the boil of the props.

I ran across to the dredge, stood on it and looked over the side. "Kelley?" I said very quietly. Then I dived over the side.

Only when I was in the air did I become afraid of the sharks, and realize that Kelley had probably been sucked into the propellers, which would mean there was no point in trying to save him.

I began to yell and continued yelling when I hit the waves, the scream filling my mouth with salt water.

The sea was warm on the top but cool and dark at the depth of my dive.

I rose to the surface still howling, spat water from my mouth and looked around for Kelley.

The hull of the *Gray Ghost* looked vast as it heaved up in my face. Rust stains trickled from the scuppers. The rigging rose up tall and black like the trunk of a dead tree.

Then it was past me and the gasoline-tasting wake butted me away in a series of waves growing smaller.

I kicked off my boots and wriggled out of my oilers.

I caught sight of Howard climbing the ladder to the bridge. He disappeared into the wheelhouse.

Gil ran out onto the bridge and pointed at me.

I shivered, feeling my legs dangle down in the cool water beneath the surface. I waited for the gray shapes to rise up and pull me down.

Then I saw Kelley off to one side, screaming and thrashing. I swam to him, slow moving and heavy in my jeans. The plastic bread bags I'd been using for socks still clung to my feet.

Kelley punched at the water, trying to stay afloat.

"Take off your boots and your oilers!" I treaded water in front of him.

He stopped thrashing suddenly and looked at me. He seemed surprised that I was there. A gash ran half the length of his forehead at the hairline. It bled and the sea washed it clean and it bled again.

I waved to him, spitting out another mouthful of water.

He sank under the next wave.

I swam to where I'd last seen him, getting ready to dive. In the distance I heard the boat's engines change pitch as it wheeled around.

Kelley popped up right in front of me, still screaming and thrashing.

I thought he was a shark.

He grabbed hold of my neck and bellowed for me to save him. We sank under and he started trying to climb on top of me as if I were some kind of raft. His boots were gone but he still wallowed in his oilers. I tried to get loose but he wouldn't let go, so I bit him on the hand.

I choked for my breath, swimming a few strokes away from him.

"Don't leave me!" His eyes were open wide.

I had a pressure in my throat from swallowing too much water. "If you don't calm down, you're going to drown and I'm going to let you!"

"I don't think I can swim!"

"Well either you can or you can't. If you took your oilers off, you'd be all right."

"Save me, Pfeif!" His face was crumpled and afraid.

I tried to hold his head above water so he could breathe. The only way I could keep him from thrashing was by saying I'd let go if he didn't stay calm.

The *Gray Ghost* idled as it pulled near. The whole crew stood on deck. They threw me a rope that had been tied in a loop at the end. When I tried to get it around Kelley's waist, he panicked again and shoved me under, yelling that the sharks were here.

I came up spluttering and shaking. I pounded on his head a few times to settle him down, then slipped the rope around his waist. Pittsley winched him on deck. In the air, he looked like an inflated balloon in the shape of a man, the kind used in parades.

In the last seconds of waiting, I was most afraid, feeling what I thought were the bodies of fish brushing past my legs.

I held on to the hook and it lifted me from the water, straining the muscles in my arms. For a moment, as I dangled above the boat, I looked down on the crew as they tended to Kelley. Water dripped from my jeans onto their backs. Then I settled my feet on the warm iron deck.

Franklin tore apart a scallop bag and used it as a bandage for Kelley's head.

Kelley breathed in a way that I knew he was crying, even though his face didn't show it.

Gil didn't seem angry. He said we might as well go into port before the whole idiot pack of us killed ourselves.

Kelley sat on the floor of the bunk room, clumsily trying to pull off his shirt. He looked like a clown in his scallop bag hat.

He made a few more swipes at the buttons on his shirt, then burst into tears.

I sat on my bunk and pretended not to see him cry.

He said he owed me and he'd pay me back. He leaned over and tried to hug me, but I pushed him away. "It was only a stupid thing, Kelley. It's not something to be crying about in front of everybody."

"I owe you, Pfeif. I'll make it up to you for saving me."

"If you hadn't freaked, you wouldn't have needed saving."

He cried for a while longer, then crawled into his bunk, still wet, and fell asleep.

I climbed up to the bow and sat in the late afternoon sun.

Franklin came out with a bowl of chocolate pudding and whipped cream. He said it was Gil's private stock and Gil wanted me to have some.

Gil nodded to me from the wheelhouse, where he sat in his chair.

I tried to enjoy the pudding and the time of sitting on the bow as we rode home, but it was spoiled by the thought of Kelley panicked and crying. I never wanted to see him that way.

11

THE DOCTOR opened my mouth and said, "Jesus."

I had gone to the Newport General Hospital as soon as we reached land. The nurse there said the wound on my chin was already starting to heal. There'd be no sense in cutting it open again in order to try and make the scar any smaller.

The doctor felt along the rim of my jaw to see if the bone was broken. He told me there didn't seem to be any infection and that the bone appeared only to be dented. "Like a piece of wood!" He chopped the edge of one hand into the palm of his other. Then he handed me a small tube of anti-bacterial cream and walked out.

I sat in the little examining room, looking at glass jars of tongue depressors and long sticks with cotton swabs at the end. On the wall was a diagram of a man's body with the flesh peeled away, showing the twine of muscles around his bones. He stood with his weight shifted onto one hip, hands open as if waiting for an explanation why someone had torn off his flesh.

When the doctor didn't return, I swung back the curtain and walked across to a nurse. I asked her the name of a good dentist in town and she looked surprised that I was still waiting around. "Try Dr. Bailey up on Bellevue. I go to him. He'll fix you right up."

So I nodded and smiled and left.

I checked the balance in my savings account at the bank on

my way up to Bellevue. Then I called Dr. Bailey's office from a phone booth. His assistant said to come right over.

I sat for a while in the waiting room reading the cover of a magazine. The inside part had been taken out. I stared at the cover so as not to have to watch other people in the room. Their eyes shifted back and forth, twisting painfully around in their sockets, spying on whoever sat next to them.

A girl about my age walked into the room and said, "James?" She wore a stiff white dress with white stockings and shoes. From the way she spoke, I thought for a moment she might be an old friend whose face I had forgotten.

Dr. Bailey had a crew cut and big hands.

I didn't think a dentist could work with hands that big.

After looking at the damage, he whispered to the girl and she left.

I peered at her as she walked out, still not sure whether I'd seen her before.

"She's pretty, isn't she?" He sat on a padded stool next to my chair.

The pressure and taste of his fingers in my mouth remained. I started to speak and he cut me off.

"She's my daughter."

"I thought maybe I knew her from someplace."

The girl came back with a tray. We didn't speak of her again. The doctor lowered my chair and turned on an overhead light, which blinded me. He injected the roof of my mouth. Bitter liquid poured down the sides of my tongue. Then he injected me in the gums and in my cheek.

He said I had damaged five teeth. All of them would require surgery.

He said he'd work on them now or I wouldn't be able to eat.

I didn't tell him they had been this way almost a week already.

With two of the teeth, he said, it was possible I had cracked them all the way up to the jawbone, and they would require root canals. He asked me how I did it and I told him.

"I've worked on fishermen before, but never any as young as you. How's your insurance? Does it cover this? Where are your parents?"

My mouth felt heavy, as if my cheeks had turned to canvas. I told him it was my responsibility to pay for the damage. I said there was no insurance. I had gone out to sea against my parents' wishes and would not be asking them to bail me out.

I made up my mind about this when I was still at sea. It didn't seem right that they should pay. If I asked my father for help, I knew he'd change his mind about letting me work on a boat. Then my mother would use his change of mood to try and talk me out of it again.

I reached for the wallet in my back pocket, ready to tell Dr. Bailey the balance in my bank account.

He set his hand on my shoulder. The overhead light made his spiked hair shine like copper wire. "I'll get you a figure soon enough on what this will cost. It has to be done in several stages, anyway, which spreads out the expense. But you should know that it will be several thousand dollars."

I imagined myself rising up from the novocaine slump, grabbing him by his sterilized shirt and yelling, "What the hell are you talking about? Franklin told me fifty bucks!"

But I stayed slumped in the chair. The numbness stretched my face out of shape and left me floating in bubbles.

I had the strange and ugly feeling of being dependent, as if I would be coming back here for the rest of my life while he slowly put me together again.

I vaguely felt the scrape of bone on broken bone as he took hold of a tooth and snapped it in half.

Then things became even more vague as he rattled around

my gums with stainless steel spikes, breaking off chips of tooth and clicking his tongue.

By the time he got to the root canal, I barely knew what was happening. I felt heat and something rubber in my mouth and a suction pipe the assistant used to drain my spit.

I fell away into darkness inside me, walked up and down gray corridors in my head, realizing that by the time I'd paid for the damage, the money I'd earned on the boats so far would be gone.

The picture of my lobster boat went blank. I thought about the energy I'd stored away, like rations, for the difficult time of getting started. It was energy built into walls against the criticism I knew would keep trickling in from people until I succeeded, until the same people would suddenly no longer criticize and would act as if they'd always been behind me. All of it shot out of focus and seemed suddenly unreachable as I lay in the chair hearing the dentist pick at my teeth.

It took all afternoon.

When it was over, Dr. Bailey said he had put in some temporary fillings. I could eat and drink what I wanted, except things like peanut brittle and extremely hot or cold liquids. "You'll have to come back and get the temporaries removed. Then I'll grind down the original teeth into little pegs." He held a tiny space between his thumb and index finger to show how small the pegs would be. "These will be anchors for the permanent caps. I estimate a total cost of twenty-five hundred dollars. Are you sure you don't want to get in touch with your parents about this?"

"No. No, thank you." The blur of words still pushed clumsily from my mouth. "Thanks for seeing to me right away."

I took a room at the Y, not yet ready to go home. I wanted to wait until the anesthetic wore off and I no longer smelled of chemicals. Since the damage was all at the back of my mouth and didn't show, I decided not to tell my parents about it.

In the same room as before, I opened my window and sat on the bed. Then I pulled the blanket over my head and thought about having no money.

Kelley appeared in the evening. He tried to twist the door handle and walk into my room in one movement. The door was locked and he slammed into it. He said he had something to show me.

When he came in, I was still under the blanket, humming a song to myself. "What do you have to show me?"

"Huh?" He breathed rum in my face.

"You said you had something to show me." I pulled off the blanket and blinked at him.

Kelley smiled, remembering why he had come. He led me out of the Y and down to the State Pier. He showed me a lobster boat painted blue. There was a light on inside and the sound of a radio playing.

Warm wind blew across the packed earth of the parking lot.

Kelley had Band-Aids on his forehead. The skin around the wound was stained by iodine. "See my boat?"

"Yours?" Spit welled up in my mouth as I got ready to tell him I had heard enough of his lies.

"Soon enough."

"What do you mean? Is it yours or isn't it?"

"I put a down payment on it and I'm paying off the rest in installments."

"Like Nelson with his car?"

"No, not like Nelson."

"And where did the money come from?" I felt my nose fizz. Then I sneezed in the dust.

"I saved it. I been living at the Y or on the *Ghost* for months now. If you don't believe me, ask Bucket."

An old man had appeared from the cabin. He wore baggy

204

overalls and stood with his hands in his pockets, waiting for a pause in our talk so he could speak.

"This is my boat, isn't it, Bucket?" Kelley pointed to me. "Tell this man whose boat we're on right now."

"Mine." Bucket took his hands out of his pockets. He held them in a knot over his stomach.

"Well, if I was to give you the rest of the money right this minute, whose would it be?"

"Yours."

"See!" Kelley laughed up at me.

"Do you have the money?" Bucket took a piece of chewing tobacco from a package with an Indian head on the front. He set the black strip in his mouth.

I watched the stretched shadow of his face in the cabin's light.

"No, Bucket." Kelley stepped down onto the boat. "I don't have the whole payment right yet. I got other debts to pay. I was trying to show my friend here that the boat is at least partly mine. Mostly mine."

"It isn't yours until I get all the money." He looked up at me. "Are you the one he wants to work with on my boat?"

"I didn't tell him yet, Bucket." Kelley set his hand on the thin bone of Bucket's shoulder and squeezed until I could see Bucket was in pain. "It was going to be a surprise."

Bucket picked at Kelley's fingers until Kelley let go.

"I want you to work with me on my boat." Kelley climbed onto the dock, still smelling of rum.

"I don't have the money, Kelley. Either to give or to lend. I'm paying to get my teeth fixed up. It's good of you, but I don't have the money."

"I'm not asking for money. I owe you. I said I'd pay you back."

"And I told you that was stupid."

"I know you want to work in-shore. You told me as much. I need a crewman because I don't want to run the boat by myself. You won't be making the same money as on Gil's boat, but I'll take you on as an equal partner. We can split the money for lobster pots and whatever costs come up after I've bought the boat. Then in time when you start your own boat, you can take half the pots with you."

"I can't even afford the pots, Kelley."

"So owe me. Pay me when you can. I'm asking you to work with me."

"You know well enough I want to work a boat like this. You know the only reason I'm working Gil's boat is so I can earn enough to have my own business."

"If you'd rather work by yourself, it's all right."

"I'll work with you, Kelley. You know that." I still didn't believe what he said.

"I'm old and tired." Bucket sat down on the deck and began cutting his nails with a clipper.

"Why didn't you tell me you had a boat, Kelley?"

"I told you I'd be quitting Gil's ship soon enough. Besides, after what you said about the people at Gunther's, I thought I'd better show you."

"You never even mentioned it."

"I'm all tired out." Bucket pulled a lunch box from one of the boat's cabinets, took out a package of raisins and ate them, inspecting each raisin before he put it in his mouth.

"I didn't need to mention it. Wasn't anything anybody could tell me that I didn't already know."

After telling us again that he was tired, Bucket climbed out of the boat, handed Kelley the key and walked home.

It stayed quiet for a while. A police siren sounded from across the bay. Water sucked at the dock pilings.

"I'm going to hang around." Kelley clicked the key against his fingernail. "You stay too if you want."

I could tell from his voice that he wanted me to leave. "I'll go back to the Y and sleep. How come that man's name is Bucket?"

"It's not. His name is Burkett, but I don't remember anyone ever calling him that."

I thought I would be up all night.

My teeth were aching and I didn't want to set much store in Kelley's offer. I wanted far too much to believe it, and I couldn't have stood him letting me down.

I lay face-down on the bed. I felt my muscles shudder and relax. My breathing came level and deep and my thoughts scattered into the black.

At five in the morning, I walked down to Kelley's boat.

I brought him a cup of coffee, but he wasn't there to drink it.

Sitting on the bow, I watched the lobstermen head out to check their pots.

I stayed there until the afternoon, counting them off as they returned, making sure they reached home safely.

Pittsley stood in front of the pinball machine at Mary's.

When the last ball went away behind the flippers, his face shifted from drunk to angry to raging. He gripped the sides of the machine, swung his face down and cracked the plastic cover with his forehead.

I saw the bartender reach for a special phone he used for calling the police whenever there was trouble. He reached down slowly, in case anyone saw him and began a stampede for the door. A fight would break out in the stampede, the way it always happened at Mary's. Men would be sent cartwheeling over tables and sometimes through windows into the street, their shouts mixed with the sound of breaking glass.

I left through the back door and stood for a minute in the dark on the gridiron steps.

Strong and sudden gusts of wind had been blowing through the streets all evening. The sky broke now and then into lightning but I heard no sound of thunder. Cables whipped against masts in the harbor.

Gil had told us all to be on the boat and ready to leave by ten o'clock, but Pittsley said we wouldn't be going out in the storm. Just to be sure, I walked down to our boat, thinking I'd raid the fridge before heading back to the Y.

Standing in the galley, I listened over the murmur of generators for a sound of anyone on board.

I climbed up to the wheelhouse. It was dark. For a second, I thought I was alone. Then I made out the shapes of arms and legs and heads. The small room was crowded with people. The whole crew was here except for Pittsley.

The hair stood up on my head.

Nobody spoke.

The ship-to-shore radio talked quietly from its place on the ceiling.

They were all listening.

"What's the matter?" I breathed in the stuffy air.

The silhouette of Gil's hand cut in front of me and I kept quiet.

Kelley whispered to me, his hand cupped over my ear. The words barely formed on his lips. "There's a boat going down off the Cape. It's a Fall River boat. Reynolds is on board."

"Reynolds the mate?" I couldn't help speaking.

Again Gil's hand sliced close to my face. He turned up the radio.

"This is Coast Guard Station Howard Point. Come back."

"This is Fishing Vessel *Essex*. Where've you been? You changed channels on me. I've been waiting."

"What is the nature of your distress, over?"

"Engine room is flooded. My boat is sinking. Crew standing by to abandon ship."

"Are you in control of the vessel, over?"

"The water's up to my shins! How much control do you want?"

"Relay your coordinates, over."

"Loran coordinates five-seven-one-two and four-oh-seven-two-oh. Did you hear me? Do you want me to repeat? I am standing by to abandon ship, over."

"Wait, over."

"I've been waiting! I've been on the mike an hour already. I'm not asking you to come out here and salvage it. I'm telling you the fucker's sinking."

"Repeat coordinates, over."

"Five-seven-one-two, four-oh-seven-two-oh. I am going to give you a telephone number and I would like you please to call that number. I would like you to get in touch with my wife. Her name is Helen and she lives in Gloucester, Mass. Reynolds, get your ass back in the Givens. Don't be worrying about food now. All right, take the bologna too."

"Repeat, over."

"Talking to my crew. Listen, I am requesting emergency assistance. I am requesting a helicopter. Are you coming out here or not?"

"Stand by, over. Release the button on your mike when you are not transmitting to us. Otherwise we can't communicate, over."

"Standing by . . . hours . . . time."

"Keep talking, *Essex*. Your signal is fading. We are trying to get a fix on you, over."

"Coast Guard, I have waves fifteen to twenty. I have a wind at forty knots. My engine room is flooded and in fifteen minutes my stern will be under water. Shut the door, Reynolds, and get back in the Givens. Jesus Christ, this water's cold. I don't know where Henry is. He's with you. I'm on the radio. You find him. They're trying to get a fix on me. A fix is a fix. I don't know. I saw him! I just saw him! He's overboard! Coast Guard, I have a man overboard! I require immediate emergency assistance, over. Do you hear me? Can you hear what I'm saying?"

"Fishing Vessel *Essex,* we have located your position. We are unable to dispatch a helicopter due to high winds. Rescue vessel is in launch procedure at this time, over."

"What's the ETA?"

"Stand by."

"Did you hear me? I asked what the ETA was. Come back."

"Fishing Vessel *Essex.* ETA two hours, over."

"I'm not going to be here in two hours. I'm not going to be here in one."

"*Essex,* stay with your vessel as long as possible. Do not launch flares until rescue vessel is in sight. Do not abandon ship until absolutely necessary, over."

"Now what the hell do you call absolutely necessary? No, Reynolds, we aren't getting a helicopter. Stand by with the Givens. I don't give a damn about Henry. It was his own stupid fault. Just please get in the Givens."

"Fishing Vessel *Essex.* Release the microphone lever when you are not communicating with us. We cannot reach you when the mike button is pressed, over."

"Coast Guard, this is the *Essex.* I am preparing to abandon ship. I have water covering my stern. I am about to lose all emergency power. I'm going to light up the sky with those rescue flares just so I can see my own boat go down."

"Fishing Vessel *Essex.* Fishing Vessel *Essex.*"

Gil sat back in his chair. Then he rammed his foot against the control panel.

Once more the Coast Guard called for the *Essex.*

Gil slapped the front of the CB and turned it off. "They're gone."

For a while nobody said anything.

"How long do you think they can last out there?" I blinked at the silhouettes around me.

An empty beer can carried by the wind bounced across the dock planks and into the sea. Hard gusts bumped our windows, stirring up the harbor.

Gil turned to me.

I felt his breath on my face.

"They can last a while. Longer than you'd think, maybe. But not long enough, unless there's another boat nearby. And if there was, they'd have called in by now."

Howard climbed down the ladder into the galley. Kelley followed him.

Now it was just Gil and Franklin and me.

Franklin touched Gil on the arm. "You can't blame yourself for that."

Gil didn't answer. He got up from his chair and took hold of the wheel. He turned it one way and then the other, steering the boat as if riding out to help the *Essex.* He whispered orders to himself, quietly and through clenched teeth.

Franklin stood next to him, looking out through the wheelhouse windows.

I stayed hidden in shadows, not daring to move. I imagined red flares arcing down into the water. I saw Reynolds floundering in the sea. His hands gripped at the rubber of the swamped survival raft. But not for long. Not in the cold water off Cape Cod. The huge waves covered him up. I felt my own breath choked out of me as the last picture rattled through my skull of Reynolds dead and falling slowly down into the pressured black.

The storm kept up for days.

Newport Harbor was jammed with boats.

I stayed at the Y. In the daytime, I wandered through the blustery streets, chin tucked against my chest.

The rest of the crew stayed drunk at Mary's.

Everybody knew about the mate. The story spread in whispers. No one mentioned it to Gil. For him, this was worse than if they did bring up the subject. He sat with Franklin and played cards while the bar clattered and shuffled around them.

I remembered those days as a time of lowered voices and staring eyes quickly turned away.

Many times I stood at the end of the dock. I listened to wind moan through the rigging of boats and watched the ragged waves in the harbor, wondering when this storm would end so we could leave the land again.

Kelley broke a pool cue over a man's head at Mary's.

Then someone knocked Kelley out with a bottle of melon liqueur.

He sat unconscious in a little red chair in the corner until the police arrived, by which time the bar was empty.

At three in the morning, he called at the Y and asked for me.

The watchman shook me awake. He found me sleeping on the linoleum floor. I must have fallen out of bed and stayed asleep. The watchman asked me to tell my friends they shouldn't call after ten.

It cost me a hundred dollars, not including taxi fare, to bail him out of jail and get him back to the boat. He had a room at the Y, but I knew they wouldn't let him in drunk.

The cabby wanted me to pay extra because Kelley made the cab smell of rotten melon.

Kelley sang all the way to the dock and held on to a lamppost while I paid the fare. When the taxi drove away, I turned around and found him lying on his back, looking up at the sky.

"I've never seen so many stars."

"You're lucky to have me for a friend, Kelley. I hardly have a dollar to my name, and what I do have I end up spending on you." I pulled at his arm but he had passed out.

I couldn't drag him to the boat. He weighed at least twice as much as I did, most of the weight in his gut.

I used a fork lift from Sabatini's fishhouse to bring Kelley from the lamppost to the *Gray Ghost*. I dropped him on the deck, on a pile of stuffed garbage bags. And I left him there because I was annoyed at getting hardly any sleep and because I had begun to wonder what it would be like if he got drunk like this every night while we were working together on his boat.

It was too late to go back to the Y and I didn't want to lie in the stuffy bunk room. The good bars had shut and only the bad ones were open. The Gatsby boys had gone away up the hill to their mansions and the streets were empty now except for drunks and punks, who used the roads all night as alleyways for their skateboards.

I went to the refrigerator and found a live lobster lying in a pot of salt water. Red rubber bands held its claws shut. I boiled it with garlic and cayenne pepper, thinking I could buy another one for whoever had brought it to the boat.

I ate the lobster sitting on the bow, cracking the shell with a pair of pliers and dipping the meat in melted butter.

The storm died away. The harbor was foggy and quiet.

Kelley told the crew, one by one as they arrived at the dock, how he brought a girl back to the boat and how she had begged him to marry her.

"She had tuts out to here!"

"The way I heard it, Pfeif brought you back from jail and you spent the night lying on a pile of garbage." Howard had gone to the police station a little while after me, since he'd heard from a friend about Kelley being arrested.

"He never did! Pfeif is pulling your leg!"

I spat on the deck. "Let's just say I have a hundred dollars coming to me and I don't care how you think you came to owe it."

Kelley sat on a dredge and scowled while we made fun of his "tuts out to here."

Howard's wife drove by, rolled down the window and yelled

at him for not coming home. We turned from our circle, where we squatted like children, and stared.

"Howard, where was you last night?" She screamed at him over the rumble of her car's engine.

Howard scratched his beard with thin fingers, pointy knees showing through holes in his jeans. "Up at the bar."

"You was not!"

"I was. Ask Pfeif!" He pointed to me.

"That where he was at, Pfeif?" She slapped the car door with her arms.

"Yes, ma'am." I hadn't seen Howard at all the day before and didn't know why she would take my word over anyone else's.

"You're all lying to me! Howard, you better come home tonight."

"Can't. We're going out."

"Well, good. I hope you sink on a reef!"

Kelley stood, puffed out his chest and yelled after her not to curse the boat. Then he ordered me to get some beer from the liquor store. He said it was my turn to buy.

"No." I shook my head. "You go to the store, buy some beer and deduct it from what you owe me." I shooed him along. "Hurry now."

Kelley looked in his wallet, pulled out a twenty-dollar bill and stuffed it in my hand. "Buy a case from the bartender at Mary's. He won't card you and he'll sell it to you cheap. Use the change to have your coffee break." Then he leaned close and whispered, "I can't even walk that far. I feel like hell. I need the beer to soften my hangover. Make sure it's light beer. Please."

I sat in my window seat at the café, reading a paper and wishing Emily would stop by. The coffee made my nerves chatter.

Then with a case of beer held against my ribs and freezing

them, I walked back to our boat, feeling the asphalt already hot from the sun.

The crew was repairing a dredge.

I shielded my eyes from the welding torch.

Nelson stopped welding, lifted the heat visor from his face and stared at me. All of them stared at me.

I set down the beer, looking at each of them in turn. "What's the matter?" My nerves still squabbled from the coffee.

"Gil wants a word with you." Howard unhooked a can from the webbing of a six-pack.

"A word about what? What did I do?" I jerked my hands up, wanting an answer.

"He just wants a word, Pfeif." Howard turned back to the dredge.

They all returned to their work and now none of them looked at me.

"The lobster!" I shouted as I walked into the galley. "I'll buy a new one! I wasn't just going to *steal* your lobster, Gil!"

He sat under the beer clock, drinking ice tea from his blue plastic cup. "What are you doing inside?"

"Howard said you wanted to talk with me." My palms were sweating. "I ate the lobster and I'm sorry. I'll buy a new one."

"Howard told you to come in here?" No expression showed on his face.

Franklin giggled over by the stove.

Gil turned to him. "Shut up, Franklin."

"So they were kidding me?" I stood up to leave.

"No. They weren't kidding you. I'm kidding you." He smiled and held out his cup. "Want some ice tea?"

"Are you mad because I ate the lobster?"

"I was going to eat that for breakfast, but that's not why I called you in here."

"I'll buy a new one from Gunther's. I promise."

"Never mind about the damn lobster. I want you to stay on shore this trip."

"Why?" The word dragged out of my mouth.

"I'm not going to give you a reason right now. I just want you to know that your job is safe and you can work on the boat again as soon as we get back. I'll even advance you some money if you need it for the next week or so." He reached in his shirt pocket and pulled out a wallet. "You need a loan?"

"Am I fired?" I smoothed sweat from my hands onto the roughness of my jeans.

"I'm trying to tell you your job is safe. You just can't come out with us this time." He put his wallet away, the fat black fist of leather stuffed with bills.

"I deserve an explanation, at least." For the first time since I walked in, I took my gaze away from his eyes. "Don't I? I do!"

"That's too bad. Now go home and take a break and I'll get Kelley to call you the day we get in. It's just the way it is, Pfeif. Just keep nice and quiet and rest easy at home."

Outside, the crew had stopped work and were drinking the beer. Nelson sat with the welding torch across his knee, the visor pulled up to his forehead. It looked like the bill of a huge duck.

They eyed me when I walked on deck. Kelley threw me a beer. I caught it and set it down, not wanting to drink. I had nothing to say to them. They were all in on it. I didn't understand and I got no explanation and now I was pissed off.

Kelley followed me up the dock road to Severn Street. He finished his beer and dropped the can in one of Sabatini's orange parking barrels. "Gil's only looking out for you, Pfeif."

I stopped, thinking of something to say, then decided that he didn't deserve an answer. They were blaming the flipped dredges on me. They were getting rid of the odd man on the crew, telling me my job was safe in case they decided to keep me on. But now they were testing out whether they could get along

216

without me. Or worse, they didn't like my company. I knew these things would be rattling through my head all week.

"I swear you'll get your job back, Pfeif."

"Then give me my job now! I'm ready to go out *now*. I'm all set to go! I bought new gloves and new boots and a new toothbrush and I'm all geared up to leave. What kind of a joke are you pulling on me?"

"Quiet down." He held up his hand. "There's a reason, but Gil asked us not to tell you for your own good."

"So don't tell me. Do what you're told. I just think it's a cheap shot, kicking me off the crew for no reason you have the guts to tell me about."

"All right." He smiled a sarcastic smile, took hold of my arm at the elbow and led me over toward the empty refrigeration trucks that Sabatini used to transport the catches up to Boston or down to New York. Kelley made me climb into the back of a truck and then walked me along the damp metal corridor to the end. We crouched down in the gloom. The place smelled of detergent. "Now don't let Gil or anyone else know that I told you or we'll probably lose both our jobs. All right?" He gripped the joint of my wrist and shook it. He talked in a whisper, which rasped out of his throat. "We have a special job this time, a job that will make us a great deal of money if it goes right. That's the thing, though. If. If it goes wrong we are all in hell. Except you."

I suddenly realized what he was talking about. "You're going out to run drugs." I sat back against the wall of the truck. "You sons of bitches are running drugs."

"We're picking up some stuff from a beach in Maine and we're dropping it off someplace in New Jersey. On the way out and on the way back we're going to fish."

"How often does Gil do this? Have you done this before?" I looked at the brightness at the end of the truck, where it opened onto the scrap heap of Sabatini's dockyard. It was a place where old shreds of net lay piled on broken dredges and lobster pots. People came here to buy joints from a thin black man named Stevens, who wore sunglasses even at night.

"I never have, but Gil has and so have the others. It's not a regular thing. He just has friends who know what they're doing and who make him an offer once a year or once every other year. Alls I know is that it's going to happen, and Gil and the rest of us decided that you were too young and wouldn't know what you were getting into. I said I didn't think you'd want to come even if he offered you a place."

"Aren't you afraid? I'm always reading about fishing boats getting caught running drugs."

"You read about the tiny fraction that get caught. How the hell do you think most of the stuff gets up north? The Coast Guard searches ships coming up from the South. They searched Gil's when he motored up from Virginia. So the way people get through with the stuff is they fly it up north, land it in places like Maine, then ship it down to Long Island and New Jersey and it gets distributed from there. You see how it works? Pfeif, it's so much money that I can't afford to turn the offer down. If Gil doesn't do it, someone else sure as hell will. I can cover all my old debts and get back to paying off the boat."

"And what do you get if you're caught?" The nervousness in me traveled from my stomach to my throat. It pulsed against the muscles in my neck.

Kelley laughed and looked at the floor. Then he looked up and was no longer laughing. "Ten years, maybe. Tops. Probably get off after four. People get out after three sometimes. Gil wouldn't. Gil'd be in there for a while longer, but that's his business. He's raking in a lot more money than the rest of us because the risk is that much greater for him."

"You don't give a shit what you're doing as long as it brings in the money, do you?" The cold of the truck fanned goosebumps along my arms.

218

Kelley smoothed his hands over his face. "I figure I'm taking enough chances out here as it is."

I stood and helped him to his feet. "What the hell am I supposed to do when you and everyone on that boat gets put away?"

"Be glad you weren't with us. Don't give me a hard time, Pfeif. You're too young and you haven't seen enough to be giving me a hard time about something like this."

"Give me a call when you get in." I started walking toward the end of the truck.

He caught up with me. "Sure enough." He slapped me on both arms at the same time, then stood back. "And keep it dark. If you talk, the wrong person might hear."

I jumped down into the heat of the dockyard. "Ripping off black bass from Gunther is one thing. But you should have drawn the line before this, Kelley."

"Enough." Kelley clicked his tongue.

Stevens sat on a pile of old netting. His clothes were black. His shoes and his hat and his glasses all were black. He didn't seem to have any pockets, and I wondered where he kept what he had to sell. He nodded to Kelley. "Are you here for me?"

"Not today, Stevens." Kelley tucked in his shirt.

"Then tomorrow, maybe." Stevens picked at a strand of fishnet twine.

Kelley slapped me on the arm again and walked away.

For a second I stared at Stevens. Stevens stared back.

He tapped the toes of his black basketball sneakers together, blank-eyed like a fish in his sunglasses. "You want something from me?"

I met Joseph on his way down to the Narragansett post office with a stack of packaged records. He gave me half the pile. "I thought you were out on the water."

"I'm not going this time." I didn't expect the records to be as heavy as they were. Joseph had typed the names of the buyers on small white stickers and attached them to the brown wrapping paper. He had a rubber stamp made for the new business. It said "World Wide Record Company" and gave his rented post office box number. Each package was stamped at the top left corner.

"Did they fire you?"

"I'm taking a rest. No, that's not true. They said they didn't want me to come out this trip."

"Sounds like they fired you."

"The captain promised me my job when they get back."

We walked up the post office steps and Joseph paid for the stamps.

On the walk home I told him the truth, that the boat was running drugs.

He didn't seem very surprised. He mumbled but said nothing else.

I didn't like his quiet, and wished I hadn't told him. "If you were working on a boat and someone made you an offer like that, would you go?"

"It depends on how badly I needed the money." He gouged a finger in his ear. "Truth is, I've thought about breaking the law to get myself out of debt."

"What were you going to do?"

He shrugged. "I don't know exactly. I only opened the possibility to myself if something came along."

It didn't surprise me to hear what he said. I may not have known where Kelley would draw the line, but I knew for sure that Joseph didn't even have a line to draw.

"I ought to tell you something, James." He stopped at the breakwater, jumped it and landed on the low-tide sand. "You want to take a walk?"

Surf scudded up the beach and crossed our feet in foam and shreds of seaweed.

Mothers helped their children build sand castles. They

slapped down walls against the tide, which filled the moats and took away decorations of shells along the battlements.

A boy and a girl buried another boy up to his neck in the sand. The boy in the sand had a look on his face as if he might have enjoyed the game when it started but wished it was over now. The girl draped seaweed around his neck like a scarf. "You bums!" The buried boy shook his head as tiny shrimp in the seaweed tickled his neck.

I wandered with Joseph past the area of beach crowded with people. We walked all the way to the end, where a fast-running stream fed into a salt marsh.

Joseph walked into the stream and water piled around his knees, soaking his rolled-up trousers. "You may already know what I'm going to tell you."

I knelt down in the sand, feeling it hot on my shins. "Go ahead."

"Dad's been running drugs for years." He waited to see what I'd say.

I kept quiet. My guts curdled.

Joseph kept talking. "All the time I was in college, he made runs to pay the bills and keep out of debt. He made a better business of that than he ever did of fishing."

I looked down at my knees.

"You didn't know, did you?" He spoke over the sound of running water.

I shook my head and said very quietly, "How could I?" Then I looked up and barked at him. "And how the hell do you know about it?"

"Dad told me."

"So he's a crook." I wished I didn't have his blood in me. "All his talk about hard and honest work and he's a crook."

"He's a crook all right, but don't you damn him so fast."

"Does Mom know?" I squinted at him over the water's shifting light.

"No."

"Why didn't he tell her?"

"Because he wanted to keep her away from it as much as he wants to keep us away. He might have quit fishing years ago if the people he dealt with had let him. He made a couple of runs and they wanted him to keep working at it. At first he said no, but then they muscled him and he had to say yes. The thing is that these people, the ones who pay him to pick stuff up and drop it off someplace else, would have no problem at all seeing to it that he had an accident or one of us had an accident, just to keep him in line and keep him working for them. He once told me a story about a New Bedford fisherman named Gulak, who made a run and when the people came back asking him to make another, he told them to fuck off. They asked him again nicely and offered him some more money but he still didn't want to go. He came back from his next fishing trip and found his wife and kids hanging from barbed wire nooses in his front yard." Joseph bent down and studied his face in the stream. Then he looked up at me again. "That's what happens as soon as you start dealing with these people. They keep coming back with little favors they want doing, and they pay you less and the favors get bigger until you either have to leave town or do what they say. So he did what they told him to do. That's why he hates the fishing, why he wants us out of it. At least then if we got mixed up in something, he couldn't blame himself. I know he's happy that you want to work in-shore, because you're no use to the people who've been screwing him all this time. They only need fishermen who operate off-shore. And besides all that, he's happy you found something you want to do. I'm happy for you too, James. I'm happier for you than I am for myself."

"So he's a crook who got screwed by other crooks." The sharp sand dug into my knees.

"You're getting it wrong, James." He picked a stone from the stream and threw it hard at the water near where I sat.

I saw then how angry I had made him.

He smoothed his hands together, squeezing out drops of water. "You shouldn't hate him for what he did. You should get down on your stupid little knees and thank him. You see" — he shook his head, eyes narrowed — "you stayed in school just long enough to learn about fairness and honesty and decency. But you don't know yet what that counts for out here. Here!" He pointed at the ground. "I thought maybe you'd have learned some of that from when you got kicked out of college."

"Learned some of what?"

"Learned something about what works, James. Not what *should* work. You went after that boy with your little sense of schoolboy honor and look where it landed you. But the other guy was smarter. He wanted your job and he got it and at the same time he got rid of you. Think about it."

"I think about it too much already."

"Now Dad saw what he wanted and he saw what he thought he had to do to get it. He doesn't want you to know. If he did, he'd have told you about it. He's still a crook, but he's also your father and what he did wasn't for himself." Joseph stood in the stream, jangling the change in his pockets. "You won't ever say I told you any of this. Understand? Maybe someday Dad will tell you. Look at me. This is important. Do you understand?"

I stared at the sand and nodded, wondering whether Gil lived under the same pressure as my father, whether people muscled him into doing what they wanted and whether he always had to give in.

Mother hugged us together with her big arms. "I'm so pleased to have both my boys home." Then she stepped back and held on to our hands, smiling, lower lip bit between her teeth.

I looked at her and thought, You'd forgive him, wouldn't you? Surely you'd forgive him if you knew.

12

~~~~~~
~~~~~~

THE MAILMAN delivered a package.

It was addressed to me, my name written in heavy black marker on the wrapping.

I sat on the front doorstep and tore off the paper.

Mother wandered through her rose garden, singing to herself and clipping off dead flowers with a scissors.

Beneath the wrapping was a box, half gold and half black, the box for a Leica. It was a brand-new M6 with a built-in light meter.

I opened the box and looked at the shiny camera. It was wrapped in a small plastic bag and cushioned between two pieces of molded Styrofoam. I caught the smell of new steel. Tucked in the side of the box were registration documents and a guarantee. I carefully unfolded the wrapping and looked for some kind of letter, anything to confirm what I was thinking. I knew the camera came from Bartlett. It was the same model as his own.

A picture of Bartlett returned to me. I saw his face, red in the glow of developing lights in the darkroom.

I picked the camera from the Styrofoam and weighed it in my hands.

I knew Bartlett was expecting to see me again in the fall. I wondered if he would have said anything about the camera. Perhaps he couldn't stand the thought of working alongside me in the darkroom for another three years without making some kind of peace. Maybe he thought we could return to being friends.

For a while as I sat on my doorstep under the midday August sun, I thought how easy it would be to go back in the fall. I could have quit the boats that day. No one would have come looking for me. They'd hire a new crewman. That sort of thing happened all the time. Pictures of school invaded my thoughts. The package of memories I had stashed away came unraveled in front of my eyes.

It didn't last long. The pictures fell into the dark at the back of my head. I had already made up my mind.

"What's that, dear?" Mother stood up from the tangle of her rose bushes. She wore a blue scarf on her head.

"A camera."

"How nice! Did you send away for it?" She picked a Japanese beetle off one of the bushes and flicked it into the street.

"I think it's from Bartlett. I know it is."

"Bartlett." Mother wiggled her fingers in her heavy work gloves. "Is he that old friend of yours who sold forest land that didn't belong to him to the Boy Scouts and told them they could cut down all the little pine trees for their Christmas fund raiser?"

I didn't answer.

She went back to cutting her roses.

My father ran his boat up on the rocks at Galilee.

He was the only one on board when it happened. He jumped from the *Glory B* as it keeled over into the surf and didn't have to swim more than a hundred feet to reach the shore.

The owner of the Fishermen's Co-op told the Narragansett newspaper he'd never forget the sight of Russell Pfeiffer walking barefoot down the middle of the road, soaked wet and wearing a life jacket on a foul, stormy day in August.

My father told everyone the steering jammed. The boat had just left port to go on another trip. Half an hour out to sea, he told his crew he thought the engine might be overheating, and headed back to dock to check the problem. He unloaded the crew and told them to go buy some lunch. He even advanced them some money, which was something he'd never done before. Then, on the excuse of running his boat a short distance to see if the engines were going to overheat again, he left the dock and motored a half mile out. He told the Coast Guard and the papers that the wheel and rudder locked just as he approached the breakwater leading back into Galilee.

The *Glory B* rammed against the granite slabs that made up the breakwater. People who saw the wreck said its bow plowed against the rocks until it was pointing almost straight up in the air. Then it toppled over and began to take on water.

The whole breakwater was lined with people who had come to see the *Glory B* break itself apart in the surf. They stood in bright-colored rain slickers, forced gradually back toward land by waves that rushed in harder and harder from the gray boil of the storm.

I stood with Joseph at the front of the crowd. He had come straight down from Providence and didn't have time to change out of his suit. I held my oiler jacket over the both of us, rain patting the rubber and pouring off the empty sleeves.

My mother and father stood with a policeman and another man in a suit whose umbrella had been blown inside out by the wind. He was the insurance claims officer and had already fallen in the water trying to get a closer look at the *Glory B*'s hull. Now the suit hung across his shoulders and clung to his buttocks like a mass of dead leaves.

Mother looked from my father to the police officer to the insurance man, her eyes almost closed against needles of rain, which cut across the rocks and dappled the water. My father went through the accident again, pausing now and then while the other two men nodded to show they understood what he was saying. Then he shook his head and stuffed his hands in his pockets. Suddenly he pulled his hands out again and talked some more. The policeman turned away and coughed. A wave smashed on the hull and hissed across the breakwater.

An ambulance arrived at the dock and two men with a stretcher ran out along the uneven rocks, pushing past the crowd.

They reached the end of the line and looked around. One of them turned to Joseph. "Where's the injured man?"

"I don't think there is one."

"We had a call that a man fell in the water and broke his arm."

"Well, the only person who fell in the water was that man over there."

The two medics approached the group.

The insurance man shook his head and held up his arm. The sleeve was torn. His wrist had been cut against the barnacles.

After a minute of talk, the insurance man took another look at his arm and bent it back and forth. Then he followed the two medics along the breakwater to their ambulance.

With each wave, the ruin of the trawler rose up and smashed down on the rocks. The sound of metal grinding against stone reached us over the rumble of the sea. Junk from the boat washed past in the channel. A yellow bucket. Life jackets. The ice hatch and wooden planks from the ice hold pens. A shirt, billowing with the current.

I shivered as the boat hammered itself to pieces on the breakwater. I knew that by the time the storm died down there would be almost nothing to salvage. The whine of scraping metal and the clink of broken glass sounded to me like something alive and in pain.

Joseph sniffed at the coat I held over his head, catching the stench of monkfish and grease from the *Gray Ghost*. "They asked him for one too many favors."

"You're sure it wasn't an accident?" I saw the long straightness of Joseph's nose in the corner of my eye. I didn't turn to face him.

"I know it wasn't. They pushed him too far with their muscling. They were trying to do a run sometime next week. You don't just run your boat up on the rocks after twenty years of fishing."

"It could happen. The steering could lock." I felt the spray of another wave touch my face.

"It could, all right. That's why he'll get the insurance money. I'm only saying what I'm sure half the fishermen on the dock already know."

I unclipped the lens cap from my camera, which I'd been carrying with me most places since I got it. I took some pictures of the *Glory B*.

A blur passed in front of the viewfinder, and when I looked up, I saw it was my father and mother and the policeman.

The policeman shook my father's hand. He wore what looked like a shower cap on the top of his hat and an orange coat that came down to his shins. "See you, Russ." He edged through the crowd back to land.

"Right!" My father raised his hand slightly, smiled for a second and then stopped smiling. "See you." He turned to me and pointed at the camera. "I want a big print when you get those developed."

I thought for a moment he might be angry that I'd brought the camera, but he grinned, his head turned from the crowd. "If it had to go down, it may as well be in my own back yard."

"I'm sorry for you, Dad." Joseph pulled the oiler jacket off his head and draped it over my mother, whose little rain hat only redirected the water down the front of her coat.

My mother buttoned the oiler. "At least no one was hurt."

"Except the insurance man." I hid the camera under my shirt to keep it dry.

"Well, that little fool deserved what he got." Mother peered out from the black rubber hood. "We told him not to get close to the boat but he did anyway. He's lucky he didn't get crushed between the hull and the rocks. As it is, he ruined a two-hundred-dollar suit."

The *Glory B* lurched and slipped down with the next wave. Its wheelhouse sank under the surface. The dirty hull showed now above the foam. I made out the fat blades of its propeller.

The crowd of people had begun to thin out. Through the mist, I watched red and blue and yellow rain slickers file across the parking lot and stop at cars or disappear into dockside restaurants. The ambulance was gone.

Mother started walking back along the breakwater. Then she turned and motioned for us to follow. "I have to say, some days I've thought about coming out here and sinking the boat by myself."

Father stood still for a moment and pressed his thumbs against his temples. "I'll be taking some time off while the insurance is settled."

"You haven't mowed the lawn in about six years, so you can start with that." Mother smiled at him.

I stepped off the breakwater and onto the gravel of the parking lot. "Dad, you lost your hat."

He touched the rough pads of his fingertips against his forehead. "So I did."

Four men were waiting by my father's truck. I recognized them as his crew. One man, whose last name was Kitteridge, stepped forward. "We're going home now, Russ. You want us to call you in the morning?"

"I'll be at the Co-op at seven. I'll try and fix you all up on other boats within twenty-four hours."

"I guess you'll be working alongside us as a crewman from now on."

"Maybe so. In time."

"If you get yourself another boat, you know where to find us. We're sorry it happened, Russ."

They must know why he wrecked the boat, I thought to myself. They're only going through the motions of apology for Joseph and Mother and me.

"This is the first time I ever seen you without a hat on, Russ." Kitteridge grinned. "We've been meaning to ask you, Mrs. Pfeiffer. Does your husband sleep with his hat on at home too?"

"Oh, he takes it off before he goes to bed. But then I think sometimes he waits until I'm asleep and puts it on again."

The noise of the boat breaking apart made us turn our heads.

Kitteridge took down his hood, showing his straggly blond hair. "I can't take much more of that sound."

We were quiet as my father looked at his shoes, hiding any expression on his face. Then everybody began talking again as we got into the truck and my father started the engine.

I sat in front, watching the breakwater appear and disappear in the sweep of our windshield wipers.

The phone rang.

My father set his fists on the kitchen table. "I am not here! Do you understand? I am not here!"

Mother picked up the receiver. "Yes. May I ask who's calling, please?" She held her hand over the mouthpiece and nodded at me. "It's someone named Kelley."

My guts jolted.

Mother held out the receiver on the flat of her palm. "Isn't he one of your friends from the boat?"

I stirred my spoon in the mush of my drowned breakfast cereal. All week I had been thinking about when he would call. If he would call. Or whether the police would arrive at my door to ask questions.

"Did everything go all right?" I paced back and forth in the kitchen, winding myself in the phone's extension cord.

"Everything's fine."

"Well, are you going to tell me about it or not?"

"I'll tell you when I see you. Meet me on Jamestown."

"Where exactly?" I heard a car ride past in the background. Then a boat horn blasted twice.

"Just get on the bus. You'll see me."

"When, Kelley?"

"Now. I'm already here."

He met me at the bus stop on Jamestown, an island between Newport and Narragansett. He waved to me from the wooden bus stop shelter. The old ladies waiting for their ride to Newport didn't like the look of Kelley and stood in the sun rather than sit next to him.

We walked out of town to the cliffs at Fort Wetherill. The fort was built during the Second World War to guard the harbor against German ships and submarines. The ruins lay buried in poison ivy and brambles, huge gun pits empty now, the concrete parapets crisscrossed with graffiti.

Kelley and I sat at the edge of the cliff, warm in the sun, watching bright-spinnakered boats tilt in the wind and move fast out to sea.

Far below I heard the waves, slugging the cliff wall and sliding back down.

Kelley told me how the run had gone. He spoke in a murmur, raising his voice only when the hammer of waves covered his words.

"On the fifth day out, we stopped fishing and moved north. Up until then, it was just like every other trip we'd made. But as soon as we changed course for the north, that's when I started getting scared. We torched holes in the outriggers and removed part of the ice room wall. We took the bulbs out of the deck lights. These were all places Gil said we'd be hiding the cargo.

"We took turns looking at the radar. Somebody had to be

watching it the whole time while Gil steered the boat. We had to tell him whenever a blip showed on the screen. I'd be sitting there six hours at a time, watching the screen, turning the distance dial from five miles to ten to twenty and never seeing anything.

"When the holes were burned in the walls and outriggers, we welded the plates back in place but only weakly so they could be knocked out again with a hammer. On the outriggers, we smoked the weld marks so they wouldn't stand out from the rest of the metal. I was glad we had work to do. Otherwise, I'd have gone out of my head.

"On the afternoon of the sixth day, I saw trees and little stretches of beach. Gil said we were someplace off Port Clyde, Maine.

"Gil brought a Zodiac out of the lazarette. We took turns blowing it up with a bicycle pump, and when that was done we fixed an outboard motor on a wooden panel at the back."

"How scared were you?" I watched him very closely.

"Later I was scared. At the time I'm telling you about, there was too much going on to be worried. It was only in the times when nothing happened that I started worrying.

"We dropped anchor a third of a mile off shore, no running lights, no deck lights. Gil turned the engines off, and you know how it is after days of hearing the engine and then suddenly having quiet. Your ears start ringing.

"Franklin came out on deck with two rifles, old Army ones. One of them had an extension on it like a bottle made out of metal. Do you know what it was? A grenade launcher. Pittsley brought it back from Vietnam. I asked Franklin what on earth we'd need those for and he told me you didn't ever know what the other man was going to be carrying.

"Then Gil handed me the rifle without the extension and took the other one for himself. There were plastic bread bags over the rifle barrels to keep out sea water. We set the Zodiac in the water and jumped into it. All I could think about when we were riding in low to the water was how this whole plan didn't have a hope of working. I wished I was you then. I wished I was on land. I couldn't think of any amount of money that was worth this.

"It was twilight when we made the beach. I jumped out in waist-deep water and waded up to the dry sand. Then I lay down in the weeds at the high-tide mark, watching for anyone nearby. Gil dragged the boat up above the water line and we waited for them to show. I couldn't see a thing in the fog.

"We were in some kind of picnic area with thick woods on either side and a dirt road running inland. I saw a couple of old tables and some barbecue grills and a hut with one side fallen in.

"Then a man showed up. He was walking down the middle of the road, wearing a camouflage jacket. Gil went across and shook his hand. I figured he knew the man from another time.

"'Suddenly another two men stood up from the bushes. Both of them had shotguns. I pointed the gun at one and then at the other and then back to the first one. I still had the damn bread bag on the end and so I couldn't aim straight. I was ready to kill him. I was ready to kill both of them. Then Gil waved me up and told me to follow these two men into the woods.

"They walked on either side of me. I was trying to stay a little bit behind so I could watch what they were doing. They walked over to the hut and set their shotguns on the floor, so I set mine down too. Then one of them asked me if it was rough out there on the water and he reached out his hand to shake. I was so scared at that point I started laughing, and then they were laughing too. We were all so nervous that somebody would start shooting. And there's Gil walking around with a grenade launcher. As soon as we figured we might actually get away with the job, we couldn't help ourselves from laughing. They said their names were Emmett and Will and I told them my name was Rudolph. We couldn't stop laughing after that."

"Where was Gil while this was going on?"

"He was in the hut with the other man, sharing a smoke. It's funny, you know. I remember every fucking detail. I don't think I closed my eyes once. I can account for every hour of this last week. Every minute."

"'So what were those two men doing? Emmett and Will?'"

"They jogged back to a truck they had parked in the woods. Then they drove it in reverse down to the edge of the sand. The back of the truck was loaded with packages wrapped in black plastic garbage bags and sealed with electrical tape. We loaded the Zodiac with as many as it could take, and we took off out to sea again.

"I threw the packages onto the deck of the *Gray Ghost* while Gil tried to hold our Zodiac steady. Howard was up on the bow in his underwear, eating a box of crackers. He didn't look worried at all. Franklin stacked the packages in the galley, and Pittsley stamped around all mad at me and Gil because we'd set our guns down. He was shaking his fist at me and asking me whose side I was on. Dumb fuck thought he was back in the jungle.

"By the time we made it to the beach again, Emmett and Will had stacked the other packages on the sand. They opened a thermos of hot soup and we passed the little plastic cup around and drank from it. I kept wanting just to talk to them and ask them where they were from, but then I figured they'd only lie the way we all did about our names.

"Gil and I made another trip out to the boat, and before we left the third time with the last packages, we all shook hands again but didn't say much. I remembered thinking if I ever saw them again, even years from now, I'd still recognize them.

"We reached the boat and Pittsley shouted to us that he saw something on the radar. Gil and I jumped up on board, hauled in the Zodiac, and the next thing I know I'm lying flat on the deck with my rifle, ready to shoot out the scupper. For a long time, we just waited in the dark. Fog was rolling all around us. All I could hear was the water.

"Gil said whatever had been on the screen wasn't there now,

and if it had been anybody but Pittsley who said they saw it, Gil might have been more worried. Franklin and Howard pulled in the anchor, Howard still in his underwear and looking like a bird with its feathers pulled off. Then we motored fast out to sea. I sat with Pittsley at the stern, watching for a boat to come out of the fog. All the time I was back to thinking there'd be no way we could get away with this. I was dead sure of it. But nothing showed up on the screen again, and after a while Gil came out on deck with a cup of coffee for each of us, said we were clear and let us get dry clothes on.

"We deflated our Zodiac and stuffed it back in the lazarette with the putt-putt motor. Then we knocked out the loose panels in the outriggers and down in the ice room. We stuffed the spaces with as many packages as we could and put the rest up in work lights, way up in the rigging. We welded the plates in once more and smoked them and dirtied them so no one would notice. Then we went back to fishing as if nothing had ever happened.

"I guess we fished for another couple of days, heading gradually south until we were off Cape May.

"We put in at Cape May and unloaded what scallops we had at a place called the Southport Fisheries. I stayed down in the ice room. I didn't want to show my face. When that was done and we'd settled with the scallop buyers, Gil tied up the boat at a warehouse dock next to the fisheries place. He gave us each a couple of hundred dollars and told us to be back on the dock by seven in the morning.

"I spent the whole night in a motel watching MTV. The whole time, I was thinking if it was going to go wrong, it would be now, and I had dreams of people busting into the room and putting handcuffs on me. I must have dreamt it six or seven times, and each time more and more people would be there and my parents were there, and my old schoolteacher. They were all piling into my room to watch the police put handcuffs on me.

"When we showed up at the boat next day all the stuff had

been taken away by whoever made the deal with Gil. And as soon as we could, we left the dock and steamed back to Sabatini's. While we were still out to sea, he handed out our pay. All cash. All old bills in fifties and twenties and tens. He told us not to spend any of it for a couple of months and then only a little at a time. He said we couldn't keep it in a bank account, but that didn't matter, since I don't have one anyway. Then he told me to give you a call and for us all to be on the boat in two days. So I called you. And here we are."

"What did you do with the money?"

"I stashed it in the same place I stashed all my other money."

"How much did you get?"

"Never you mind. I got what I expected to get, and that doesn't make me rich but it keeps my head above water for a while."

"Are you going to keep working for Gil?"

"Sure. It's a good boat to work on. He doesn't cheat us and he makes a good catch when his dredges aren't flipping. It's a decent wage. I'd be a fool to quit before I had enough to cover any kind of mess up that might happen when we start lobstering. I'll be fishing with Gil up until Christmas. Then I'll quit and start setting out lobster pots in the spring."

"I guess I'll do the same."

"I've never had the feeling of being able to rest easy the way I do now. Now I have enough money not to think about money for a while."

All week I had been thinking about the *Gray Ghost* and the run they were making. I no longer knew whether I'd have gone if Gil asked me. I thought of the months of work it would take to bring me even near what Kelley had made in a week. The tiredness and the dirt. It felt as if all the rest I'd had in my time at home would be drawn out of me in the first day back on the *Ghost*. Nowadays I slept better out to sea. "Aren't you still worried about getting caught?"

"Not now. Those packages get run onto the market faster than you'd ever believe. By the time they reach the streets and the little dealers like Stevens, nobody knows where it's come from." Kelley took off his shoes and picked at his toes, the way he did when he was nervous. He didn't really know the way the business worked and was only trying to convince himself.

I walked to the edge of the cliff and looked down, gripping the rock with my feet to keep steady. It was a fifty-foot drop. Joseph and I used to come here and jump, feeling the air shoved out of our lungs, the slap against our feet as we hit the water and a rush of bubbles that took us back to the surface.

I breathed in deep and stepped off the edge, hearing Kelley shout as I slipped out of view. Pressure, like a pair of hands held against my face. My guts jolted up into my ribs. The wind spread my fingers apart. I tried to yell something but had no air in my lungs. Then the sudden clap as I struck the water, and a rushing sound as I curved down into the cold. I rose slowly, feet first, to the top.

My hands stung and there was pain in the arches of my feet. I let myself be carried toward the rocks by a wave and gripped at the barnacles. The wave sucked back and pulled me away, ducking me under for a second.

Kelley looked down, hands on his head. "You did that on purpose!"

I waved at him and swam again at the rocks, this time finding a grip and climbing above the level of the waves. I rested on a ledge, sharp light breaking off the water and jabbing at my eyes.

"Where are you?" Kelley called down from the top. "Are you all right?"

"Jump, Kelley!"

"Never!"

Then I heard him mumble to himself. A few seconds later I saw his flapping arms, open mouth and the blur of his big pink belly strike the water. He disappeared, leaving an arc of spray in the air. For a moment, the only trace of him was a ring of white froth folding away in the sweep of a wave. Then a rush of bubbles hissed to the surface. In the middle of them I saw the soles of his shoes.

He dog-paddled across to where I sat, the salt already drying on my skin. He took in mouthfuls of water and spat them out again. His hands raked along the barnacles, searching for a grip, and twice the waves dragged him back before he left the water. "You knew I'd have to jump. You made it so I didn't have a choice." He shook the sting from his red hands.

We missed the last bus back to Newport, so Kelley called a taxi.

When the man arrived, I recognized him as one of the cabbies that sat on the hoods of their cars outside the Y.

He leaned out the window. "How come your clothes are wet?"

"We went swimming." I felt the salt crusty in my eyebrows.

"I can't take you in my cab with wet clothes." He pulled at his nose and then sniffed.

"We're almost dry." Kelley slapped the soaked thighs of his jeans. "It won't matter."

The driver shook his head. "I just finished cleaning up the car from last week. I gave a ride to some fisherman who got soaked in melon-flavored alcohol."

I remembered him now from the night Kelley was thrown in jail.

We asked him to wait, then ran across the road to a surf shop. We bought swimming trunks called Baggies, which came down to our knees. Kelley's had palm trees done in pink and red and orange. Mine had pelicans in blue and green and purple.

As we crossed the bridge, Kelley asked the driver if it was true that all the cabbies who worked near the Y had gone in for vasectomies.

The cabby blinked at us in his rearview mirror. "I'd kill the man who started that rumor if I could find him." He was fat enough that his belly button would honk the horn if he stopped suddenly.

"Is it true?" Kelley hugged the headrest of the passenger seat.

"I'd kill him stone dead, and you can tell him if you know him."

Their voices blew past my ears. I wasn't really listening. Instead, I thought about heading out to sea again. I had been on land too long. I closed my eyes and listened to the even rattle of our tires crossing the spacers of the bridge.

13

A SHARK came up in the dredge, almost dead by the time it reached our deck.

We were three days out to sea.

The shark was a mako, about seven feet long with flat eyes the size of golf balls. The gray of its back gave way to pale white on the belly.

Gil grabbed the mako by its sickle-shaped tail and dragged it to the center of the deck. He kicked it in the gills to see if it was still alive.

The mako quivered under the leather of its skin, then opened its mouth and showed us some teeth.

I brought out my camera, which I kept carefully packed away in its Styrofoam box. Then everyone wanted their picture taken with the fish.

Pittsley and Nelson knelt on either side of the mako and smiled. Pittsley wanted to point at it.

"If anybody looks at the photo, they're going to know where the fish is without you pointing at it." I crouched down and loaded a roll of film.

Pittsley pointed at the mako anyway, and Nelson stood with his foot on the thing's head as if it were a shot lion.

Gil picked up the shark and hugged it, his fingers pressed hard into the rough skin to stop it from thrashing around. Franklin stood in the background, his head appearing first over one of Gil's shoulders and then over the other as Gil staggered across the deck, trying to keep the mako steady while I took the picture.

Kelley crouched next to the fish and lifted its snout to show the teeth: small white triangles on top and inward-pointing spikes below. Kelley opened his mouth to show his own teeth.

Then the shark bit him.

Kelley lost his grip on the snout, the shark closed its mouth and Kelley's fingers got in the way.

Slowly and carefully, Kelley pried open the mako's jaws and removed his hand. At first there was no blood. Then slits made by the teeth opened up and dark drops spilled from his hand onto the fish's head.

Kelley walked to the ice hatch and picked up a crowbar used to dislodge stones jammed in the dredges. He began beating the shark on the head. He swung the heavy iron bar the same way a person swings an ax. The first few strikes left dents in the gray skin. After several more, we could see the pink meat underneath.

The rest of us stood watching, afraid to get close as Kelley took out his anger on the mako.

Eventually Gil told him to set the crowbar down before he hurt himself. When Kelley didn't stop, Gil shook his finger and yelled, "I mean it now!"

Franklin bandaged the hand with cloth from a scallop bag, the same as he had done before with Kelley's head.

"Is it deep? Is it a mess?" Kelley shouted in Franklin's ear.

Gil brought a machete down from the wheelhouse. He carried it on the boat for removing tangles of fishing net that sometimes snagged on the dredges. He cut off the shark's head and staggered back, swearing from the smell. He tied a rope to its tail and dragged the body to the stern. The fish's bored-looking eyes gaped from its severed head.

Gil threw its body overboard and attached the rope to a holding bar above the lazarette.

"What about my picture?" Howard hadn't wanted to get near the shark when it first came on board, but now that it was in bits and pieces and half of it over the side, he decided to make a fuss.

I took a photo of him sitting on the ice hatch, hands held over his groin the way he always sat. The shark's head lay next to him, smelly and bleeding on the wooden hatch.

When we pulled up the carcass a half hour later, there was almost nothing left. Bites the size of footballs had been ripped from the belly and back.

Howard cut the teeth from its head and cleaned the jaws in a bucket of salt water and bleach. Then he tied them on the bow rail to harden in the sun.

I had seen trawlers docked at Galilee with shark jaws racked up along the bow. I used to watch fishermen unload the huge bodies, heads and fins cut off. They sometimes sold the meat as swordfish, since it tasted nearly the same and fetched a better price.

Kelley said a shop in New Bedford had a pair of jaws on display that a person could crawl through.

I told him I already knew. Father took me to see the jaws years before. We went there on a family trip, stood by the window of a run-down bar where the jaws were on display and then drove home. My father talked about them for a week. "Jesus. Did you see them? Did you ever see a thing like that in your life?"

It rained in the night.

The clean path of daydreams through my head shut down. A twisting grayness took its place.

Kelley wore a work glove over his bandage. The fit was too tight and he worked poorly. The scallops piled up on his side of the pen, and when I reached my hand across to scoop some into my section, he shoved me away and said he'd do his share.

I could tell he'd found some way to blame me for the accident, since it was me who brought out the camera. Somehow he had shifted the fault away from himself.

Howard had stomach cramps. Every couple of minutes, he threw down his gloves and stamped off to the toilet. He reappeared a while later looking drained and pale, and worked until the cramps sent him back inside.

Kelley's moping tired me out. I pressed my knife against the metal basin of the scallop pen until it snapped.

"Oh, I knew it would break sooner or later." I held up the stub of the blade and looked at Kelley from the corner of my eye.

He was too busy with his bandaged hand to bother with me.

I climbed the ladder up to the bridge. Gil had a box of new scallop knives under his bed. I had seen them the night I tried on his survival suit. All I wanted was a couple of minutes' rest. I'd sit on the dry floor of the wheelhouse, winding tape onto the new knife handle, and maybe Gil would be eating potato chips and maybe he would give me some.

Gil slapped a knife on the control panel next to where I stood. Water dripped from the sleeves of my oilers onto the floor.

I had on a hopeful smile, scanning the room for signs of his special reserves of food.

I picked up the knife and still had on my hopeful smile.

Gil watched me, eyes screwed almost shut. "Fuck off." The depth gauge blinked and the radar blinked and Gil's fingernails shone like eyes. Gil hit a lever that started the cable drums turning, to bring in the dredges. The whole boat moaned with the sound.

I walked out under the work lights. The warm smell of the wheelhouse was pulled from my lungs in one breath and replaced with salt air.

I held the greasy rungs tightly as I climbed down the ladder to the deck. Dead crabs not swept overboard lay on their backs, legs slowly scraping at nothing. Skates flapped their wings on the metal plates.

Howard still sat in the toilet. Through a small window in the door, I could see his head bowed over and resting in his hands.

It was Kelley's turn to cut up the monkfish and he still hadn't finished the job. They lay in a pile at the stern, mouths locked open and filled with sand. "I'll help you just this once, Kelley!" I shouted over the rumble of cable drums, pulling Kelley's fish knife from his whale-bone seat, where he stuck the blade. "But I want you to be grateful! I want to see some gratitude!" Then I turned and shook my finger at him, imitating Gil. "I mean it now!"

Kelley stood by the cable drums, looking at me, teeth bared in a smile.

I picked up a monk and sliced off its tail, wishing I hadn't picked Kelley's knife to work with because it wasn't sharp and made a mess of the fish. I raised my head from the jumble of meat and skin and wiry bones. A pinkness showed on the horizon. Perhaps it was the glow of a city, perhaps New York City, scorching the sky with its millions of lights. Silver dots of rain cut down through the shine of work lights into my face. I imagined walking down Fifth Avenue in my oilers, my hair sticking up like a hedgehog from not being brushed, moving with the shuffling steps I always took on the boat.

After stabbing at a couple of fish, I gave up working with Kelley's knife and decided to find my own. I held up the blade, shook it at Kelley and mouthed the word "useless."

Then I saw that he had not been smiling.

He stood beside the cable drum, teeth still bared, face frozen and open-eyed. His right arm was torn off above the elbow. The rest of it lay stuck between the cables winding in.

I dragged him over to the ice hatch and lay him down. Blood poured from him like folds of silk.

244

I climbed very carefully up to the wheelhouse. "Kelley is hurt." I said each word loud and very clear in the stuffy space of the cabin.

Gil slopped out of his chair and ran down to see.

Then everything went from being what I remembered as very slow and calm to shouting and panic and pointless orders barked across the deck.

The rest of the crew piled out half asleep from the bunk room.

From the bridge I watched the cluster of naked legs and arms and Gil's back over the place where Kelley lay.

In the middle of their shouting I heard Kelley cry out in a high-pitched voice.

He had been cleaning grease from his gloves by gripping the cable as it wound in. I knew it. All of us did that when we couldn't find a cloth to clean away the blood and oil that collected on the rubber. The bandage must have caught on a snag in the cable wire and dragged his arm in before he could pull free.

I climbed down from the bridge and helped carry him into the galley. We held him so high that we banged the stump of his arm against the door frame, and the spit from his screaming came down on us. I held him by the shoulder and blood dripped in my eyes and pooled in the dip of my collar bone.

We set him on the table and stared at his pale face. His lips formed words with no sound.

Then we tore the sleeve off a shirt and wrapped it in a tourniquet around the stump.

Gil called for the Coast Guard on the radio but couldn't raise anyone.

Franklin pushed us out on deck and said not to come back in.

I sat with Howard on the ice hatch. He held his hands to his stomach and groaned with pain from the cramps. His dirty beard looked like brambles growing out of his skin.

Nelson and Pittsley were still in their underwear. They

crouched against the stern, hidden from waves that slapped the hull and crashed across our deck.

Gil appeared on the bridge and told us to finish hauling back the dredges. No one had answered on the radio. We'd have to steam to the nearest port, which was Block Island.

"What about his arm?" Howard croaked up into the work lights. His eyes were bloodshot smudges.

"Get it. Put it in the ice room. Right now."

"Make Pfeif do it. I can hardly move."

"I don't care who does it, but get it done now."

I had begun to shake in my knees and elbows. Shivers walked up my back so violently they were painful.

Gil let out the cable until Kelley's arm came loose from the drum. It fell on the deck.

I picked it up by the hand and carried it down to the ice room.

Howard opened the hatch and stood in front of the hole, hidden in steam rising from the ice below.

I swung the arm down onto a pile of new ice. Then Howard and I shut the hatch again.

Gil hauled in the cables.

A minute later, the dredges appeared and clanked against the sides.

We brought them on deck and I followed the movements of hooks and chains until both dredges lay flat on the iron plates. Then I rummaged through the pile with my basket until the scallops were gathered and ready for cutting.

And since there was nothing else to do, I cut out the scallops and bagged them and left them in the washer pen. I didn't want to go down in the hold.

Howard and I cleaned away the crabs and skates and sand. Anything that looked out of place I threw overboard or dropped into the lazarette.

*

Franklin had wrapped Kelley in blankets and given him a life jacket for a pillow. There were no painkillers on the boat. Not even aspirin.

I walked into the galley expecting to be thrown out again, but no one bothered me.

I touched Kelley's dirty boots as I moved past, seeing the heels worn out and the treads rubbed off his soles.

Franklin sat at the galley table with Kelley's head in his hands. He wiped Kelley's face with a damp cloth and talked to him in a quiet voice, sometimes drawing the cloth across Kelley's forehead. It sounded as if Franklin was telling him a story.

I bowed my head forward to listen, watching Kelley's face to see if he'd open his eyes or move his lips. Then I felt Franklin's hand on my shoulder.

He waved me away. The skin was chapped and white on his knuckles.

Before I left, I smoothed Kelley's hair back on his head.

It took five hours to reach Block Island.

When land showed on radar, I went down to the bunk room and sat in the dark by myself. I took off my diesel-smelling clothes for the first time since leaving land. From the bottom of my pack, I took clean trousers and a shirt.

I was asleep when we came into port.

Franklin turned on the bunk room light and I swung out of bed thinking it must be time to go on watch. I reached for my trousers hanging on a brass hook, then saw Kelley, ugly white, and his blood dried black on the galley table.

All around us in the dark were moored boats and land and the flashing light of an ambulance waiting at the dock, since Gil had finally raised someone on the radio.

I stood on our bow with the heavy mooring rope, a staleness in my body I had never felt before.

One of the ambulance men caught the rope and slipped it over a dock piling.

The medics carried Kelley out like a plank and laid him on a stretcher. They banged his head on the door frame but he didn't make a sound. Gil was made to go with them. Before he left, he told me to go down to the ice room and bring up Kelley's arm.

Holding my breath, I reached across the bloody ice and took hold of the arm. It was almost frozen. I handed it up to the same man who had caught the mooring line. His round glasses had steamed up in foggy air rising from the ice room. I couldn't see his eyes. His mouth twitched as he closed his fingers around the stump.

In the time before dawn when the Block Island streets were still empty, I stole a child's bicycle, which I found leaning against a telephone pole.

Gray light filtered through the clouds.

I cycled out of town, across the island to Mohegan Bluffs. Hundreds of years ago a tribe of Mohegan Indians had canoed across from the mainland to attack the local natives, but they were tired from canoeing and the locals drove them back over the edge of this cliff.

Yellow nylon rope had been stretched across the last hundred feet of ground. Cracks showed in the earth. Erosion was pulling the cliff wall into the sea.

I ducked under the rope and walked over the cracked earth to the place where I knew my grandfather was buried.

The plaque lay twenty feet from the edge. I saw boulders and dirt in long slides down to the water.

When my mother and grandmother used to bring me here, I never came close to the grave, since I didn't know exactly where his body rested. I didn't want to tread on him.

First my mother said he was buried with his head under the plaque and his feet pointing out to sea. After that, she said it was the other way around. Then she thought his body might be on the land side of the plaque. Finally she admitted that she couldn't remember.

248

My grandmother had also forgotten, the way she forgot everything else in the months before she died.

I was afraid that the coffin underneath would collapse if I trod on it, and the grass would fold up over me.

In the end, my mother persuaded me to come close enough to read the plaque. She swore that they had buried him standing up so he could look out to sea.

I used to dream that my grandfather lifted the plaque after dark and rested with his elbows propped on the ground, watching trawlers run past into Newport and Galilee.

If the cliff eroded much more, he and his bones and his plaque would all go down to the sea for good. With the toe of my boot, I pushed back grass from the rim of the plaque. The bronze was crusted turquoise with decay.

I broke the bike's chain as I pedaled into town. I put the dirty links in a purple plastic basket hooked between the handlebars and coasted the rest of the way. Then I set the bike back against the telephone pole.

Gil sat on the rusty dredge. He was showered and shaved and alone on the deck.

I heard the sound of Franklin scrubbing out the galley. Breaths of bleach and soap reached me where I stood on the wood planks of the dock.

Gil said Pittsley and Howard had wandered off down the beach. Nelson was lying in his bunk.

"How's Kelley?" I eased myself down on the planks.

"He's dead." Gil stared at the palm of his hand. "I think maybe he was dead when they took him off the boat. I didn't ask."

I already knew. I had seen Kelley's face when they carried him out.

Gil pulled a rubber band from his pocket and used it to make a cat's cradle. "The police were pretty good about it. They aren't impounding my boat or the scallops. The Coast Guard'll send someone around in a couple of days to inspect." He pulled the rubber band out and back around his fingers. "I have to find out where his parents live. I have to call them and let them know."

"Are we sailing back to Newport today?" The staleness still ached in my body. I wanted to be home in my room, where I could think straight.

"Not for a while. I have accident reports to fill out."

"Is it all right if I take the ferry home? There's one that runs to Galilee." Beads of dew on the dock planks soaked through my trousers.

He squinted up at me. "Are you quitting?"

"I just want to get some rest. I don't think I could sleep on the boat right now."

"Sure. Then go. Just be at Sabatini's by seven tomorrow morning, for when we unload the scallops."

"What are you going to tell Kelley's folks?"

Gil slid his lower jaw back and forth. "If you're going home, go home."

The only other people on the ferry were a group my age. Three boys and five girls. They wore clean khaki trousers, penny loafers and aviator sunglasses.

I sat on a bench sipping coffee from a paper cup, leaning forward to hear what they said. They spoke of the hotel they'd been working at since June. They talked about going back to school, about the courses they would sign up for and the money they had made. Their faces were smooth and tanned.

Pale, late summer sky rose up above the flimsy huts of Galilee as we came into the harbor.

I wondered if my parents would even bother to ask me about returning to college. I hoped they would leave it alone. With pictures of Kelley still burning like sunspots on my eyes, I didn't know how much talking it would take to make me change my mind. I didn't want to change my mind. I wanted it to be too late.

I walked home from the ferry. Warm mist clogged the hedges. A strong smell of honeysuckle blew in from the fields. Little frogs swam in the ditch water.

Nobody was home and the house was locked, so I fell asleep spread-eagled on my face in the front yard. A while later, I woke and found the neighbor's dog sniffing at me. He licked my ear, then lay down and used my leg for a pillow. I put my face back in the grass and slept again.

Kelley's parents drove down from Kennebunk.

They buried him in a cemetery just outside Newport.

I didn't see the funeral. Gil told us the parents wanted to have only family members present. He said we should all be at Mary's on Monday morning, the service having taken place on Saturday. He told us to wear jacket and tie.

My mother and father fought when I told them about the death. He explained to her how that accident wouldn't happen in the work I intended to do. She said she didn't care. She said she had stopped caring. Then she took it back and asked to know each detail of Kelley's death, stopping me every couple of seconds to ask if I knew never to do such a thing.

I had no trouble remembering what happened. The details seemed clear and separate and passed through my head without leaving me sick or sad or afraid. What bothered me was that I didn't feel as sad as I thought I should. Several times a day, I caught myself planning the business with Kelley and not realizing that he was dead. And each time I remembered, the neat screen where my plans played out went blank.

On Monday, I dressed in jacket and tie and took the bus to Newport.

At Mary's, I met Pittsley and Howard and Nelson, who had just come back from a clothes shop.

Howard explained how Pittsley refused to listen to the shop lady and bought a jacket with the sleeves too short. He also bought a ready-made tie with plastic clips for attaching to the collar.

Gil walked into the bar wearing a suit from the fifties with wide lapels and a western design stiched onto the pockets. I thought to myself that he must always have been this fat.

He drove us to the cemetery in his truck. We sat in the back with the wind whipping at our neatly combed hair. By the time we arrived, it looked as if we'd been at sea a week.

We stood around Kelley's grave with our hands double-fisted on our chests while Gil read prayers from a book he borrowed from the Seamen's Mission. Then, by himself and with no music, he sang a hymn about the darkness that deepens, which had as a chorus the words "abide with me."

Even as Gil sang, I looked around the stone-crowded church-yard, expecting to see Kelley's head poking up from behind one of the grave markers, thumbless hand held over his smiling face and the sound of his snorting giggles waking us all from our mourning.

Bunches of flowers lay stacked beside a white wooden cross. Gil said the cross would be replaced by a headstone when the carving had been done for it. Earth was piled high on the grave. Gil told us this was for when the coffin caved in. He made us all promise to drop by now and then to pay respects.

On the way back to Mary's, I sat in the front next to Gil.

He didn't speak for a while. He drummed on the steering wheel with his chubby fingers, then played with the rearview mirror. "Look at them."

"Who?" I raised my head. I'd been studying my fingernails.

Gil pointed at the reflection of Nelson and Pittsley and Howard in the back of the truck. "What a mangy bunch, eh?"

I nodded.

"Mangy bunch," he said again, and slumped back in his seat. "I guess they're all going to quit on me now."

"I don't think so, Gil."

"What about you? Are you going to quit?"

"No, Gil."

He nodded and chewed at his lower lip. "I won't hire a new man if I don't have to. At least not for a while. You and Howard can handle your watch. I'll keep Franklin out on deck with Nelson. We'll all help with the cooking. Truth is, I'm not sure I could find a crewman right now. Not once the word gets out about what happened. People are superstitious."

"What did the Coast Guard say to you?"

He looked at me out of the corner of his eye, as if it were none of my business. "They made me replace the Givens Buoys. Made me go into a pharmacy and buy just about one of everything. My boat's more like a floating hospital than a trawler. Of course, it should have been that way before. I just have to live with that."

I heard Howard and Pittsley and Nelson talking in the back. "How old was Kelley?"

"I don't know, Pfeif. I guess maybe thirty-five. Thirty-eight. I don't know." He cleared his throat. "Let me ask you something, Pfeif. Do you know where Kelley kept his money?"

"All I know is that he stored it in a Tupperware box and not in a bank."

"Did he keep it on the boat?"

"I don't know."

"I've had Franklin search the whole ship and he's found nothing. You'd do yourself a favor to remember where it is, Pfeif."

"I swear I don't know."

"There's thousands of dollars in that little box, and no one's ever going to find it. Not if I know Kelley. You two were going in on a boat together. Is that right?"

"He told you."

"He told me when he was drunk and then he forgot he told me. He figured he owed you for jumping in after him when he got knocked overboard."

"I told him he didn't owe me a thing except the hundred dollars for bailing him out of jail."

"Are you still going to try and get a boat?"

"I was always going to get myself a small boat. I took Kelley's offer so I could learn the work."

"Do you have Kelley's boat?"

"I doubt that. Not now."

"So you want to fish in-shore? Don't like it out there, do you?"

"I think I'd just prefer to run my business and live close to the land."

"You work for me until you have the money. I'll keep your paychecks coming. You and Howard will handle that watch by yourselves. I don't need to hire a new man." Quiet. A bug splatted on the windshield. Gil squirted wiper fluid on the glass and set the wipers going. "Ever had a friend die on you before?"

"No. Grandparents but not friends."

"It messes you up for a while."

After a few days, the clear and painless memory of how Kelley died fell apart into an ugliness that sent echoes through me of his scream and the exact feeling of how it was to stand on the bridge looking down at the crew grouped over his body, all of them treading in his blood. Sometimes, in the middle of a conversation, the pictures returned so violently that I forgot what I was saying and had to be reminded. I shook the way I had shaken when I carried his arm down to the ice room. I felt as if I'd never get away from it, that I'd be shaking the rest of my life.

I met Bucket in the dusty parking lot of his dockyard as he shuffled toward the bus stop.

We walked back to his boat and sat in the cabin. He opened his lunch box, which had a picture of Donny Osmond printed on the front, and took out a sandwich.

I told him Kelley was dead and he said he already knew. I had nothing else to tell him. All I wanted to do was leave. I sat on the hard wooden seat and said nothing, hearing the squelch of Bucket gumming his sandwich.

"I suppose you'll be keeping up the payments on your own." He spoke with his mouth full.

I convinced myself earlier that Bucket would hold on to Kelley's money and sell the boat to someone else. I hadn't even considered that he'd let me finish off the debt and keep the business. Without speaking, I pulled out my wallet and gave him everything in it as the next down payment.

He folded the money away in his palm like a magician. Then he wrote out a contract twice on the wax paper wrapping of his sandwich. At the bottom he wrote "Legal."

I looked at the figures. I still owed him over five thousand dollars.

We signed both copies and each kept one.

"How long do you think it will take you to pay off the boat?" He clipped his lunch box shut.

"I'll keep working for Gil and give you everything I take home. In the meantime, you can show me how to work this business."

"I get tired. I can't work late in the day because of my getting tired. I'll teach you as long as I got the energy." He locked the cabin door and we walked across the parking lot. I paced slowly to keep level with him. His hands were crooked with arthritis.

At the bus stop, I asked him to lend me some money for the bus, since I'd given him all I had.

He asked the price of my fare home.

"Seventy-five cents, Mr. Bucket."

He pulled three quarters from the deep pocket of his overalls and let them fall one by one into my hand.

That evening, I heard my father pacing downstairs.

The insurance adjusters were haggling over his claim.

He was restless on land and couldn't understand why insurance men kept going back to the *Glory B* and peering at the wreck. By now, the only part that showed above the water was its mast. A big orange buoy had been attached to the hull to warn other fishermen where it lay.

Earlier in the evening, he and my mother had sat in white metal chairs at the bottom of the garden. She brought out drinks and talked while he picked his nails and nodded at what she said.

I stayed out of sight in my room, hidden behind the mosquito screen. I strained to hear what they said, but the wind took their voices away.

I woke in the middle of the night.

My mother was standing in the doorway. "Do you miss your friend who died?"

I sat up and rubbed at my face. "Why are you asking me now?"

"Who are you going to work with on your own boat now that he's gone?"

"I'll work by myself until I find a partner."

"You can't do it by yourself. That's what I came in here to tell you. I couldn't go to sleep until I told you what's on my mind. You can't do that job by yourself." Then she coughed and tapped at her chest with the tips of her fingers.

"Can't because you don't want me to, or because you don't think I can do it?" I swung my legs onto the floor and heard the blood storm in my ears. When I looked up, she was gone.

In the morning, she denied ever coming to my room.

I told her word for word what she said and she still denied it. After a while, I couldn't be sure whether she'd really been there and was only talking in her sleep or whether I had dreamt it up myself.

My father said it wouldn't be the first time she walked around and did things in her sleep. He told me that once, just after they got married, she carried their record player out of the living room in her sleep and hid it under her bed. When she woke up in the morning she called the police because she thought their house had been robbed.

After breakfast, Joseph and I piled into the bathroom the way we always did. We brushed our teeth over the same tiny sink and fought for space in front of the mirror to comb our hair.

Then he sat down on the toilet and shaved with an electric razor while I stayed at the sink with a can of shaving foam.

"Joseph, do you think Dad likes his new job?" I rinsed my plastic razor under the tap.

"Doubt it."

"Has he said anything to you?"

"Nothing," Joseph muttered over the bumble-bee hum of his shaver.

"I was going to ask him . . . I mean . . . he could work with me when I get my new boat."

"He could but he wouldn't."

"You could work with me, Joseph. I'd be happy to teach you how things work."

"Don't be preposterous." He trimmed his sideburns.

I tapped my razor against the faucet to loosen shaving cream caught between the blades. "I wouldn't hold you to it. You could quit when you wanted to."

"It would be smelly. I don't want to work where it's smelly."

"You get used to it. You don't notice it after the first couple of days."

"Would I have to touch the lobsters? I never could figure out how to touch them when they don't have those rubber bands on their claws."

"You take hold of their backs. They can't pinch you that way."

"Maybe I'd do the job if I could drive the boat. Could I drive the boat and not have to touch the lobsters?"

"I guess."

"No." He shook his head. "No. I'm not getting talked into this." He shut off the shaver and scraped at his cheek. Then he splashed after-shave on his face and walked out smelling of limes.

14

THE Gatsby people disappeared.

When I came back from my next trip on the *Gray Ghost,* the streets of Newport were almost empty.

Some of the cafés on Severn Street had closed down.

In my free days on shore, Bucket took me out in his boat to check the few pots he still kept in the water. When the lobsters had been collected and the last pots dropped back down, leaving shreds of seaweed and small crabs scattered on the deck, Bucket cut the motor and we sat drinking coffee while the boat drifted toward land.

Back at the dock, I crouched in the engine room of his boat, learning how to pull the thing apart and put it back together.

I scraped barnacles off old lobster pots and painted them with an ugly-smelling dye to keep them clean.

I rebuilt parts that had rotted out, sitting cross-legged on the dusty ground with small nails held between my teeth.

When he became too tired to work anymore, or too tired from watching me do all the work, we moved to the work shed, where other lobstermen sat reading papers or having papers read to them. The room was filled with smoke from their tobacco.

"I been looking for Kelley's money." Bucket gummed at a sandwich in the stuffy air of the work shed.

"No luck?" I kneaded my neck. It was stiff from crouching in the engine room.

"No." Bucket waved his sandwich across the room. "But every-body's in on it. The whole wharf's crawling with people every night."

I nodded, imagining the shadows seething with clumsy fish-ermen tripping over each other in the dark.

"Damn Lester's ruining it for everybody." Bucket blinked at me through the smoky air. "A couple of nights ago, when I was having a look around, he sat himself up on the roof of Sabatini's fishhouse every evening. The old fucker had himself a flash-light. He waited until I was in range, then he turned the damn thing on and yelled at me to stop or he'd shoot."

I nodded again.

"Hey." He prodded me with his sandwich. "Want a bite?"

"No, thanks."

"You aren't talking much today."

"I went to the dentist earlier."

"Oh, is that where you was?"

"I sat in his chair half the day listening to the squeal of that drill. He was grinding down my broken teeth so he could fit the permanent replacements."

"Once you lose them, you don't miss them. Let me tell you, James."

I rubbed my chin, feeling again the weight of the dentist leaning into my mouth. My spit tasted of metal. The replace-ments were made of porcelain and gold. They felt too big in my mouth.

"You don't miss them a bit." Bucket rummaged through his stale-smelling lunch box for something else to eat.

Someone kept calling our house.

When one of us answered the phone, the person on the other end stayed quiet.

They called at different hours. Breakfast time. Dinner time. The middle of the night.

Mostly I just hung up. Other times, I put my hand over the mouthpiece and listened. Faintly in the distance, I heard a radio playing, or a TV. Once I heard an ambulance whine past.

I thought it was just some kid with nothing better to do. I knew it would stop in a while.

My father couldn't stand it. Every time he heard a ring, he'd jump. He'd pick up the receiver and scream into it that the line was tapped and the police were on their way.

My mother told him to calm down. She said if the kids thought they were getting to us, then they'd keep calling.

He didn't listen.

On the third night of crank calls, the phone rang at two in the morning.

I heard the bedsprings creak in my parents' room as my father lunged for the receiver.

"Stop it!" he screamed. "For Christ's sake, can't you see I've had enough?" He slammed the phone back again.

I heard my mother's voice telling him to be calm.

He mumbled something and went downstairs.

A while later, since I couldn't sleep, I went down after him. I stepped carefully on the creaking boards of the staircase.

The lights were off.

My father sat in a chair in the living room, his bare feet on the coffee table.

He had opened the windows. The white lace curtains billowed in with the breeze.

He turned to face me. His cheeks looked hollow in the dark. "Did you hear something outside? Is that why you came down?"

"I came down to see if you were all right."

He turned away and looked out the window again. "I thought I heard someone in the garden."

"Do you want to take a look?"

We walked out on the lawn and stood looking up and down the empty road. Street lights scooped holes out of the dark.

My ankles and feet were wet with dew. I knelt down and ran my fingers through the soaked grass.

My father stood by the mailbox. He breathed in deep and scratched at the back of his neck. "This is ridiculous." He spun on his heel and walked back toward the house.

"They won't come for you now." I spoke quietly as he moved by.

He stopped. "What?"

I looked up. "I said they won't come for you now."

"Who won't?"

"You know who. They'll leave you alone from now on."

For a long time he didn't move. Then he sighed. "Maybe so." From the rustle in his throat, I thought he was about to cry.

He disappeared into the house.

I stayed kneeling in the grass after he had gone, watching fireflies spark in the hedge across the road. I wished he had talked to me then, explained how they muscled him and kept him going out to sea. I wished he could have asked me for advice. I wished I had advice to give.

"Don't answer it!" My mother held up her hand. It was coated with suds from the dishwashing liquid in the sink. "Let the damn thing keep ringing."

I let the phone ring three times. "It could be important." I picked up the receiver. "Hello?"

"Hi! Is James there?"

"This is." I nodded at my mother, showing her it was all right.

"It's Rex calling."

"Who?"

"Rex Webber. Emily's friend."

"Oh. Hello, Rex."

My mother stood next to me, pointing at the receiver and mouthing the word "who" over and over. She dripped dishwashing suds on the floor.

I waved her away.

Rex cleared his throat. "I have some great news."

"What's that?" I watched my mother go back to washing the dishes.

"Emily and I are getting married."

"You are?" My stomach boiled. I walked into the next room, pulling the phone cord tight. "Why?"

"Well." Rex laughed. "Umm . . ."

"I mean, when?" I sat down at the dining room table. "When are you getting married?"

"The day after tomorrow. It's all kind of sudden, I know. That's why I'm calling to invite you rather than sending a printed card. Besides, the damn things are too expensive."

For a while it was quiet. Mother finished with the dishes and went upstairs. I heard her run the bath water.

I dug my thumbnail into the wood of the table.

"So." Rex cleared his throat again. "Are you coming?"

I slid back until my neck rested against the edge of the chair and I was looking at the ceiling. "Sure."

"Great! It's at two o'clock. The old courthouse in Newport, the one with punishment stocks out front. Now I have to call Emily's parents. They're down in the West Indies, you know. Mr. Vogel's in the fishing business too. Did you know that?"

She didn't tell you about us, did she? I thought to myself. She didn't tell you a thing. "Yeah, Rex. I know about Vic Vogel."

"Well, of course. I forget how long you two have been friends. Well, I'd better make the call. See you at two o'clock."

"Day after tomorrow."

"You got it, buddy."

When he had hung up, I very carefully unplugged the phone from the wall and took it outside. I took a shovel from the garage and dug a deep hole at the far end of the yard, where Mother grew blackberries and pumpkins. I set the phone in the hole and buried it. I tamped the earth down with my hands.

No one said a word. My mother probably thought my father had hidden the phone. He probably thought she did. I knew it would be weeks before we bought another.

My parents came to the ceremony. They insisted.

Emily's mother and father didn't show. They were still in the West Indies, waiting to be extradited.

A man with a video camera crept up and down the aisles, jamming the lens in our faces and making the floorboards creak. His camera whirred like the beating of wings.

The priest spoke in a soft voice and I heard very little of what he said.

A woman with fake flowers on her hat blocked my view, so I had to lean out into the aisle.

Rex and Emily stood in front of the priest with their heads bowed. He wore black and she wore white.

I sat fidgeting on the bench, craning my neck around at the windows and rafters and wood floor. The memory of the time Emily and I had spent in high school and at the East Bay Plant filed past my eyes and straggled back into the past.

I tried to catch her eye as she and Rex walked out the door, into the pelting of rice thrown by others at the ceremony.

Emily smiled at everyone, her eyes tripping past us without seeing as she made her way down to a limousine with tinted windows.

The limo pulled away from the curb.

I was sure I'd never see her again.

An old lady stood next to me, holding a brown paper bag half filled with rice. She was the one with the fake flowers on her hat.

I grabbed her bag and ran down the steps. I ran after the limo, snatching handfuls of rice from the bag and throwing them after the limousine. I ran as fast as I could, my shirt coming untucked and something ripping in the arm of my suit jacket. I threw all the rice and then I crumpled the bag and threw that.

In a single flutter of confusion, everything I remembered of her and me together became antique and small and unimportant.

But the limousine looked important. Rex looked important. The pure black and pure white of their clothes looked important.

I stood by myself in the road, watching their car turn onto the highway. When it was gone, I tucked in my shirt and walked to our truck, where my mother and father sat. I climbed into the open back and slumped down.

Mother rolled down her window. "Don't get your suit dirty. You're invited to a reception in an hour."

"Hell with it." I wiped sweat off my face.

Father rolled down his window. "Don't you want to go?"

"Hell with it." The cold air cut into my throat.

Father drove home over the bridges.

I sat in the back, shivering in the wind. It cut around the cab of the truck and through the thin fabric of my suit. The railings of the bridges were plastered with ice.

Father slid back a window at the rear of the cab. "You could have sat up front with us, you know."

I looked up, my ears feeling frozen solid like little clamshells. "I could have caught the damn limo if I'd run a little faster."

He smiled weakly. "That might have been inappropriate, James."

My spine shuddered in the cold. "Inappropriate!" I shouted. "The hell with everything!" I huddled into a ball and let my teeth rattle.

Two days later, storms came down hard from the north.

Gil had planned to take us out to sea that night, but we stayed in the harbor while cold wind beat at the windows of Mary's bar.

I'd been in Mary's all afternoon. It was a place meant for summer, with light through the windows and shadows of fishing nets stretched along the walls. Now it looked dingy. I grew sick of catching sight of my shabby face in the mirror behind the bar. The jukebox broke, and no one played the pinball machine. Colored lights tiptoed up and down its screen, trying to attract attention.

Before the storm, my father had met his old crewman Kitteridge at a bar in Galilee. Kitteridge had his own boat now. For a favor, and since he didn't start as manager at the Fishermen's Co-op for several weeks, my father agreed to go out with Kitteridge as mate on a couple of trips while he broke in a new crew. Kitteridge's boat left port just as the wind started blowing.

Gil took us out to sea one day in late September.

The storm still trampled the water, but we were tired of waiting on land.

Franklin cooked hot dogs for dinner.

We all crammed into the galley to eat.

There was no room at the table, so I sat with Howard on the floor. Heat rose up from the engines below.

"What's the matter, James?" Gil called to me from across the galley. "You don't look so good. Is the storm getting to you?"

"A bit." I always felt a little seasick in the storms.

"You wait until the winter comes. Then you'll see some storms. I'll have you up in the rigging knocking off icicles with a hammer. I'll have you beating chunks of ice from the bow rail so we don't get top-heavy and capsize. Oh, it gets nasty in the winter. You wait and see."

By midnight, we were nowhere near land. It rained in sheets around the boat, making us feel as if we were surrounded by static on a television screen.

From my bunk, I heard waves explode on the hull. I found myself waking with hands pressed hard against the roof of the bunk, as if only the force of my body could stop the sea from breaking through.

I crawled down to the forward bulkhead to find new light bulbs after the ones in the galley gave out. Against the plate steel of the bow, I saw trickles of water along the weld marks. Gil laughed at me when I ran into the wheelhouse, out of breath, and told him about the droplets. He said it was only condensation, but I went back to the bulkhead and stayed for a long time, shining a flashlight on the sweating walls, made deaf by the thunder of the waves.

Howard bought himself a Walkman and kept me awake playing it while we lay in the bunk room. The tinny drumbeat sounds reached me as *ksh ksh*. When he left the room, I took the batteries out and put them in again backward. He got so mad at the machine, because he couldn't fix it, that he set it on the floor and stamped it into rubble.

At sunrise, I was walking the deck.

I gathered fish that came up in the dredges and flipped them into a basket. They were winter fluke, with thick green skin, white bellies and bubble eyes. I dug the nail of the fish pick into the meat of their backs and jerked them into a slime-covered basket.

Sun shone in dull gray strips on the water.

As I moved to pick up the basket, a big crab reached from the deck and grabbed my thumb. Its claws were black at the ends, as if they had been hardened in a fire. I cried out and shook my hand but the crab stayed on, legs tucked under its shell, mouth plates sliding back and forth. I swung the crab against the ice hatch and broke the claw off its body. The crab dropped to the floor and started crawling away. The claw still gripped at my thumb. By squeezing the muscle behind its first joint, I made the claw let go. Then I ground the crab into the deck with my heel.

We had just pulled the dredges on deck when Nelson appeared from the bunk room and walked toward the stern to take a piss. He stood with his hands on the small of his back, looking at the water. Suddenly he shouted, "It's a man! A man!"

I moved to get a better look and saw the head of the man in the water. He rose up on the crest of one wave and disappeared into the trough of another.

He wore a survival suit.

Gil had already begun to wheel the boat around.

We waved and called to the man, but as we pulled close I saw his eyes were closed, his mouth shut tight. He looked old and his eyebrows were gray.

We passed him once and couldn't reach him, so we turned and tried again.

His arms spread out from his body and the fingers waved like seaweed at the end. Glow strips on the suit reflected the sun's weak light.

Pittsley and Nelson pulled him to the boat with a rubber-tipped gaff hook, then heaved him over the side with a rope. His heels slapped hard on the deck.

"Dead man," Pittsley shouted in my ear. "We got us a corpse."

I picked up my fish basket again, not wanting to touch the man if I didn't have to.

The dead man's survival suit looked weathered. A few barnacles grew on the rubber.

We crowded around and looked down at his face. It had been hardened by the sea. His eyebrows were crusted with salt and the skin was pulled tight on the bones. Behind the closed eyelids his eyes had sunk into his head. The lips were thin strips stretched over the teeth and his nostrils two fat, shriveled holes.

Gil turned the man over with the toe of his boot.

I held my breath as I stepped close. On the back, in faded letters, I read:

Blow Whistle To Attract Attention.
Relax! Remember — You Cannot Sink.

268

"You want me to call the Coast Guard?" Howard wiped his hands on his trousers, even though he had not touched the body.

Gil rocked on his heels with the strike of a wave against the boat. "What for? He's already dead. Throw him back over."

Without a word, Pittsley and Nelson picked the man up by his arms and started dragging him toward the gap in the stern.

I took another look at the man's face and smooth shape of his forehead tucked into the survival suit's hood. Then I took another pace forward, my eyes fixed on the face. A sharp jolt punched through my ribs. "It's my dad."

"What?" Pittsley and Nelson dropped the man. His head fell with a crack on the deck.

I began to breathe very fast, feeling the same shudders that had run through me when Kelley died. "It's my dad." I knelt next to the body and put my hands on either side of his head, my thumbs against the freezing cold skin. "My dad." I looked up at the faces of the people around me. My dad, I tried to say again, but only crackled in my throat.

I wrapped my arms around his chest and began to carry him toward the galley. The body was heavier than I thought, and my knees were shaking. I fell over with the body on top of me. "Help me carry my dad." I stood up, took hold of the arm and pulled.

Gil set his hand on my shoulder and squeezed. "What are you talking about, Pfeif? What makes you think this is your dad?"

"I know him from his face." I bent over and took the man's head in my hands. My mouth locked open and I felt myself choking.

"You don't know anybody from that face."

"It's my dad." Something acid rose up from my throat and spilled down the side of my mouth.

"You told me your dad wasn't fishing anymore, Pfeif."

I breathed in and breathed in again but the air was thin and empty. "He went out a couple of days ago with a friend. He was going as mate. Just for a couple of trips." I groped behind me for the ice hatch and sat down, a painful heaviness in my guts.

"Pfeiffer." Gil's face appeared in front of me, jaw muscles in two bars down the side of his cheek. "This man has been out here for a lot longer than a couple of days. This man has been dead a long time. Now you" — his finger jabbed, out of focus, close to my sight — "you saw your dad only a day or two ago. Right?"

"Yes. Three days ago."

"Well, then."

"I know him from his eyes." I bent down and pulled back the man's eyelids with my thumb. The pupils were gone, rolled back into his head. Only the white remained. I stood up and screamed in Gil's face. "It's my dad!"

Gil took hold of my collar and lifted me onto the tips of my toes.

My nose fizzed and tears ran down my face.

Gil shook me. "Did you see him a couple of days ago or not?"

"Yes." I dabbed at my eyes with the tips of my fingers.

He turned to Pittsley. "Then get this floater out of here!" Gil faced me again. "There's barnacles on the suit! He's been out here for ages. Now it's not your father and you know it."

Pittsley took the man's arms and dragged him toward the gap in our stern.

"You can't just leave him out here!" I tried to push Gil aside but he held on to me, his hands gripping my skin through the material of my coat.

"If we put him down in the ice room and hand him over to the police when we get back, they declare the catch contaminated and we lose it. We lose the whole thing. Now this man is dead and you don't know him and you can't help him. He doesn't care where he is. He's a piece of driftwood now. Do you understand?"

"You can't leave him out here by himself." I hung in the grip of Gil's hands on my collar.

"What are you talking about?"

I shrugged my shoulders, the heaviness in my stomach pulling me down. "Can't." I looked up. The rest of the crew was watching me. I stared down at the deck, ashamed.

They threw the man over. I saw the ball of his head bob up on the wave crests. Then he was gone in the dullness of the broken sea.

"Send these dredges down." Gil snapped his fingers at us and returned to the wheelhouse.

I heard the clank of chains, the hum of cable running loose.

At the end of my watch, I set the bloated scallop bags on fresh beds of ice and got a dozen eggs for Franklin from the food storage area at the back of the ice room. I listened to the boat idle in neutral for a second before the Cats slammed into gear and gathered speed.

I handed the eggs up to Howard. They came in a pink Styrofoam box with a barnyard scene in blue ink on the front.

"You all right now?" He held the eggs to his chest. Water dripped from the sides of the ice hatch.

"I was sure, Howard. I know now, but right then I swear I was sure."

"You be glad you were wrong is all." He grinned and his head slipped away, leaving a neat square of gray sky in its place.

After he'd gone, I was very tired. I lay down next to the scallops and breathed in the peppery air, feeling my muscles go numb.

I stayed very still, having nightmares on the ice. I didn't blink in case I suddenly found myself on the top of a wave, my dead and naked body in the red survival suit, legs dangling down, owning trails of seaweed and the studs of barnacles.

I lay in the bunk room with my right arm hooked over my eyes, hearing the clatter of knives and forks as Gil and Howard ate their meal.

The door opened and someone stood in the doorway without turning on the light.

I raised my head and saw Gil.

"Not hungry, Pfeif?"

"No, thank you."

"Better now? You don't still think that man was your father?"

"No, Gil. But out there I was sure."

"I know." His bulk filled the space of the doorway. "You were spooked. Everybody gets spooked. It's usually a sign that a person needs a break. I was thinking maybe you'd want to take some time off when we get back to port. Take a couple of weeks."

"Is that a nice way of firing me?"

"No. You can have your job back any time. You still looking forward to starting your business?"

"Still, yes. I'm learning the ropes from the old man who's selling his boat."

"Listen, Pfeif." He walked into the room and shut the door. It was completely dark. "You're working to pay off that boat, aren't you?"

"Pay it off and have some money to get started with. The dentist bill has been wiping me out."

"You want to pay that boat off now? By next week?"

"Of course, if I could." Even with my eyes wide open, I could see nothing in the room.

"You remember that time I made you stay on land while the rest of us went out to sea? Do you know why that was?"

"Kelley told me." I heard his feet shuffle close by.

"I didn't think he'd keep his mouth shut to you about it." His knees cracked as he bent down. I smelled his breath in my face but still couldn't see him. "Next week we make another one of those trips. Do you want to take Kelley's place on this one? It's all right if you say no. But if you come with us, you'd pay off the boat and probably have all you need to get started."

"What would we be doing exactly?"

"Same as last time. Same place. Same people. Same chances and same pay. Fact is, I'm under a little bit of an obligation to make this trip."

"When would we leave?"

"In a week, like I said. You can't use the money all at once, so use the time off to take a break afterwards. A couple of weeks, maybe."

Gil was right. If I didn't take a rest soon, I would go out of my head. Kelley's death still kept me awake in my bunk, and I needed the sleep to be able to work well on deck. It was wearing me down each time I spoke to my father, waiting for him to tell me about what he had done in the years he put Joseph through school. I sat there wondering when he would trust me enough, the way he had trusted Joseph, to let me in on the secret I already knew. But he never spoke of it. He stayed silent and his silence was corroding my nerves. Rest. Time to sleep. Time to think. Time to lose, at least for a while, the perpetual rolling motion of the sea inside my skull.

I turned my face to where I thought Gil stood in the dark. "Good enough. I'll be ready when you say."

His knees cracked again as he stood. "Excellent. Still not hungry?"

I didn't answer. A tightness had come up in my throat.

Gil opened the bunk room door and slipped out.

Rain thrashed the streets. It had been storming since the sun went down.

I sat on my bed at the Y, dressed in my oilers.

It was the middle of the night.

I'd spent hours trying to remember what Kelley had said about the run, imagining hours spent watching the radar, the faces of Emmet and Will as they walked from the woods, nervous laughter when the men figured out they weren't going to kill each other and the weight of packages from the back of their truck. I tried to map each detail in my head, so as not to be afraid when the time came.

At three o'clock, I left the room and went outside.

Water bubbled in the gutters. It washed across the road in veils.

Rain poured down my arms and dripped from the tips of my fingers.

We were due to leave the dock at four.

The bars had closed and all the streets were empty. Cold gusts barged down the alleys. I took my time walking by the shop windows on Severn Street. Serious-faced mannequins stared through the glass.

I moved quietly past Lester's boat and around the back of Sabatini's fishhouse. Instead of going straight to the *Gray Ghost,* I crouched in one of the empty ice carts, watching for movement on the dock, listening for any break in the quiet. The bay was choppy and black. I tucked my hands into the sleeves of my oilers. Then I wiggled my toes in my boots, to keep from going numb.

Footsteps. Howard walked across the dock. The wooden planks gleamed in the wet. Rain crowded around the wharf lights. Howard stood next to the *Gray Ghost* and looked around, puffing white air through his teeth. Then he jumped down on deck and disappeared into the galley.

I stayed in the ice cart, sheltered from the wind, waiting to see who else would show.

The wheelhouse door opened. Franklin's face appeared.

I heard Gil's voice inside. "Come on, Franklin. Shut the damn door. It's too cold."

A crumpled ball of paper bounced off Franklin's head. The door closed again.

Then Pittsley and Nelson stepped onto the dock. They were both trying to shelter under one small umbrella. Pittsley tugged it away from Nelson and Nelson tugged it back. The two of them were drenched.

274

Acid washed through my stomach. My muscles tensed, ready to lift me from my crouch and shove me across to the boat. But I stayed slumped in the cart.

Wind nudged past the corrugated iron of the fishhouse roof. It gathered the strands of falling rain, spun them into shapes like people dancing, then swept them away across the water.

Shudders of tension rushed through me.

It was several minutes before I realized that I could not cross the shining planks that lay between me and the *Ghost*. Could not ride out to sea and do what my father had done.

I wanted to be gone. Wanted never to have come this far. Fatigue twisted my bones.

The twitching of my nerves died down and I crawled with cramped legs onto the dock.

I walked into the dark fishhouse.

Suddenly the blackness moved and became human.

My father stood in front of me, glaring from the deep hood of his coat. He pulled down the hood, showing the paleness of his bald head. "They're waiting for you, James."

"I'm not going, Dad."

The sound of breathing. Drum of raindrops on the roof.

He reached his hand out slowly and closed his fingers around my temples.

I didn't move, waiting for him to crush my skull like an egg.

He ran his fingers through my hair and took his hand away.

When I looked up a few seconds later he was gone, as if he had never been there. Then I saw his crooked shadow walk out into the storm.

I ran to catch up as the engines of the *Gray Ghost* thundered into life.